also by Rebecca Chace

Chautauqua Summer: Adventures of
a Late-Twentieth-Century Vaudevillian

Capture the Flag

a novel

Rebecca Chace

simon & schuster

SIMON & SCHUSTER
Rockefeller Center
1230 Avenue of the Americas
New York, NY 10020

Designed by Jeanette Olender
Manufactured in the United States of America

10 9 8 7 6 5 4 3 2 1

Library of Congress Cataloging-in-Publication Data
Chace, Rebecca.
Capture the flag: a novel / Rebecca Chace.
p. cm.
I. Title.
PS3553.H17C36 1999
813'.54—dc21 99-24078 CIP
ISBN 0-684-85758-8

23

acknowledgments

I would like to thank the following people for their support: Anne Freedgood, who provided me with crucial feedback and encouragement throughout the earliest stages of the manuscript. My editors, Laurie Chittenden and Denise Roy, have brought an infallible sense of what is right for this book that has never faltered. My thanks to all at Simon & Schuster, including Nicole Graev and Brenda Copeland for all of their help and patience. My deepest regard, as it has for over thirty years, goes to Annik LaFarge. Jennifer Rudolph Walsh has been instrumental every step of the way, and her suggestions have had a profound influence on the final shape of the book. Harvey Ginsberg, Tony Pasqualini, Steven Bernstein, Kevin Buckley, Alan Rothblatt, Abigail Halperin, Jonathan Rosenberg, Sarah Chace, Mark Warren, Kate Doyle, Tim Weiner, Silvana Paternostro, Jacob Conrad, Pesha Ona, and Jennifer Collins have all helped in ways impossible to enumerate here. I cannot imagine any of it being possible without Paul.

to my mother and father

Capture the Flag

With a variable key
you unlock the house in which
drifts the snow of that left unspoken. . . .

You vary the key, you vary the word
that is free to drift with the flakes.
What snowball will form round the word
depends on the wind that rebuffs you.

PAUL CELAN, "With a Variable Key"

the families

the Edwards
  Luke Edwards
  Ellen Billings Edwards
their daughter
  Annie Billings Edwards

the Shanlick-Masons
  Peter Shanlick
  Janis Mason Shanlick
his daughters
  Therese (Tessa) Shanlick
  Liz Shanlick
  Samantha (Sam) Shanlick
her sons
  Justin Mason
  Nick Mason

Part One

the game 1972

Annie's eyelids and cheeks were black with grease-paint camouflage. Her mother had cut her hair into a pixie cut that summer, and Annie liked it because sometimes strangers thought she was a boy. She gauged the height of the barbed wire stretched between the fence posts in front of her—and jumped.

Before the game began, she had run up the dirt driveway and cut out into the fields where her father and Justin always shot at woodchucks. Throwing herself hard on the ground, she had crawled on her belly, practicing combat moves for the game, willing herself invisible. I am a snake, she thought, a snake, a lizard, a gila monster. I am the thing no one can see. Then back down the road the screen door to the kitchen had slammed shut, and she heard them before she could see them: Peter Shanlick's rattling laugh and her father Luke's soft reply as the two captains walked up the long dirt driveway to see who would get the better field this year.

This was the sixth year their families had met for Capture the Flag. Peter was Justin's stepfather and captain of the other team. His first novel, published when he was just out of college, had been a best-seller. Now, at thirty-seven, he hadn't published anything since. He held his anger close to his body like a charm, and his menace always pulled women to him. Luke hurried to keep up, stoop-shouldered and wiry. Next to Peter, he looked like a boy. Everyone said that Luke was the smarter of the two; though he had left *his* college novel unfinished and had become an editor of historical biographies instead.

That night Annie caught the first firefly in her fist. She thought it was a good omen and took care not to hurt it as she crouched down and peeked between her fingers to watch it blink. Then, when she looked up, the sky had already got darker and she opened her hands to let the firefly loose, marking its slow, winking progress above the grass.

"Annie . . . Annie." Her father's voice rolled across the road and the field to her.

She wanted the sound to go on and on, north to Canada where they made the ale that he drank on weekends. "Annie . . . Annie . . ." She pushed off the ground, and her new sneakers sent her higher and higher as she ran down the field and landed in Luke's arms. His scratchy wool sweater pushed into her nose. The smell of him was familiar and satisfying as he spun her around and whispered, "O.K., kid, ready for your mission?"

Then her mother had come over and pulled the strings of Annie's sweatshirt together. Annie had shrugged her away, but Ellen had pretended not to notice, whispering, "Are you warm enough?"

Her mother always formed each vowel perfectly, with the odd, nonregional accent of the northeastern upper class. Annie's father said that the only way you could sound like you came from nowhere was if you came from somewhere in particular. Ellen had grown up in the family home outside of Boston and in a string of Connecticut boarding schools. She tucked a stray hair under Annie's hood. Annie loved the smell of her mother's hands. She used a special lilac soap from France.

"And look at your makeup," Ellen had said. "Is that so nobody sees you in the dark?"

"Yeah—it's camouflage, Mom, not makeup."

Too ashamed of Ellen's ignorance to stand with her, Annie had walked over to Justin, who was switching his new stopwatch on and off.

"Cool," Annie said, trying to peek over his shoulder on tiptoes.

Justin ignored her. When she looked back at Ellen, her mother had gone back down the road to talk to Justin's mother.

"Jesus, Annie. Let me see your hands." Annie stared at Justin for a moment, then out at the pasture where a herd of cows was milling about. She had cut her hands on the barbed wire as she jumped the fence. It's already been a long time since the game started, she thought to herself. Justin reached for Annie's hands gently, turning them over so that the palms faced up. Annie was a city kid, and her hands were not callused, even though it was the end of summer. The skin had pulled away from the soft center of her hands in jagged X's that seeped blood.

"Oh, Annie," Justin said, stroking the outsides of her hands softly.

It had been all right until he did that. Now she started to cry, and she couldn't stop. She tried to wipe her face with her hand, but that hurt too much, then she started to laugh as she tried to use the back of her hands like an animal's paws. Justin smiled and wiped her face with his shirttail. At least she was laughing. Justin had to admit she was tough.

"We gotta wrap these up. Get your bandanna."

They each had one around their necks, along with black hooded sweatshirts, black jeans, and black Converse high-top sneakers. Justin was fourteen, three years older than Annie, and he had insisted that Annie wear exactly what he did if she was going to join him on a mission. This was the first year her father had allowed Annie to be on the offensive team with Justin, who had been going for the flag alone ever since he was twelve.

The games had begun five years ago when Peter Shanlick had married Janis, Justin's mother. It was a second marriage for both of them, and in the first year Janis had inherited the country house in upstate New York where the annual game was played. Justin always played against his stepfather, leading the offense on Luke's team. Justin and

Peter were equally uneasy with each other. Justin was old enough to remember what it had been like before his mother had married Peter, and though he hardly ever saw his real father, he would never let Peter get too close. Justin didn't let any adult get really close except for Luke. Luke talked history with Justin, who was obsessed with the military campaigns of Western civilization, from the Holy Roman Empire to D-Day. Luke educated, tested, and joked with Justin, treating him like his son—a privilege that Peter was never allowed. Annie had always been jealous of Justin and her father, but she didn't know whether it was the attention that Luke paid to Justin, or the attention Justin paid to Luke that she longed for more.

The game was played on the two big fields above the house, with the driveway for the borderline. The flags were actually two large white T-shirts, hidden early in the day. Each team was allowed to hide its flag without being spied on; Luke and Peter were very strict about that. Then the captains would secretly divide their own teams into offense and defense. To win, the flag had to be found, captured, and brought back over the border to home territory. Since the game never began before dark, it sometimes went on until two or three in the morning.

Every year Luke and Justin synchronized their watches so they could coordinate the reconnaissance teams they sent out from the creek and the ridges that ringed the property. Justin was Luke's second-in-command and the acknowledged leader of the "Hard Core Youth Corps," as Luke liked to call the children. Annie's and Justin's families had been meeting once a year to play Capture the Flag ever since Annie was six years old, which was as far back as she could remember.

The first six years of her life were gone, as if a gray metal wall had come down in her mind in 1967. That was how she thought of it: a clean, smooth metal wall. When her parents talked about the apartment they had lived in, or the nursery school she had attended, there were no pictures in her mind to go along with the words. The earliest moment that she could actually remember was sitting with Luke on the edge of her parents' big bed inside an apartment with long hallways and high windows that faced north. Luke was telling her that her mother, Ellen—everyone called their parents by their first names then—had gone away during the night. She was sick, but she hadn't gone to the hospital. She would be fine. She would call soon from wherever they had sent her. Annie had wondered who "they" were, and if her mother and father were part of "them" or not. Annie and Luke were going to be on their own for a while, but Ellen would send for Annie when she could.

After that morning, Annie could remember everything. The farm where she visited her mother that summer. The day Ellen moved back into New York with Annie and Luke, school, summers, chicken pox, a broken wrist, a dog—everything that had been filling up the last five years of her life was there for her with absolute clarity, so she decided not to worry about the first six years and only half-believed her parents when they told stories of the things they had done when she was little. She often humored them by nodding her head, as if she knew what they were talking about when they made references to that time.

Now Justin wrapped her hands in the bandannas. They felt better wrapped up tight, and Annie thought they looked dramatic. She knew that when the game was over, she could show them to Ellen, who would wash them in hydrogen peroxide until they fizzed, and to Luke, who would be proud that she would do anything for the game. These hands might make her a hero.

Justin checked his watch. "Forty-five minutes until the charge," he said. He took off his glasses and wiped them reflexively. "We've still got time, but we gotta get to the flag."

The clouds had thinned just enough to give them some light, and Annie could see the closest tree line running north and south just beyond them.

"But you said that we were too far north, that we weren't even supposed to be in the cow pasture."

"Just hold on a minute, Annie." Justin refused to be wrong, ever.

He squatted down on the ground and handed her his flashlight. "Here, hold this steady."

It hurt Annie's hands to grip the flashlight as Justin drew a map in the dirt. This year Justin had made a relief map at school of the fields around the country house, and he and Luke had met in the city for weeks before the game, setting up two-front wars and four-pronged attacks. Phalanxes of cousins spread out in his dreams. Now he drew a large square with one curved line down the center. He had a nervous way of pushing his fine, light brown hair back from his face, now that it was long and it was always slipping out from behind his ears. He refused to tie it back in a ponytail because he thought that looked too feminine. Justin was almost always in motion, even if it was just moving his hands to his face for perpetual nail-biting and hair adjustment. Annie's hair was rough and curly. She envied everything about Justin, his perfect hair, his sureness. She watched him finish drawing the map, and he poked at it with a stick as Annie began to shiver and the small white circle of light from the flashlight trembled at the edges of the map. Justin ignored her shaking; this was war.

"That line is the driveway to the house," he said, pointing with his stick, "and the borderline between the two territories."

"Justin, I already know—"

"Listen, dipshit, I just want to check our bearings, O.K.?"

Annie kept quiet.

"If this is our side—" Justin pointed to one half, "and this is Peter's, then they've probably got their prison closer to the house, here at the bottom of the driveway. If Peter's team hid their flag up near the tree line—"

"Like they do every year," Annie said.

Justin gave her a look. "No shit, Sherlock—then the flag is on the northern edge of their field. We put our flag in the center of our field, where it can be guarded from all sides."

"Which is smarter," Annie said.

"Which is smarter, according to traditional warfare. But depending on who is guarding the flag—in this case your mother—it may or may not be well defended from the enemy. Luke always puts too many people guarding the prison and not enough people guarding the flag."

"But they always come over and tag the prisoners free as soon as we capture them," Annie said. "All they have to do is sneak up and touch one of them, then they all tag each other, and they're free. It's not fair."

"I know how it's done, Annie. It's not fair—it's the rules of the game. Hey, all we have to do is sneak up, grab their flag, and then run back over the border to our side without getting tagged. If it's so easy—"

"I didn't say it was easy, Justin." She hated it when he was sarcastic. He had learned it from her father. Luke was the kind of man who frightened people at cocktail parties.

"Good. Because it's not." Justin was cold, triumphant. Annie wanted to walk away, to change the scene in front of her by turning on the television or reading a book. That's what she did at home, but here there was nowhere to walk away to. She held the flashlight and kept quiet. Before morning this will be over, she thought, and I won't remember anything but how I got the scars on my hands. Her mother would want to know.

"Look at the map," Justin was saying, his face close to the dirt circle. "I think that we're in this cow pasture here—north of the enemy's field—so if we keep heading east, we'll come to the tree line, and then we can find the creek behind their field, and we're home free."

"Which way is east?" Annie turned off the flashlight. She wanted to be on the way to the flag so that they wouldn't have to talk anymore. "Is that the tree line you mean?" She pointed with the flashlight. "Which way is east, Justin?"

"I don't know." Justin looked past her.

"What?"

He wouldn't look at her. Annie waved an arm in front of his face. "Justin? Let's go."

Justin turned on her fast, and Annie pulled back. He looked as if he were going to hit her, but when he spoke, his voice was quiet.

"I don't know which way is east. I've never known which way anything is when I leave Manhattan. Uptown, downtown; east, west. It's so easy there. But out here . . . Who the fuck knows, Annie. I never know."

"But all these years you've been out here alone."

"I get lost every year." He grabbed her wrist suddenly and pulled her up against him. She could feel his rib cage pound against her. "Annie, you're on this mission with me because Luke made me take you, remember? Don't you dare tell. Don't you ever tell."

"I won't, Justin, I promise I won't."

"Don't tell Luke."

"No."

Justin pulled her closer and covered her mouth with his, pushing his tongue inside of her mouth. Annie couldn't breathe, and she pulled back from him. She had never been kissed like that before, never had any boy kiss her at all.

Justin kissed her again, and this time Annie let him have her mouth as if it was part of a dare she couldn't refuse, then she let him have the inside of her shirt, her barely beginning breasts. Each new part of her that he grabbed froze her into shock. I am not my body, she thought, as he pushed her onto the ground. He pulled his pants down and pulled her sweatshirt up, leaving the snap of her jeans fastened as he rubbed himself against her naked stomach. She had never even seen a man's sex before except in pictures, and she was surprised by how solid it felt against her skin. She was afraid to look down and see it, and she hoped he wouldn't make her touch it. Almost in response he grabbed her wrists and pinned her down. His breathing got stronger, and she felt disgust for the first time. She hated his desperate pushing over and over again. Each time he pushed himself along the space between her navel and her chest he erased her more and more. She began to fight him, twisting her hips to try to get out from under him, but that was when he made a sound that made her realize that he wanted her, really wanted her. Annie liked that. Her hips lifted up harder against him of their own accord, and she felt her body betray her by its response to him. This body is not mine, she thought, and hated him for being able to do that to her.

Annie was surprised that he lay so still afterwards, trembling just slightly, with his thin chest pounding against hers and his breath clouding the cold air next to her face. Annie was afraid to move. He had stopped very suddenly. Every part of her felt pounded and filthy. Her mouth had a metallic taste, and she ran her hands along the outside of her own hips roughly, ashamed at their betrayal. She had no desire to cry, and this surprised her. It felt as if a block of ice had been placed just inside her sacrum, and a new cold hardness ran from her breastbone to her pelvis. Justin rolled off of her, and she glanced quickly at his body. His sex lay there as if nothing had happened, as if nothing could ever happen there again.

"Now we've both done something we can't tell," Justin said.

So he knew; he had felt her hips lifting into him, and she hated him for that more than for grabbing her wrists or using his weight as a weapon. He knew that for a second she had liked it. Annie pulled her sweatshirt down and used it to wipe off her stomach. Her belly felt sticky and foreign, and she wished that she had soap and water to rub off the spot where he had been. As soon as the game is over, I'm going to take a shower, she thought; I'll tell them I'm cold. Below her navel Annie was still hairless. There were girls at school who had hair there, but not Annie, not yet. Rubbing hard at the place on her stomach where he had been, she felt a wave of nausea, and she leaned over and vomited violently.

Justin reached over and touched her back. "Are you O.K.?" He sounded different to Annie, not so sure of everything anymore. His face looked younger.

"No." Annie said. He reached for her again. "Don't touch me," she said softly.

She watched his face harden back into the old Justin. "Are you gonna tell," he asked, "about getting lost?"

"I'm not gonna tell."

Justin got up and walked over to the fence, hitching his pants up as he walked. The wind was picking up, breaking the clouds apart into great gray chunks, and the sky opened just long enough for Annie to watch him reach the barbed wire and clasp his hands hard around it. He came back to her and held out his bloodied hands.

"Swear?" he asked. "Blood brothers."

Annie held out her hands, and he unwrapped the bandannas. The bleeding had stopped, but it started up again when he pulled the cloth away. Annie grabbed his hands and held them tight, so that their palms were pressed hard against each other and she could see Justin wince behind his glasses. Then she let go.

"Blood brothers," she said quietly.

He helped her wrap up her hands again but said that he didn't need to wrap his, he could suck the blood off as he walked.

Annie started walking. "This way," she said.

"How do you know?" asked Justin.

"Just because I know. It feels right."

"It feels right? This isn't Central Park, Annie."

Annie sped up. Justin followed her without saying anything. She had something on him for the first time in her life. But she knew that he had something on her, too, and she wasn't exactly sure what it was. All she knew was that she wasn't going to tell.

They ran across the field without bothering to hide. If they were going in the right direction, they would hit the creek. If not, there wouldn't be time to backtrack. In fifteen minutes Luke was supposed to lead the charge up the hill to Peter's flag as a tactical diversion for Justin and Annie. If they didn't get to their positions behind the flag, ready to run for it before Luke began the charge, the entire mission would fail. When they got into the tree line, they moved under the branches, crouching and running. Justin held back the big pine branches for her so that they wouldn't snap in her face. The sound of the creek kept getting louder, so they knew that they were going the right way.

Annie slid down the bank and grabbed a tree that bent over with her into the water. The creek came up to her knees and the current sucked on her sneakers and jeans. Justin was already heading downstream. She slipped over the rocks and grabbed at the banks. Justin stopped and pulled down a branch that hung over the water, bending it back and forth until it broke. He stripped off the smaller branches with his knife and handed it to her.

"Here, use it for a walking stick as long as we're in the creek. No one will hear us down here, and we can get as far as the flag before we hit the woods again."

"Thanks."

They started moving again. At every sound, they crouched and froze, not moving until Justin gave the signal. The enemy could be patrolling the banks; the creek was the back border of their territory.

"Just stick close to the shore and they won't see us," Justin said, pulling himself up over a log.

"What if Peter's team is doing the same thing?"

"No way. They'd never think of walking the creek, it's too far away from our side. Too cold."

The bottom kept changing. The rocks were covered with scum that scraped off onto their sneakers, and the mud pulled on their heels. It was all about balance. Justin jumped from one gravel bar to another, and Annie felt the water come up to her belly button in the dark. She had to pee and secretly let herself go, wishing the warmth would stay in her crotch.

When they got to the pasture where they thought Peter's flag was hidden they heard the shouting begin, and Justin and Annie ran for the tree line, their sneakers breaking out from the water loud and clumsy. They ran almost all the way up the hill before they stopped. Annie's jeans were heavy as she squatted beside him.

Justin checked his watch. "We're late."

Then the music broke out over everything. Blasting up from the garage next to the farmhouse, the 1812 Overture, top volume. A bare bulb flicked on down below, and they saw someone waving his arms in the light.

"It's the charge!" Justin ran from the trees. "Go for the flag, Annie!"

She tried to follow him as he cut across and up the hill but he could run faster than she could, and her wet jeans slowed her down. She didn't know where Peter's flag was hidden, and everyone was running away from them, down the hill toward Luke's side. At that moment she realized it was Peter's team that was charging. She spun around and saw the enemy, moving up on her from behind. Annie stopped running and started to walk, real slow, in the other direction. She was still supposed to find Peter's flag, and where was Justin?

"Liz?" It was Tessa, Justin's stepsister.

Annie mumbled and kept moving.

"Annie!" Tessa turned and ran at her. Annie took off down the hill. Now her only hope was to make it back over to Luke's side without getting captured herself.

"They've got the flag! They've got it!" Annie heard someone yelling, and then, when they were almost to the driveway/borderline, Tessa tackled her. She pulled the hood of Annie's sweatshirt down. Annie's whole wet body was pounded into the ground.

"Annie! Got you!"

Peter Shanlick stumbled past them down the driveway, the white flag slung around his body.

"We won!"

Tessa let her go and ran after her father.

"We got it!" Peter was yelling, "Got it from you again, Luke. Come out and give yourself up!"

Justin's voice came from behind Annie, harsh and breaking as it always did these days.

"Fuck you, Shanlick! Fuck you!"

Listening to his voice Annie wanted Justin to win even more than she wanted to be the hero. Even more than she wanted Luke to win, she wanted Justin to win. She stayed where she was and watched Peter Shanlick dance down the driveway as he laughed back at

Justin. The other kids leapt and reached for the flag. Down at the house someone started the bonfire that had been prepared hours earlier, and everyone began to come out of the fields.

Annie walked to the edge of the driveway. She was going to wait until she saw Luke. She knew that Justin wouldn't want to see her, that he might not even come down to the fire for a long time. If they had won, everything would be different.

Then she saw the car. She knew it was her parents' car because of the sound of the engine; it was a VW bug. The headlights swerved as it went around the people who came down the driveway and headed for the house. Peter Shanlick stopped in front of the car and held out his arms. The flag flapped behind him, and the headlights shone through the cloth, making a warped white face in the dark.

Annie waited for the window to roll down to find out where her mother was going, maybe to the store to get cigarettes. But the window stayed up, and Peter finally sidestepped out of the way and hit the hood, then the roof of the car, as he walked past. Annie could see them both inside. Her mother was at the wheel, and she couldn't see her father's face. She ran after them. Her last chance was to catch them at the top of the hill where they always stopped to look both ways. The car stopped, and Annie could see them talking, heads close together, silhouetted in the windshield. She stopped to watch them, and she saw her mother's hand reach up to her father's face and then drift back down slowly, as if underwater. Luke got out of the car.

"Mom! Wait! I want a chocolate bar!"

The car pulled out onto the road.

"What are you doing here?" Luke asked her, as if she shouldn't have been there.

"I want Mom to bring me back a Hershey bar from the store."

He walked past her down toward the house. She ran to keep up.

"She's going back to the city early, Annie."

"Is it because we lost the game?"

Luke slowed down a minute and let her catch up. He took her hand.

"No. We'll see her tomorrow, Annie, when we get home."

Annie wondered how they would get home now that her mother had taken the car. But she didn't ask her father anything else as they walked the rest of the way down the driveway to Peter and Janis's house. Now she won't see my hands, thought Annie. If she had seen Annie's hands she would have washed them with her special soap from France, and they would have become soft and gentle like hers. Annie hated her own hands. They were ragged looking, with bitten nails and cuticles.

"Dad, look." Annie showed him her bandaged hands. He stopped walking and tried to examine them in the dark.

"What is it, what did you do?" he asked. The bandannas she and Justin had wrapped them in were wet from the stream, and he squeezed water from them as he grabbed her hands.

"Ouch! Stop it!" Annie cried. "I cut them going over a barbed wire fence. Justin and I were late and then—"

Annie stopped, remembering she couldn't tell about getting lost. "I'd better wash them in hydrogen peroxide," she murmured.

Luke put her hands down and looked back at the road, distracted, then started walking again. "I'm sure Peter and Janis have some. Ask Janis." He paused and looked down at the house. "Goddamn Shanlick, winning again. I just want to win the game again, Annie, you know? It's been three years since we won." He stabbed the air with his hands as he spoke. Luke always spoke very quickly, his mind forever outpacing his mouth, and he had a graceful way of moving. Her mother always agreed with him when he boasted of being a marvelous dancer.

"I know." Annie half-jogged alongside him to keep up. He usually wanted a full report from Annie on how the game had been; he always wanted to discuss the game. "Dad, Justin and I started out just like you said, heading north along the borderline, but then—"

"Three years . . ." Luke wasn't listening anymore. "Goddamn Shanlick."

"Yeah." Annie slowed down; they were almost at the bonfire. She let him walk ahead of her into the circle of people at the fire. "Yeah," she said. "Goddamn Shanlick."

Peter Shanlick had been Luke's best friend at college. When Peter married Janis, she had brought with her her two sons: Justin and his younger brother, Nick, who now spent the summers and weekends with Peter's three girls: Tessa, Liz, and Sam. The kids' names would be spun off, in order of age, whenever anybody talked about them, but everyone usually called them "the Boys" and "the Girls"; they even called each other that. All five of them were always there for the game, with Janis and the girls playing on their father's team and both boys playing against Peter on Luke's team.

Tessa was the oldest girl, one year older than Annie, with long straight black hair and a gap between her two front teeth. Everyone said that she was the prettiest of the three. Hitting puberty seemed effortless for her, and she had a subtle sexuality that made her seem older than twelve. Sam was the youngest, a ten-year-old who was still considered the baby. She had brown eyes so big, with lashes so long and thick, that they outsized her face and added to her waiflike demeanor. She was a pistol, who never tired of teasing her stepbrothers, and she was almost strong enough to wrestle Nick to the ground. Liz was in the middle, exactly Annie's age. She had the reputation of being the smartest of the sisters, and the plain one, but Annie thought she was the real beauty. Of the three, Liz most closely resembled their father, with Peter's square jaw and dark Germanic eyes. Her hair was chopped short above her shoulders in a thick dark mane that Annie envied. Two years ago, at Capture the Flag, Annie and Liz had cut themselves with a razor and sucked hard on the tips of each other's fingers, trying to get at more than just the little globe of blood that came out first. Liz had wanted to cut deeper, but Annie said that it didn't matter how much blood you got as long as you got some.

For the girls the summers peaked the weekend of the game. They exulted in the Shanlick victories and prepared for hours with Annie, outfitting themselves in dark clothes. The next day they led Annie to the secret places they had discovered that summer: a climbing rock or a hidden meadow. They lay there watching the sky and retelling their journeys through the night before.

As soon as Annie and Luke got to the fire he went into the house to get a drink. Nick was throwing firecrackers into the bonfire. Nick had never been committed to the game the way Justin was. What he liked was the party afterwards. Nick was a charmer. He was as quick as Justin without the mean streak, and he liked to make the girls laugh. It had been Nick who had turned on the music at the moment of the charge, glad of an excuse to leave the field and get warm in the house. Annie crouched next to Liz and Tessa, who were ripping open a bag of marshmallows.

"Beat you again, Annie." Liz grinned at her.

"Wait till next year," Annie said, narrowing her eyes at Liz and trying to look tough. Liz and Tessa laughed.

"You're never going to beat us," said Tessa. "Your plans are too complicated. Dad just waits until everybody gets drunk enough and then charges up the hill to your flag. It's easy."

"You haven't won every year," Annie said, but they knew from her voice that she was giving up.

"Where's your mom?" asked Tessa.

"She went home."

"How come?"

"I don't know. I think she was feeling sick or something." It sounded lame, and Annie knew it, but the girls weren't really that interested and they let it pass. Ellen had always kept to the periphery of Capture the Flag weekend.

"How was scouting with Justin?" asked Liz.

"You couldn't pay me to scout with Justin," Tessa said. "What a bully."

"That's just because you're not his favorite anymore, Tessa." Liz surveyed her marshmallow, blowing out the flames on its blackened head. "Last year you were singing a different tune." Nobody could get away with anything around Liz; she forgot nothing and seemed unaware of the consequences of her bluntness. To Annie, who measured and questioned every word before speaking, she seemed fearless.

"Justin's favorite! He makes me sick," said Tessa. "Go get some more sticks, Annie," she said, cramming a graham cracker into her mouth. "I lost my knife."

Annie ran out to the edge of the woods, glad to get away. She didn't want to talk about Justin. He still hadn't come down to the fire, and Annie wondered if he was going to stay away all night, go back up to the cow pasture with his stick and draw maps on the ground for next year's game. The air away from the fire felt like the water did when you swam into a cold spot in the pond. Annie shivered and pulled up her sweatshirt to see if there was any mark on her stomach from where he had been; it already seemed like a long time ago. Her stomach was covered with little translucent flakes that she rubbed off with her hands. She brought her fingers up to her mouth to taste them: They were sour and sweaty. She touched her tongue to her palm again and didn't know if that taste was her or Justin since she had been sweating so much going up the stream. If their sweat had mingled, did that mean anything? And what he had done to her, or with her, would it change everything too? She pulled at a pile of wood that was waiting to go into the fire, picking four small sticks, just for the girls to roast with. Running back to the fire she passed them out to Tessa and Liz—Sam didn't want to move from Janis's lap, where she sat wrapped in an army blanket. Every time a firecracker went off she cheered. Annie hated marshmallows, but she loved to play with candles and matches—anything to do with fire—so she roasted them for everybody else. She made them perfect, so that they burned her fingers as she pulled them off the stick, and then she put them on top of the chocolate bar and graham cracker balanced on her knee.

Justin walked into the circle quietly, from the same direction she had just come from, and Annie felt a line of nerves go from the base of her spine to her skull in one clean shot. He squatted near the fire without looking at her, and she worried that he had been spying on her at the woodpile. Now she watched him talking to Nick, poking the fire, and was surprised that he still acted exactly like Justin. She felt as if her skin had been exchanged for someone else's, and was almost surprised that no one had noticed.

She put another graham cracker on top of a stratification of burned marshmallow and chocolate and passed it to Justin, who was squatting next to Liz. He took it as if it was his by right, without looking at her. Annie hated him for that, even though it wasn't unusual—Justin had a way of making people want to do things for him; of all the kids he had made himself the arbiter of cool. Each of his stepsisters had had a crush on Justin more than once. The only person who had never worshipped him was Nick.

The graham cracker snapped in Justin's mouth and crumbled down the front of his sweatshirt. "Why can't *you* make them like this, Tessa?"

"Shut up, Justin."

Tessa only made them for herself. Nick sat next to her, and they talked quietly, giggles rising occasionally. Nick was small for twelve, with bright green eyes and clear, almost transparent skin. Janis said that Nick looked like his father and Justin looked like her, but Annie had never met their father and the boys didn't talk about him. She only knew that he lived somewhere out West, farther from New York than Annie had ever been.

The brothers' alliances with their stepsisters seemed to change every year: This summer it was Tessa and Nick. Annie and Liz both hated their little tent of conversation, as if there was nobody else around.

"You want another?" Annie asked Justin. "I'll make you another."

"You're gonna make me throw up," Justin said, finishing it off. He smiled at her for the first time, and Annie realized that she had been holding her breath.

Sam was asleep on Janis's lap; her thumb had snuck inside of her mouth, and her breath made little clouds of white in the air. Janis was leaning back and talking to somebody Annie didn't know, a neighbor with straight brown hair that was cut like a man's; she constantly blew the smoke from her cigarette into her drink. Janis was a rangy woman whose hair was dyed auburn. Her fingers were covered with gaudy rings that Annie loved. They clicked against each other in the dark, and Annie watched her as she threw her head back and laughed hard and loud; her laugh was always recognizable. Janis didn't care about being loud, and she was one of Annie's favorite grown-ups. She never seemed to care whose kid it was that she was kissing and hugging, or whose face she was cleaning with a spit-moistened Kleenex. She flipped the sleeping Sam easily from one side of her body to another as she got more comfortable and leaned in to talk more intimately with her neighbor.

Peter Shanlick threw an empty bottle onto the rock pile behind the bonfire. Everybody turned to watch, and Peter threw another, then another, stepping farther back each time and sending the bottle spinning in a perfect arc.

Nick left the bonfire circle, ran over to the garage, and came out with the football. He threw it to Peter. Peter was in a good mood after winning the game, and he grabbed the ball and ran off into the dark. Nick flipped on the light outside the kitchen door and the bugs swarmed where the grass lit up.

"Girls against boys!" Peter shouted. "Janis, you be captain!"

Janis laughed at him, but Justin jumped up and ran over to Nick and Peter, hitting each of the three girls lightly on the head as he ran by. Standing just outside the fire circle Justin jutted his skinny hips to one side and stuck out his lower lip at them.

"Chickens . . ." he drawled, then turned and shook his butt in their direction. Luke was already up, and he grabbed Justin by the shoulder, whispering something in his ear that Annie couldn't catch, but they laughed together like equals. Annie and Liz looked at each other, then Janis sighed dramatically and passed the still sleeping Sam over to the woman with the man's haircut. Janis put out her cigarette and walked slowly over to the lawn, the three girls following behind. Janis looked at Peter, Luke, and the boys yelling and tossing the ball back and forth, and she laughed once, very loudly, then pulled Annie, Tessa, and Liz into a huddle. She grinned at all of them, heads pulled together so that the light leaked in around their cheekbones and over the tops of their heads like a diffused electric halo.

"Anyone have a plan?" Janis asked.

"Get the ball and run," said Tessa. "Then go back to the fire and make more marshmallows." Janis nodded so seriously that they all broke up laughing, clapped their hands just like the boys always did, and split up. Liz passed the ball off to Tessa just before Nick tackled her and sent her screaming into the wet grass. Luke tried to intercept it and slipped. Annie was behind him and went for the ball but fumbled. It bounced off her bandaged fingers, bending them back, and rolled into the fire.

"Get it, Annie! Get it!" Luke yelled at her from the lawn.

Annie grabbed a stick, but the fire was too hot, and Annie only managed to push the ball farther and farther into the fire. It hurt her hands to hold the stick, and the fire was burning the edges of her bandanna wrappings.

"Get it, Annie! Just get it!" Luke yelled.

Luke's arm reached right past her into the fire, knocking her down onto the old ash gray rocks that made the bonfire circle. She heard the crack of her skull on the rocks inside of her own ears and saw his fingers grab the football, not slipping, and scoop it out of the hot center. She felt for her head with her hand and then her wrist, since she couldn't feel anything with her hands. When she brought her wrist down from her head it was wet with blood, and she started to cry.

"Oh, Christ." Luke picked her up, kissed her, and she felt the football pressing into her back. It was hot from the fire and there was the smell of burnt leather.

"Where does it hurt?"

"My head."

He tried to put her down and look into her face. She didn't want him to let go of her and buried her head in the sheepskin collar of his coat, making Luke kneel down with her on the ground. She couldn't stop crying, and the wind was blowing smoke from the bonfire right at them, making her father's features look blurred, underwater. Luke had to let go of her and rub his eyes to be able to see her, and this suddenly terrified Annie.

"I'm here, Daddy. I'm here," she yelled, as if she were a little child.

Luke stared at her. "What?"

Annie felt herself starting to blush, every part of her neck and face flushed bright red, and she couldn't answer, so she hid her head in the warm lapel of Luke's jacket again. He held her silently, and she knew that he really didn't need an answer anymore; he was letting her hide.

The football game had stopped as soon as she fumbled the ball into the fire, and she slowly became aware that everyone had gathered around her father and her.

"What a baby," she heard Justin say, from far away.

"Is she all right?" Liz asked. Then Janis came up and took her hand.

"She'll be O.K." Janis stopped and looked down. "Jesus, Annie, what is this on your hands?"

"I climbed a barbed wire fence."

"Well, let's go into the house and wash up. You're all right, aren't you, Annie?"

"I guess so." Annie took in huge gulps of wood smoke between each word. She blinked and panted.

Janis picked her up and carried her toward the house. Looking over the top of Janis's shoulder, Annie watched her father slowly sit down in the dirt and pull the football into his stomach, not bothering to move out of the way of the smoke. He stayed that way, rocking the football back and forth in the cup of his body, until Janis carried her through the screen door to the kitchen and she couldn't see him anymore. The water from the sink ran warm over her head, and she watched it go from red to pink.

"Not so bad," Janis said, tucking a towel around Annie's neck, "not so bad."

• • •

Luke and Annie took the train from Albany to New York City the next morning. Luke gave her money for chips and Coke from the dining car and settled down with the paper. Annie sat on the seat opposite him so that she could ride in the same direction that the train was going. She was armed with another book in the series from *Little House on the Prairie.* Ellen had always told her never to go anywhere without a sweater and a book. As Annie watched the fields of upstate New York glide by the window, she pretended that she and Luke were heading out to homestead an unknown land together.

Annie missed the drive down to the city on the highway. She loved the bare roads up north when they would be the only car for a while, and she and Ellen counted the out-of-state license plates. As they got closer to the city they always turned onto the Saw Mill River Parkway, with its wooden tollbooths like fairy-tale cottages. Luke would pull the car up so that Annie could throw a quarter from the back window into the basket that made the arm from the tollbooth rise like a drawbridge to let them pass. Her father always told stories on the long drive. Luke attached great importance to his own history and repeated it to everyone, assuming that it must be of interest to them as well. Annie loved the stories and made him repeat them over and over again so that she could memorize them—not that he needed much urging. There was the story of his parents' summer cottage on the Rhode Island shore being swept away by the hurricane of '38, leaving only the straw wastebasket untouched. There was the day he had gone alone with a gun and shot a snake on Copperhead Hill.

Annie knew that her father wanted to imprint his history upon her until it became part of her body. The stories made Annie feel important and safe. She secretly copied his style of handwriting and his signature, as if copying everything about him would make her belong more and more to him, becoming an integral part of him. The more she imitated him, the prouder he became of her, and he let everyone know it. Then, once he started to include Annie herself in his repertoire of stories, she felt that she had begun to make certain that he wouldn't be able to leave her behind.

While Annie's mother loved to read aloud and tell stories to Annie, she never talked about her side of the family, and visits to Ellen's relatives were infrequent. When Ellen wasn't there, Luke would make remarks about her side of the family, hinting at grand fortunes that Ellen would never see and a distant relative locked up in an asylum in western Connecticut. It was true that Ellen had no money of her own to speak of, but she did have some good pieces of furniture, and once she had told Annie that her side of the family was related to a witch who was burned in Salem. This outdid Luke's side by far, and Annie wanted to know everything, but her mother had forgotten the details of the story, only that she was certain it was true.

Last night, her mother had driven all the way back to the city alone, with no one to throw quarters for her. Annie worried about her. She put down her book and asked Luke again if they should have called this morning, to make sure she had gotten home all right. But Luke said that he was sure she had, and he hadn't wanted to wake her up if she was sleeping.

"If there was bad news, we'd hear about it," he said. "They always know how to find you if anything really bad happens. She's fine, Annie." He went back to the paper, and Annie stared out the window, hating him now. She heard him put the paper down again, and knew he was looking at her; she stayed with the fields and the cows.

"Did you bring along *Treasure Island*?" he asked.

Of course she had. Even though she was old enough to read anything to herself by now, she had brought the book along just in case she could get Luke or Ellen to read to her. She usually had each of her parents reading simultaneously from a different book. *Treasure Island* was a cliff-hanger, and Annie hadn't been able to wait for Luke to finish reading, as their plan of one chapter per night was often postponed for one reason or another. So she had gone on and read ahead to find out what happened to Jim Hawkins and Long John Silver—but she did not admit this to Luke, and when he asked her where they had left off she told him to begin at her favorite part: when Jim sneaks away from the safety of the stockade on Treasure Island and goes off on his own adventure to save the ship.

Luke leaned back with the battered copy of the book that had been his own and draped his long legs gracefully across one another. He held out an arm. Annie wouldn't smile yet, but she came over to sit next to him on the leather banquette of the old train. He put one arm around her, allowing her to look at the page, as he had always done, and began to read:

"I was a fool, if you like, and certainly I was going to do a foolish, over-bold act; but I was determined to do it with all the precautions in my power."

Luke threw himself into it. His voice was deep and resonant, and he punctuated the reading with guttural laughter for the drunken mutineers on board the boat, then dropped to almost a whisper as he described Jim Hawkins rowing up close to the ship in his tiny coracle, climbing aboard to be alone with the mutineers, then grasping the anchor line and sawing it through with his knife, letting the great ship loose from her moorings. Even though Annie and Luke both knew how everything ended up, Jim's long drift around Treasure Island with the schooner in sight, shipping water into the coracle and almost drifting out to sea forever, seemed interminable. His coracle, the only means of escape, was smashed by the ship, and Jim had to defend himself against Israel Hands, the bloodthirsty buccaneer who finally fell to his own death after trying to murder Jim. At the end of this adventure lay Long John Silver, and the parrot saying "pieces-of-eight," but Luke stopped just before Jim was caught by Silver and his success in bringing the great schooner ashore was still intact.

"More tonight," said Luke, looking out the window at the approaching tenements of the South Bronx.

Annie begged him for more, just one more chapter, and she felt him waver, but then the train tracks suddenly got rough and the car swayed back and forth as she caught sight of the George Washington

Bridge, which dipped and swung in time, the high white lights anchoring New Jersey, the Great Plains, and the Wild Wild West to Manhattan. Annie knew that she was home, that somewhere against the shore the Little Red Lighthouse was talking to the bridge in code. Then the train shot underground and everything went black. Luke got up, and everyone in the car began to gather their things from the racks overhead.

"New York City. Grand Central Station!" called the conductor as he walked through; his brimmed hat shone, his pants were pressed to an immovable crease, and his shoes gleamed. He looked too clean to work in New York City, thought Annie; he would go on through the city to other, cleaner places: Maryland, North Carolina, Florida: the South. He never looked at their faces as he flipped tickets from the metal strip above their seats. "Grand Central Station!"

"How did it go?" Ellen asked as she opened the apartment door. She looked consciously put together. Her slender figure was shown off by a white cardigan, which clung to her torso, and fashionable peg-legged plaid pants, which matched the scarf she had tied around her reddish-brown curls. Her eyes were not made up; they were aquamarine blue, even looking violet in some lights, like Elizabeth Taylor's, as Luke was fond of pointing out, and she didn't need anything to make them stand out from her face. In any case, her skin was so pale that it seemed as if she were always wearing a light blue eye shadow, the color of her eyes showing through the translucence of her eyelids. Annie had inherited her hair but not her eyes, and what good was one without the other? she thought. People were always saying how beautiful her mother was, and then looking at her with slight disappointment. Annie took after her father, except for the hair. She was frail, with shoulders that already stooped over like his, despite her teachers nagging her to stand up straight. She didn't feel small, however, and was always surprised when she heard people describe her as short. They must not know many eleven-year-olds, she would think, for in her mind she was as tall, or taller, than her classmates.

"Shanlick won." Annie started to drag her bag down the hallway to her bedroom.

"I'm sorry," Ellen said. She took one handle of the bag and helped her.

Please don't pretend to care who wins, thought Annie. She kept her eyes fixed on the woodwork of the hallway floor and tried to toss it off: "We'll get them next year."

Ellen heaved Annie's bag onto the bed. She took Annie's face between her hands and made her look her in the eye. Annie's small, narrow eyes from Luke's side of the family. Ellen held her there a moment, then hugged her hard. "What was it like scouting with Justin?"

"It was pretty good. I had to climb a barbed wire fence, see?"

Annie showed her hands, which looked disappointingly better today. She had wanted to be able to show Ellen the dried blood. She wasn't going to tell Ellen about falling into the fire during the football game; she knew that Luke wouldn't want her to tell. Still, her mother seemed quite impressed with the marks on her hands and gave Annie permission to use some of her hand cream on them until they healed. Then the buzzer to the apartment door sounded, and Annie ran to let Luke inside. Ellen let Annie get the door, then went up and took some luggage from Luke. Annie carefully watched her father watching Ellen, who was asking about the end of the game as if she was sorry she had to miss it, but it was unavoidable. She was feeling much better now and she hoped that everyone understood.

"Of course, of course," her father was saying, kissing her more than once. "Don't even think about it."

Annie wasn't going to ask why Ellen had left the game. She didn't want to ruin everything. Ellen's disappearances had been happening for as long as Annie could remember, and it was a mistake to bring them up once they were all together again. They usually told Annie that it was a migraine, and that Ellen had to lie in her room with all of the shades drawn and keep perfectly quiet. Sometimes Annie wouldn't see her for days at a time except when Luke brought her in for a goodnight kiss. She knew enough now to stop believing in a migraine after the first day or so, though she still kept quiet and avoided her parents' bedroom, where the window shades were dark red with little tassels, and there were always too many water glasses and scattered blue-and-red capsules on the nightstand. On those days their room felt as if all of the air had been sucked out of it.

But whatever it had been last night, Ellen made Annie laugh at everything tonight and told her that they were just alike. Annie knew this wasn't really true, since Ellen was beautiful and she was not. But she didn't mind hearing it. She wanted to be like Ellen, who laughed and draped her feet with red painted toenails over the side of the armchair. Tonight Luke would make a martini for Ellen and a scotch and soda for himself. They would watch the news on television until the report came on about that day in Vietnam. Then Luke would shut off the television and say that there were always more American casualties than they said on TV: They were lying about the numbers. Ellen would agree, finish her drink, and then go to cook up minute steaks and Minute rice. Everything would be all right.

Three weeks later, school began again, and Annie wouldn't see Justin or the girls for a long time. The day after the game Justin had been nice to her again, more like the old Justin, and now she thought about him almost every day but never called him or the girls. She felt it was up to Luke to call Peter and Janis and make a plan that she would naturally be a part of, but when she asked her father about it he just gave her the girls' phone number again, and she hadn't called. She saw less and less of Luke during the fall. Last spring they had moved into a new apartment on Central Park West, and Luke had two jobs now, editing a magazine of military history as well as working at the publishing house. He stayed late almost every day, complaining about it when he came home, but Annie and Ellen both knew that he liked to complain. Sometimes he spent the night at the office, calling home around bedtime to say that he had to keep working on changes on a new manuscript from one of his authors or he would never make his deadline. He was just vague enough that Annie was never sure whether to believe him or not, though Ellen registered no emotion at the news, and he often spoke only to Annie, leaving her to pass on the message to her mother. Then Annie wouldn't see him until dinner the next night, when he came home wearing the same clothes but in a better mood.

Ellen started something new that fall with Annie: kite-flying. Ellen had taken Annie to buy a kite the day after Annie had returned from Capture the Flag. She had said that she wanted to start a new tradition that didn't involve so many people. Luke had then asked her why she didn't like his friends, and Ellen had said that was just it, they were *his* friends and she wouldn't go up to Shanlick's place next year. Luke kept pushing her for details about who she didn't like and why, then told her how much those people liked her. In the end only Annie had gone to buy the kite with Ellen, though Luke said he knew kites better than anyone. But he did approve of the kite when they brought it home, and he had even come to fly it with them once this fall. On good days, when the sky was as blue as ice and everyone on the street was wearing their jackets open to the wind, Annie would take the bus after school two more stops to Columbia University on upper Broadway, where Ellen taught part-time. Ellen kept the kite at her office, and they would walk over to the park next to the Hudson River, where the wind blew steadily all day off the water. On the way to the river, Ellen showed Annie how to split open the seed pods that came floating down from maple trees and covered the paving stones like tiny winged hearts. Ellen and Annie broke them in the middle and stuck them onto the ends of their noses with sticky sap from the pods, making long Pulcinella noses out of the wings.

Halloween fell on a Thursday that year, and Annie decided that she was too old to go trick-or-treating around their building. When she told Ellen that she didn't want to dress up for school or join her friends at a Halloween party, Ellen proposed that they go kite-flying instead. But when she got off the bus near Columbia that afternoon there were horses in the middle of Broadway, and Annie didn't know if she could get to her mother's office. The horses were being ridden by police, and there were more of them than Annie had ever seen before. She had grown up seeing one or two mounted police trotting down the street occasionally. The police officers on horseback were friendly and would let Annie stroke the horse's nose, or at least smile at her as they rode by. But the police in front of the gates of Columbia today were different. They carried metal shields emblazoned with the insignia of the city. They had helmets and wooden batons that they spun next to their horses' flanks. The horses seemed spooked, nervous at being so close together, and the officers constantly jerked at the reins, pulling their heads around and forcing them to walk in tight circles. The gates of Columbia were draped with makeshift banners made from bedsheets painted with slogans about Nixon and the war. "McGovern for President."

People were everywhere. Loud music was playing out one of the windows, and students danced inside the gates. The people on the street outside stared at them, shouted at them, or simply walked by—impenetrable New Yorkers. The mounted police fidgeted in their saddles, bored and nervous.

Annie had been to antiwar demonstrations with her parents before, but she had never seen Columbia look like this. Is this the revolution? she wondered, as she walked by people stretched out lazily on the university lawns. She wished that this revolution was like the one in *A Tale of Two Cities* (the new book that Luke was reading to her), with blood running in the streets and a mysterious woman knitting your fate into a scarf. Things were certainly different on campus, but it didn't feel dangerous enough. It was more exciting near the gate, with the police horses. Maybe the police would fire on the demonstrators—if Annie was there she could run to the fallen students and staunch their wounds with her shirt. She would rip her clothing into strips and bind their arms with tourniquets, save their lives until the ambulance came. If only it was that kind of revolution she could be a hero, then disappear without a trace and no one would know who she was. She could see the headline in the *New York Post:* The Child Who Saved the Revolution.

She wondered if her mother would still be in her office. What if she had left early? Would they still go to the park today? Things had been back and forth at home all week. Twice Ellen had woken Annie up for school and made breakfast, once she had even walked her to the bus stop. The other days Annie had woken up by herself, and there had been no sign of Luke or Ellen. When she looked into their bedroom, Ellen had been alone in bed, asleep with the red shades drawn, and Annie had made her own breakfast and gotten to school late. Ellen had been up this morning, though, and had told Annie to meet her after work for kite-flying. There had been no word at school for Annie that there was a change of plans, and, besides, there was a good wind and it was a warm autumn day. The trees inside the campus were aureoled in yellow and red, and all of the leaves seemed perfect and brittle, on the verge of falling. Annie had keys to the apartment and it would be easy to go home, but she wanted to get inside Columbia whether Ellen was there or not. She didn't really care about kite-flying today; she wanted to get to the dancers and the music and the pots of red paint that were being splashed onto bedsheets spread out on the grass by an important-looking young man with wire-rimmed glasses.

She threw her book bag over her shoulder and walked up to the edge of the gate, where a very worried-looking student stood with a walkie-talkie. Despite the patchy hair on his chin, which was trying very hard to be a beard, he was managing to look official, like the police. Annie decided to put on her most innocent face:

"I'm supposed to meet my mother here. She works in the English department."

"The English department is closed for the demonstration. All of the teachers have gone home."

Annie tried to look lost. "But I've been home and she's not there," she lied. "I always meet her here after school. Please, let me go look."

Annie could tell that he was wavering. He didn't know what to do with her; he didn't want to take on the responsibility. Annie pressed him.

"I know where the office is. If she's not there, I'll go right home."

He looked at the police, back at her, and let her through. He had more to worry about than a kid on campus. His walkie-talkie rattled and he picked it up from his belt. Annie was free.

"Make sure you go straight home if she's not there," he said to Annie as she scooted by. She nodded without looking at him and headed for the English building.

The building was open and everything seemed very peaceful. Two students were smoking a joint on the front steps; that was the most unusual thing Annie had seen since she entered the gates.

"If McGovern's elected it's going to change everything," one of the students said to the other. "Think about it."

"Things didn't change in Paris, not permanently. Things didn't change here after sixty-eight."

"It's not over yet."

Annie ran up the steps past them, slowing down as they exhaled, trying to catch the smoke through her nose. She knew about pot and wished that she could try it, but no one had ever offered her any. She knew that everyone probably thought she was too young, even though she knew she wasn't. She ran up the two flights of stairs to her mother's office. The building was mostly deserted, and she could hear the sound of women's voices and a typewriter from the end of the hallway. Ellen was there. Annie could hear her talking, and she stopped walking to listen.

"If too much time goes by, then I stop having any desire to talk about the little things." Annie thought that Ellen must be talking to Patricia, the teacher who shared the office with her and who was also a close friend and neighbor. Patricia lived only three blocks away, and she had been going in and out of Annie's kitchen ever since she could remember. "The details of what happened yesterday or the day before are gone forever by the time I see him. The post office, work, what Annie said at dinner, it's all mundane—nothing about art or even politics really—but these are the things that make up my life, after all."

"And once you stop including each other in the day-to-day . . . ," Patricia said slowly, sounding a bit distracted.

"Exactly," Ellen said. "It's so easy, almost like a habit, to stop including each other in anything."

"Amazing how fast it happens." Annie heard Patricia light a cigarette.

"It doesn't feel fast to me," Ellen said quietly, so that Annie could barely hear her.

"What do you mean?"

"It's like we've been sitting in one place forever. The landscape doesn't change."

"Mmm . . ." Patricia took another long drag of her cigarette, and the typing started up again. Annie couldn't tell if it was her mother or Patricia going back to work, but then the second typewriter started up and Annie breathed again. She got her most casual walk going in advance and went into the office. Ellen stopped typing and gave her a fantastic smile. She pushed her chair out and gave Annie a hug.

"You made it! I knew you would." She turned to Patricia. "See, I told you my kid could make it here. This demonstration is a joke compared to sixty-eight."

"Maybe so." Patricia put out her cigarette and squinted up at Annie, smiling. "How're you doing, kid? So you made it through the barriers, huh?"

"There weren't any barriers," Annie said. "I wanted to see what was going on."

"What *is* going on?" Ellen asked.

"Not much. Just looked like a lot of people sitting around to me."

"That's the revolution for you." Ellen laughed, giving Patricia a look. "Classes will be back on schedule tomorrow, you wait."

"Well . . ." Patricia grinned at Annie. "Remember, Annie, come the revolution—"

"You're the first to go!" Annie, Ellen, and Patricia all finished together.

"Come on, Annie, let's go to the river." Ellen picked up the plastic kite bag and handed it to Annie.

"What about the demonstration?"

"I don't think it's going to amount to much, really." Annie looked disappointed. "I wouldn't want to miss anything either, honey, but I really think we're better off going to the park. There may not be many more days like this."

"Indian summer," Patricia murmured in her gravelly voice, as if it were a charm.

"Come on, kid. Let's go."

Ellen threw her bag over her shoulder, and Patricia waved them out of the office. The dope smokers were gone from the front steps, and when Annie told her mother about them, she laughed. "It's going to be a very forgetful revolution, I guess." Nothing seemed to have changed at the gate except for a new student manning a walkie-talkie. There were still a lot of mounted police outside, but now they were bantering with the students and letting the horses graze at the short grass on the cement islands in the middle of Broadway. Ellen stopped to talk to a student who told her that the demonstration would probably be over that evening.

"So it goes," Ellen remarked, partly to herself. "Columbia University: 1974."

Annie couldn't think of anything to say to that, and she was sick of hearing about how nothing was as good as it used to be. The paths in Riverside Park were strewn with amber leaves and long brown seed pods that fell from some tree whose name Annie didn't know. There were after-school teams playing in every available field, fresh and clean in their uniforms, as if the fall could impart new life, another chance.

School was different this fall. Some of the girls in Annie's class had started their periods, and there was a new atmosphere of mistrust; friendships were formed or broken over a weekend. Bull Sessions and Truth were the new games—even if you didn't want to say anything you were still expected to play, so Annie would sit in a circle with her friends and each girl would take a turn telling the others what she hated most about them. The new games hurt, and the old, dependable hierarchies were changing. Girls who weren't any good at sports became popular because boys from other schools liked them. Academics didn't seem to count for much anymore. Annie, a jock with no figure or monthly bleeding, didn't know where she stood. Last week at gym class she had pinned down and straddled Jenny Andrews, just to prove that she could still be tougher than anyone else in the class. But it didn't seem to impress anyone, and Annie didn't know what to do to get a reaction from the girls around them, any reaction. She had pounded Jenny's head repeatedly onto the gym floor, something she had never done before, slamming her down over and over again until the gym teacher ran over and stopped her. The punishment she received didn't faze her, but Jenny had cried so much that Annie felt only shame, none of the exaltation and power she used to feel after showing off. Afterward, the other girls avoided Annie.

"Let's keep going down to the river path," Ellen said. Sometimes they flew the kite in one of the long, narrow fields above the river where there were more people and it felt safer. But today Ellen led them down broad slate steps that were covered with leaves and graffiti, through a dark tunnel that smelled of urine and out to the baseball fields next to the river. Annie wasn't allowed to go to this section of the park by herself, though she had been here before with Ellen and the kite. There was a ball game going on, with coaches yelling at their kids. But the kids were out of uniform, and Annie felt as if they had crossed the street into the tough neighborhood, leaving the private school field hockey teams up above. Ellen was oblivious, however, and Annie stuck close to her as they crossed under the highway, under another bridge with spray paint covering carved marble detail work, and came up next to the Hudson River.

They laid out Annie's "bat kite," a plastic kite with a simple design that almost always flew easily.

"Do you want to run with it first?" Ellen asked. She was unrolling the kite and Annie popped the wooden wing-spreader into place. "Or do you want to set it up?"

"You run first," Annie said. Ellen smiled at her and pulled the lapels of her black pea coat together. The wind was coming up off the river and the sky seemed more white than blue, with gray clouds rapidly filling in the gaps of clear sky.

"O.K.," Ellen said. "Thanks. You run the next time up." Annie liked that about her mother. She didn't fake it about liking something just because she thought you liked it. She really loved running with the kite, and Annie knew it.

Annie took the kite and walked with the wind behind her about twenty feet down the cement walkway that went along the river. She turned to face Ellen, who was holding the string on a stick, slowly paying it out. Ellen gave her a serious little nod, and Annie held up the kite so that the wind could catch it. The wind pulled, Annie threw it as high up as she could, and Ellen started to run. She ran full out, past the drunks asleep on the benches and the men in shiny shirts who were fishing in the dirty river. The kite went up and up and up. Ellen was letting the string go free as she ran, and Annie knew she wouldn't stop until the string was completely out: 150 feet up. The string bowed as the kite kept climbing, but Ellen never looked back, just kept running.

The kite found the high air currents and stayed steadily up there. Annie and Ellen traded off holding the stick. It was like being right out on the edge of everything, Annie thought, holding onto the last piece of string. All she would have to do would be to let go of the stick and the kite would be free; it would never come back. Ellen wanted to do it. They had never had the kite out that far, and Ellen wanted to let it go.

"Think about it, Annie," she said. "If I let go right now," she pretended to drop the stick, and Annie leapt for it. Ellen laughed. "I let go of it right now, and it sails way up the Hudson, over the Adirondacks, maybe even up into New Hampshire and Vermont . . . then Canada, Newfoundland, Nova Scotia, the Bay of Fundy!" She pretended to let go of it again and teased Annie, holding onto it with just a thumb and forefinger.

"No!" Annie shouted, grabbing the stick from Ellen. "It'll just hit a tree or something, in New Jersey, and die there. I want to keep it, Mom."

Ellen smiled at her, but in a different way, more distant. "How did I raise such a practical child?" she asked flatly. Annie shrugged and stared up at the kite. The lights went on at the Palisades Amusement Park across the river and on the Maxwell House Coffee sign over Hoboken.

"Come on. We've got to get home," Ellen said, looking around. "It's late and we don't want to be down here after dark."

She rushed Annie along, pulling in the kite string herself because she said that Annie was too slow at it. The fishermen, picking up their buckets to go home, gave Annie and Ellen sidelong glances as they went by. One of them stopped and showed Annie a small gray fish swimming around in slow circles against the yellow plastic walls of his bucket. The man pointed to his mouth and laughed, then rubbed his stomach with a meaningful look.

"Fish. Good. O.K.?" he said.

"O.K.," said Annie, and he walked off laughing.

Ellen and Annie rushed up through the rancid tunnels to the top half of the park. Annie could tell that her mother was nervous to be in the park at dusk.

"We should have left sooner," she muttered, looking around and pushing Annie ahead of her. "This is just stupid. There's that soccer team; we'll walk out with them. Hurry up."

It's not my fault we're late, thought Annie as Ellen pushed her ahead. It made her want to drag her feet, but she was just as frightened of the park after nightfall as her mother was. If it had been just me, thought Annie, I would've left before the lights came on in Hoboken.

Ellen relaxed once they got to Broadway, which was well populated with neighborhood people walking their dogs or doing their evening shopping. Children were walking in small costumed packs for Halloween, with black capes for the boys and witch's hats for the girls. They hauled shopping bags of loot and raced each other into the storefronts to ask for candy. Ellen asked Annie if she wanted to go home and dress up after all, but Annie said no, and she was a little surprised to find that she meant it.

Ellen didn't seem to care what time Annie got to bed that night. She let her watch television for an extra hour, and by the time Annie finally stopped reading in bed, at about eleven, Luke still wasn't home. Ellen said that he was probably going to stay at the office overnight and Annie shouldn't wait up anymore. Annie fell asleep listening to the talk-radio in the kitchen, where Ellen sat writing and smoking.

When she woke up the radio was still on, announcing the weather. Annie rolled over, wanting to sleep more. The clock next to her bed read seven o'clock, which was late. She was supposed to be at school by seven forty-five. Annie knew she was on her own. It was going to be one of those mornings when Ellen didn't get out of bed.

"Shit," she said to herself, knowing there was no escape from school, and no escape from being late to her first class.

The first thing she saw from the hallway were Ellen's feet, bare and sticking out of the kitchen door. Annie waited, to see if anything moved. She started to call her mother's name but stopped herself just as the sound was reaching her throat. She rushed into the kitchen and saw Ellen on the floor in her silky mauve nightgown, which was pulled up a bit, as if she had fallen, not simply lain down to sleep there. Annie remembered what happened on television when they thought that someone was dead. She leaned over and put her head down to Ellen's chest. Her chest was moving and she was breathing.

Annie knew that she was alive even without touching her, but it gave her something to do. Annie knew that Luke wasn't home. It wasn't even worth looking in the bedroom. She looked again at her mother and wondered why there wasn't any blood if she had fallen.

It seemed as if the room got brighter the more she looked at Ellen. She saw her mother's body outlined perfectly in black like a paper cutout. She moved her eyes away from her mother and anchored them on ordinary things, like the toaster resting in a pool of crumbs on the Formica counter. The disc jockey was still talking about traffic, and she walked over to shut off the radio. Then she picked up the telephone on the wall, looking again at Ellen, whose mouth was slightly open. Except for the strangeness of her position, with her legs splayed out oddly, she could simply have been sleeping on the kitchen floor. Actually, she looked quite comfortable, and for a brief second Annie contemplated lying down there with her.

She dialed her father's office number: There was no answer; it was too early for a switchboard operator. Should she call 911? The operator? She wanted Luke, and she pictured him asleep on the black vinyl couch in his office surrounded by long yellow legal pads.

She looked at the list of phone numbers tacked up next to the telephone. Patricia's number was there. She lived closer than anyone else. Annie dialed her number, and Patricia answered the phone sounding grumpy, as if Annie had woken her up. Her morning voice was even harsher than usual, and Annie felt frightened to speak to her and was silent at first.

"Hello? Hello? Who is this?"

"Patricia. It's me. Annie."

"Annie? Oh, Annie. What is it? What time is it?"

"Seven. Patricia—it's Mom." She couldn't talk suddenly, and she fought to keep breathing.

"Annie? What is it? Where are you?"

"I'm home," whispered Annie, starting to cry at last. She hated to cry. She hated sounding like a child. Each word came separately, wrung out of her. "Mom is on the floor."

"Where is your father?" Patricia was completely practical. Annie was relieved.

"He's at work, I think. Nobody answered at the office."

"Annie. Stay there. I'm coming. It's going to be all right. Do you hear me, Annie?"

"Yes." She wished Patricia hadn't said that. She knew everything would be all right. Ellen was breathing, wasn't she? She thought of Luke again. "Patricia—find my dad."

"I will. Don't worry. I'll be right there. O.K., Annie? O.K.?"

"O.K." Annie hung up.

She went back to her room and got dressed for school. She pulled on her blazer, checked her book bag for all of the homework she needed to bring into class that day, and waited in her room. She wasn't crying anymore.

Everything moved very quickly after Patricia arrived, and they called an ambulance. Luke arrived twenty minutes after Patricia did, and he came in like a great river of practicality and held Annie for a long time while she hid in his shoulder. Patricia made tea and all of the right phone calls. Then Luke called the school and after speaking with them privately from the bedroom, he told Annie that she should go in to school, even though it was too late for her first class, and that he would pick her up at three o'clock that day. Annie was shocked that only forty-five minutes had passed since she called Patricia. Luke held her again and said that her mother was going to be all right. She had taken too many pills by mistake, but she was going to the hospital and she would be all right. Annie said nothing. She knew that it was a lie, about the pills being taken by accident. She hated Luke and Patricia for lying and treating her like a child, but she wanted Luke to take over, so she was quiet. She knew that her father would be there to pick her up at three o'clock from school.

"Can't I stay with you today?" she asked, thinking that just maybe he would let her. Luke went over to his bureau and picked up a coin from a little wooden bowl Annie had made and given to him from her woodworking class two years go. He put it into her hand and told her that he had been saving it for her birthday. It was a silver coin almost as big as a half-dollar with a fish swimming on one side and a harp on the other.

"It's from Ireland," Luke said, pulling her against him again. "For luck." Luke turned it over so that the fish was facing up. "It's a salmon," he said, tracing its outline with his index finger, which was blackened on the inside from years of leaky fountain pens. The doorbell rang and Patricia called out for him. He looked up slowly, as if he was hearing her from a long way off. "That'll be the ambulance. Now, go to school, and I'll see you at three." Annie, along with other tenants from the building, watched her mother being put into the ambulance. Ellen was still sleeping, filled with a sort of peace.

Ellen spent two weeks in the hospital, and Luke took Annie up to see her on the weekends. The hospital was in Westchester County, just north of the city, and to get there they drove over the same bridge they always took to go up to the Game. It felt as if they were making a wrong turn when her father took the exit that led to the hospital instead of continuing north.

Annie didn't think that the hospital looked much like a hospital. The plaque at the bottom of the long driveway said it was an "institute," but the whole place looked more like a wealthy private home. Poplars lined the drive, and they swayed nakedly in the November wind. Luke remarked on the poplars, how he had loved driving along roads like this in France, where he had lived for three years after his college graduation. But the trees looked so tall and lean that Annie kept expecting one to come crashing down in a strong gust, and she was relieved when they came out of that long allée and parked in front of the large brick building that was covered with ivy.

The first time they had come she had wondered if her mother would be in a locked room, wearing a hospital gown. She had been told almost nothing about what was really wrong with Ellen. All anyone would say was that Ellen was in the hospital because she needed a rest. Everyone seemed so concerned about reassuring her that her mother was going to be all right that Annie didn't feel she could ask any questions. Like, why did she want to die?

There was a song that had been playing on the radio a lot last summer:

> They're coming to take me away!
> Ha Ha, Hee Hee, Ho Ho, Ha Ha!
> To the Funny Farm!
> Where everything's beautiful all the time!

The song kept going through Annie's head. The singer sounded like a demented clown and she imagined his face covered with white makeup and a big smeared red mouth. She had gone around singing the song last summer with all of her friends, but now she hated it. It was as if the clown had decided to live with her for the rest of her life, always singing and laughing that stupid laugh. She had tried to trick the clown by acting as if she didn't care. She told her friends at school that her mother was at the "funny farm" and got them to laugh about it. She even sang it to them herself to show how tough she was. But it was the worst when she was alone in bed at night, trying to sleep; all she could hear was that same relentless chorus over and over again, and she slept with her pillow over her head, thinking how pathetic she was to be obsessed with a song from AM radio.

The visit had been nothing like she had expected. Her mother was dressed in her regular clothes and was wearing sneakers. There were no nurses or doctors in white coats anywhere, and when they went in the front door and announced themselves to the receptionist, it felt more like she was visiting her mother at a nice hotel.

When Ellen came downstairs she gave Annie a big hug and smiled at her. Annie smiled back, but felt strangely formal. Her mother had a different smell. Clean, but harsh. Cheap soap, Annie thought to herself, and wondered if she could bring Ellen her own soap from home. She would ask later. Ellen looked different, too, with no makeup, not even lipstick, and her hair was flattened at the back, as if she had been lying down for a long time. Annie knew that her mother never even went down to the laundry room without putting on lipstick, and her face looked unnatural without it. Then Annie realized that she hadn't seen any mirrors anywhere, even when she used the bathroom. Her mother must not know how she looked, Annie thought.

The three of them sat together in a small glassed-in patio that faced the lawn. There were comfortable chairs here and an unfinished jigsaw puzzle on the table. Ellen smoked and asked Annie about school. She tried to think of what to say, but what had happened to Ellen had been the biggest thing at school the week before. She tried talking about some of the sports teams. Annie was captain of the sixth-grade athletic team this year, and they had been killing the other teams in an unstoppable winning streak.

Ellen seemed interested at first, but pretty soon she stopped looking at Annie and began to look just past her in a way that Annie recognized, and her stomach tightened. Annie began to talk faster, but eventually she stopped talking altogether, unable to think of anything to say. Nothing seemed interesting enough. Luke asked her mother for a cigarette, and Ellen offered him the pack. Annie was surprised; Luke almost never smoked. When he did, he smoked the way he walked—fast. There was a brief silence, then Ellen prompted her again to tell her about school, though Annie knew she wasn't really interested. She was "trying," and Annie hated it. Halfway through the visit Annie could only shrug her shoulders, and then Ellen got angry. She didn't say she was, but Annie knew it, and she knew that Luke knew it. The three of them sat in silence. The only sound was the slap of wet leaves flying against the glass and the deep drags Ellen took on her cigarette. Annie wondered if anyone was allowed to have a turntable, or a radio. The whole place seemed unnaturally quiet.

"They've been letting me leave work early this week," Luke said.

"Good," Ellen said, smiling without emotion.

"They're being very good about it. Sidney knows how much I've been working."

"You've always worked late," she said, and lit a new cigarette with the burning end of her old one. Annie wondered if they were only allowed to smoke when visitors were there, and so she had to get in as many as she could.

"I had to put in a lot of time this month. Things were piling up at the magazine," Luke said.

Ellen's eyes flickered over his face once. "Oh, I know. They pile up."

All three of them looked out at the lawn, and a metal lawn chair, painted white, suddenly tipped over in the wind.

There was a pause.

"It's interesting," Ellen said, then stopped. "It's interesting that that particular chair would blow over, but none of the others have. Look."

She was right. Only one chair had gone over out of a group of about five.

"Must have been an especially strong gust," Luke said.

Ellen looked at him as if he were stupid. "Of course," she said. "It's not really interesting at all, is it?" Her voice was pitched slightly higher, the way it always was when Ellen was in one of her moods.

"That's not what I meant," Luke said. Then he stopped and looked out at the lawn again.

"Well, it could be the chair, couldn't it?" Ellen asked, looking at both of them as if daring them to interrupt her. "How the chair was placed—carelessly—when the others were put down really well. I mean, those others can withstand the winter, just look at them." She got up and walked to the edge of the room and pressed her face against the glass. Annie saw Luke start to get up, as if to stop Ellen, but instead he stopped himself.

"What's interesting is whether it is due to the nature of the chair, or to the nature of the wind, that the chair gets blown over," she said triumphantly, turning back to Luke.

"Clearly it's the wind," Luke said, recrossing his legs nervously. "The chairs are all the same."

"Clearly? Clearly?" Ellen went back to her chair and lit another cigarette. "They all *look* the same, that's all you know."

"Right," Luke said heavily. "That's all I know."

"Patricia's coming by for dinner this week," he said after a few moments. "I figured I'd make her a chicken pot pie. We're not sick of them yet, are we Annie?"

"Nope." Annie scuffed her sneakers under the edge of her chair and wished that Luke would just shut up and take them home.

"And Annie's been going to soccer practice or to Ally's place after school."

Ally Schwartz was in Annie's class and lived a block and a half away. Her mother was never home, but there was a housekeeper who was small and old. She opened the door for them when they came home from school and then sat in the kitchen watching a black-and-white television set all afternoon. Ally Schwartz's house was always well stocked with Yodels and Cheez Doodles. There was never any real snack food at Annie's house, and she couldn't get enough of it at Ally Schwartz's. Ally Schwartz wasn't allowed to go to the park alone, or even with a friend, which Annie thought was ridiculous. She had been going alone to the sections of the park that her parents set up as boundaries since she was nine. Annie liked Ally Schwartz for short stretches of time, but she had been spending too much time with her this week, waiting until Luke got home from work. There wasn't much to do except eat at Ally Schwartz's apartment. Lately she had been wanting to take a pair of scissors and cut off Ally Schwartz's long single braid of black hair when her back was turned.

At last a woman who was better dressed than Ellen came to the door and announced that visiting hours were over. Annie snuck a quick look at her father. He looked visibly relieved, and Ellen seemed exactly the same as she had been since Annie had stopped answering her. She gave Annie a quick, dry kiss and said good-bye to Luke in her angry voice. He didn't even try to kiss her.

"She hates me," Annie said, as soon as they got in the car. The windshield wipers on the VW bug were clogged with leaves and could hardly lift themselves. Luke rolled down the window as they drove down the driveway and pulled the leaves away with his hand.

"She doesn't," he yelled against the rain that was whipping in the open window.

"Well, I hate her," Annie said quietly, pretty sure he couldn't hear her.

Luke rolled up the window and rubbed the inside of the windshield with his sleeve so that he could see. The heater was broken and the car felt cold and damp inside. Annie sat with her shoulders hunched up and her coat pulled tight around her.

"She doesn't hate you," he said again, after he had maneuvered the car onto the parkway.

"Well, she sure hates you," Annie said.

Luke just smiled, his eyes still fixed on the road. "She seems to," he said, and he sounded very tired. "She's depressed, Annie."

"That's all anyone says," she said, pulling her knees to her chest and kicking her feet against the glove compartment door. "Why? What's so awful?"

"I don't know," he said. The rain began coming down in sheets now, and the edges of the road were already flooded. He pulled the knob that turned on the headlights and rubbed again at the fogged-up windshield. "Maybe it's me. Maybe it's the city."

"We could live somewhere else," Annie said. But she didn't really mean it. She knew they would never live anywhere but New York. But Luke answered her seriously.

"I can't really leave, because of my job," he said. "But your mother could live somewhere else. Some of the doctors think it might be a good idea."

"Yeah?" Annie kicked again at the glove compartment. "Those

doctors are the crazy ones. They don't know her. They don't know us." Luke didn't say anything. "Mom loves New York," Annie said, turning to look at him.

"We'll see," Luke said. "We've gotta wait and see what happens."

"I know what's gonna happen." Annie pressed her nose against the window and squinted her eyes so that the passing trees looked as if they were part of a watercolor. "You and Mom will get divorced and we'll have to move out of our apartment."

Luke didn't say anything.

Annie kicked harder against the glove compartment. "Right?" she asked. "Right?" She kicked again, and this time the glove compartment popped open and millions of little pieces of paper came flying out. Old receipts, parking tickets, shopping lists.

"Goddamnit, Annie. What the hell are you doing?"

He pulled over to the side of the road. The other cars swooshed past them, drenching the side of the car with the spray from their tires. He turned the key in the ignition and the car shuddered several times before shutting down. Luke reached over and hit her hard on the top of her head. "Goddamnit!" He hit her again and again.

"I'm sorry, Dad. I'm sorry."

"Clean it up," he said, shoving her down toward the floor of the car where most of the papers had landed. The floorboards leaked, and some of the papers were stuck to the wet rubber matting. Annie began to gather them up, and the papers tore and disintegrated in her hands.

Luke watched her. "We're going to sit here until it's done," he said. Annie began to put them in a neat pile on her lap, matching torn pieces together. She didn't want Luke to see her cry, and she turned her head away. Luke watched her for a minute, then he suddenly grabbed all of the papers out of her lap and squeezed them into a ball in his fist. He clenched his fingers so tight that water dripped out between his fingers onto the floor of the car. Annie stared at him. He dug the toe of his shoe into a crack that ran the length of the floorboard on his side, wedging the rusted metal wide open so that Annie could see the river of dirty water running on the pavement underneath them.

He threw the ball of papers down through the crack, then moved his foot so that the floorboard covered it up again.

He turned and pulled Annie close to him. He kissed the top of her head, where it was still tender from his hitting her. "I'm sorry, Annie," he said. "I love you, you know that. I just didn't want you messing up the car." He pushed at the floorboard again, looking through the crack to the wet pavement. "As if it makes any difference." He looked back at Annie. "Sorry I clipped you. Are you all right?"

Annie nodded.

"Scout's honor?"

Annie smiled a little. "It didn't really hurt."

He held out his hand and they gave each other their secret handshake, which was really the Black Panther handshake. Annie had learned the gesture from a man at one of the political meetings her parents had taken her to last year. She had been bored, and a young black man had felt sorry for her, or maybe he was just bored too. Anyway, he taught her the handshake. She had showed it to Luke later, and he loved to do it with her—especially the last two moves, when you brought your fist to your heart and then raised it into the air shouting, "Power to the People!"

Ellen disapproved of Luke doing it because he always said the final chant with an air of cynicism.

"You're everything they are against," she would say. "It's one thing for Annie, she's a kid, but you . . . It's embarrassing."

"Power to the People!" he would always respond. "I've always been a Friend of the People."

"Oh God, Luke, who do you think you are? Roosevelt?" Ellen had asked him one day.

"Yes," he answered. "FDR, not Teddy."

"What about Eleanor?" Annie had asked, and that made him laugh, she remembered.

"You be Eleanor," he said. "I expect nothing less."

Now they did the Panther handshake over the smooth, gray, plastic gearshift handle, and when Luke raised his fist in the air he shouted "Power to the People!" louder than ever, to make Annie laugh. She held her fist up in the air but remained silent.

"Are you embarrassed?" he asked.

"No," she said. He raised his eyebrows at her, challenging her.

"Power to the People!" she shouted. It was so loud inside the car that she surprised herself. They both laughed.

"You cold?" he asked her. She nodded. Luke reached into the back and grabbed the army blanket they always kept there and wrapped it around her. "Better?"

"Uh huh."

Luke started the car again and peered out the window at his mirror; the rain had finally let up a bit. He flipped on his turn signal.

"What about those papers?" Annie said. "There were some parking tickets in there."

"They'll find me, don't worry," Luke snorted. "It doesn't matter."

"Are you and Mom going to break up?" Annie asked.

He turned back to her. "I don't know," he said, and then waited, looking at her.

She shrugged. "It's just, everyone's parents are divorced."

He smiled briefly and then turned back to look at the road. He pulled out onto the parkway again and rubbed the inside of the windshield with his sleeve. "But no matter what happens, we're gonna get a new car. Deal?"

Annie thought a minute; she loved the old car. She had drawn pictures in crayon all over the inside carpeting in the way-back. Her father glanced over at her, worried.

"O.K.," she said quickly. "Deal."

"Have you ever been to Times Square on New Year's Eve, Dad?"

"Christ, no." Luke pressed the buzzer for the elevator.

"I think it'd be fun." Annie pulled her peacoat close. It was just as cold in the entryway to Peter and Janis's building as it had been out on Great Jones Street.

"Watch it on TV."

"Can we? Tonight? Do you think we can?"

"Why not?"

The elevator arrived, and Luke pulled open the door. Annie loved this elevator. It had a big iron gate that you had to pull back by hand, and there was a smooth metal cable that ran right through the ceiling and the floor. He let Annie press the button, and the elevator started up the shaft. She wanted to reach her hands out through the gate and touch the cement walls going by, but she didn't because Luke was there, and he would never let her do it. He leaned against the back wall of the elevator in his big sheepskin coat and blue jeans.

Peter and Janis's loft was on the top floor, and about halfway up the shaft they heard the music: "Satisfaction." Annie knew all the words. Her bedroom walls were covered with posters of Mick Jagger, his white jumpsuit undone to the pubic bone.

Luke grinned at her, pushed himself off the wall, and started to dance, shuffling across the floor of the elevator. Annie started to twist along with him. She giggled at her father's dancing, and when the chorus came around they both shouted as loud as they could:

> " 'Cause I try! And I try! And I try! And I try!
> I can't get no—"

The music got louder and louder as they got closer to the top floor, and the elevator suddenly stopped. Luke grabbed Annie so that she wouldn't fall, and they stayed together for a minute, breathing hard.

Luke pulled open the elevator gate and pushed Annie into the loft ahead of him. She hadn't seen the girls since last summer. Her school was uptown and the Shanlick girls went to school downtown. The two worlds never overlapped. Annie had no idea what subway to take to get downtown, and she wasn't allowed to take the subway alone anyway. It was the same for the Shanlick girls, who never went north of Fourteenth Street. Annie didn't know why Peter and Luke never saw each other during the school year. Sometimes Luke would mention that he had seen Peter for a drink after work, but they never got together on the weekends. It was almost as if the two families lived in different states, and Annie and her father would take the long journey downtown only once a year, for New Year's Eve. Ellen never went to the New Year's party, and for the first time it occurred to Annie that maybe Ellen didn't like Janis and Peter.

Ellen had gone to Vermont directly from the hospital. Luke packed a suitcase full of her things and drove her up there. She was going to live at another institute of some sort—another looney bin, Annie told herself—and Luke couldn't tell her how long Ellen might be staying there. He had said that they would be visiting her, but they hadn't gone once in the month and a half since she had left the hospital in Westchester. Annie had hoped for Thanksgiving, but Luke said she wasn't ready for them yet, and that Thanksgiving was an unimportant holiday—he had never liked it. Annie knew she wasn't supposed to like it either, but she had thought they could at least go and visit Ellen since it was a long weekend. They had celebrated Thanksgiving with a friend of Luke's, and Annie hadn't liked it, which she knew pleased Luke in a certain way. Then Christmas had come and gone, with its obligatory attendance of *The Nutcracker.* Luke loved the ballet and had made it a family tradition. Annie had still only spoken on the phone to Ellen. The connection always made it sound as if they were speaking to someone in another country, and on Christmas day Annie had been jealous of Ellen because she said there was snow up where she was. It had only rained in the city. They didn't discuss on the phone why Annie and Luke couldn't come for Christmas, but Luke told her that all the holidays were difficult for her mother.

Ellen had sent her and Luke identical Christmas presents from Vermont, which Annie thought was strange. They both got maple sugar candy in the shape of a leaf.

"She didn't even get us different shapes," Annie had said to her father when they unwrapped the small cardboard box with her mother's handwriting on the address sticker.

"Maybe she can't get anything else up there," Luke said. "It is the country, after all."

"But not even different shapes. And no wrapping paper. Don't they even have wrapping paper in Vermont?"

Luke hadn't said anything.

The apartment was also changing with Ellen gone. Luke had his books piled everywhere, since now he came home at night to be with Annie, and he had to keep working after she went to sleep. There were books on the dining room table, and he and Annie always ate at one end, so that he wouldn't have to rearrange everything. They also started reading through dinner, which Annie had never been allowed to do before her mother went away. She loved it. Luke would put down the plates of food (fish sticks or chicken pot pie), and then they would each take out a book. It was very companionable.

Annie had thought about calling Liz and Tessa after Halloween, when her mother went into the hospital. She wasn't sure what she would say to them if she called, and she wondered what they already knew. She was sure they would have heard something. If the girls knew the truth, she hoped Justin and Nick didn't. Justin was always ragging on the grown-ups, saying that one friend of their parents was a drunk, or somebody else was a lech. He called all the homosexuals in the crowd perverts and said they were always after him. Maybe Ellen was a whacko. She hoped he didn't know. He hadn't really talked to her after the game last summer. He had acted as if the whole thing had never happened, but she remembered that feeling of importance it had given her when Justin was on top of her. Annie had started masturbating that fall, and at first she would try to think of Justin as she touched herself, remembering the night of the game. But other times thinking of Justin made it impossible for her, and after her mother left she found herself doing it more and more, but it only worked when she could make herself think of nothing at all.

She wondered if the Shanlick girls had ever masturbated, and she thought that if she could be alone with Liz for a moment tonight, maybe she could find a way to ask her. She wasn't sure what she would say about her mother, or what she'd do if Justin started ragging on Ellen tonight. He was always so funny when he was mean it was hard to fight back. Now that they were actually at the party she was glad that she hadn't called the girls.

Peter and Janis's loft was huge, the entire floor of a building, and they had divided the back half into many bedrooms that came off a long hallway. The big living room at the other end of the hall was divided into two rooms by French doors whose glass panes were covered with chipped white paint. The television was turned on in the room closer to the kitchen, and the music was playing from the other half, which looked out on Great Jones Street. Justin and Sam were lying on their stomachs watching TV. There were two sofas that had been pushed against the walls and covered with Indian-print bedspreads, and piles of books lay on the floor like end tables next to them. Nick's rabbit cage was on top of the television set, and the rabbit gently kicked wood shavings into the back.

The sound from the record player and the television bounced back and forth so loudly that Justin and Sam didn't hear them walk in. Luke nudged Justin with the toe of his black loafer.

"Luke!" Justin rolled over and tried to kick back, but Luke jumped out of the way. They laughed.

"Why aren't you reading your history?" Luke smiled.

"Ever heard of Christmas vacation, Luke? No, I know—Talleyrand never took Christmas vacation." Luke laughed and so did Justin. Then Justin nudged Annie with his sneaker.

"Hi, Annie." He smiled at her, and Annie felt ready to do anything for him again.

She smiled back. "Hi, Justin. Hi, Sam."

Sam turned from the set and grinned at her. "Wanna watch?"

"O.K."

Janis walked in with bowls of canned spaghetti and slices of orange on a tray. "Luke! Great, you're here. How are you sweetheart? Annie, are you hungry?"

"Janis." Luke kissed her on the cheek. "More beautiful than ever."

Janis laughed and kissed him back. "I'm glad you got here early. Want some SpaghettiOs, Annie?" Janis put the tray down on the floor in front of Justin and Sam. "Just grab one of these bowls—do Tessa and Liz know you're here? Tessa! Liz!"

She walked to the glass doors and opened them. "Peter! Turn it down! Luke's here!"

"Mom! Close the door! We can't hear the TV!" Justin shouted from the floor. Janis looked at Luke. "You get him to turn it down. I've got to get these kids some food."

Luke dropped his coat on the couch and walked into the front room, closing the door behind him and winking at Justin.

"Now, I want you to eat the oranges too," Janis said halfheartedly. "Vitamin C."

Tessa and Liz came in carrying a big can of Hawaiian Punch and a stack of Dixie cups. Liz smiled at Annie. She was wearing her usual paint-stained T-shirt and blue jeans, an outfit that hid the figure Annie was envious of. Tessa had gained some weight, but it only made her look more grown up. She was wearing some of Janis's eye makeup.

"How are you, Tess?"

"Good, I guess. Hate school."

"Yeah. School sucks."

Annie wished that she went to school with the Shanlick sisters. Annie's school was all girls, and they had to wear uniforms every day except Friday. Tessa, Liz, and Sam went to public school in the Village. They had boys in their class, and they had never had to wear uniforms.

The downstairs buzzer was ringing, and people kept arriving and walking through the TV room to the dance floor where Luke and Peter were sitting. They said hello to the kids as they walked through, and Annie pretended to know the ones she couldn't remember. Nick came back from playing basketball, and they all sat on the floor eating silently and watching the TV. Every time the music got louder, Justin turned up the TV set. The party was just getting started in the front room.

"I'm bored—I'm bored—I'm bored." Nick said, rolling over toward Tessa.

Tessa smiled at him. Nick reached out and pushed her onto her back, tickling her until she started to scream and hit him. So Tessa was still his favorite, thought Annie.

"Will you guys cut it out? I'm trying to watch," Justin said as they knocked into him.

Nick turned toward the other room and lay his head on the floor so that he could see under the door, watching the feet stomping and crisscrossing in shadows. He turned back to Tessa. "Let's watch them."

He opened the French doors just enough to peek through. Tessa squeezed in next to him, and Liz and Annie shoved their way in at the bottom. The music was so loud that they could hardly hear what anyone was saying; watching the party was like seeing a silent movie with Peter's record collection for the soundtrack.

Peter was still being the DJ, and Janis was dancing with a tall man in a yellow T-shirt. She was wearing purple tights with black fishnets over them and a black leather miniskirt that hiked almost all the way up when she did the twist. Her copper hair looked freshly dyed for the new year. Red neon blinked in the window and reflected onto the floor: "Billiards—Open All Night."

A man in a checked suit danced by himself, in and out of the red light, smoking and moving very slowly. A girl in a black turtleneck pulled Peter onto the dance floor, her fingers snapping tight off her hips.

"Great place!" she shouted at him over the music.

"Thanks. Wanna fuck?"

The girl in the turtleneck stared at him for a minute, as if unsure that she had really heard him say that. Then she laughed suddenly and turned away. She danced to the bar on the other side of the room.

Peter was sweating so much that his white T-shirt was almost transparent, and his black hair was cut close to his head, which looked almost violent in that room full of long, loose hair. He walked over to Janis and pulled her up against him. He kept his wallet in the back pocket of his blue jeans, the wallet shape outlined in a faded blue line that was almost white. Janis grabbed his hips and then they twisted together slowly. The best dancers in the room.

A skinny girl in a miniskirt was smoking and looking out the open window. She leaned over to a man in a hat and corduroy jacket who wouldn't look up from the joints he was rolling on an album cover. She spoke so loudly that Annie could hear her over the music.

"I don't know. The idea of living in the country really makes me nervous."

"How come?"

"I don't know. It just seems so apolitical somehow."

"I know what you mean."

The skinny girl climbed up onto the windowsill and started to dance, grinding up against the top half of the windowpane. The man in the hat stopped rolling joints briefly and looked up her skirt in a perfunctory manner. Two women sat on the couch near the door, smoking. They shouted at each other over the music.

"I know that California is where the money is, but I can't live somewhere where nobody reads books."

"I finally had to make a list of all the reasons we got married. In nineteen fifty-four I actually thought he could teach me to enjoy sex."

"That's so depressing."

They both laughed, lit each other's cigarettes, and reached for their drinks as if they were part of the same body. The room was smoke and sweat all around them and everybody danced except Luke.

Luke was not yet drunk enough to dance. He liked listening to rock 'n' roll but said he didn't know how to dance to it. Jazz, he understood. Swing music. Peter and Janis grabbed his empty hands and pulled him out onto the dance floor. He and Peter locked arms, and

Janis left them, moving around the room, gathering paper cups, and joking.

A woman's fingers hooked onto Luke's belt loops from behind. He kept looking at Peter as she pulled up tight against him, then Peter let go, suddenly, with a laugh that cracked out over the music, and Luke fell back into her. She gasped with his weight, and he turned. She was a frail, blond woman in a short skirt. Luke smiled, and so did she. He grabbed for her waist and steered her around the room in a very fast waltz.

Nick pulled Tessa away from the door, and they all fell into a heap.

"Come on, Nick—"

"Shut the fucking door. I can't hear!" Justin's face was inches away from the TV screen. Annie was starting to hate Justin; he hadn't spoken to her again since she'd arrived.

"Dance marathon!" Nick shouted, jumping up on the couch and starting to twist. Tessa jumped onto the other couch, her feet slipping between the cushions. Sam jumped up next to Nick and tried to push him over, but he was bigger and she fell onto the floor. Liz and Annie let her swing dance with them in the center of the room.

"How long do we go for?" Sam asked, losing her feet in a spin.

"The one who dances the longest—wins!" Nick yelled back.

Liz and Annie dropped out first, and sat back against the wall, passing the can of Hawaiian Punch back and forth. It tasted cold, sweet, and metallic.

"Where's your mom?" Liz asked.

"She's living in Vermont."

"You're staying with your dad?"

"Yeah, but I'm going up to see her next weekend." That's what Annie always said, since she never knew when they would really go. It sounded better, she thought.

"Is she still sick?"

"No."

"So why is she living up there?"

"I don't know. Because she wants to, I guess. My dad says she likes living in the country."

Liz swished the punch inside her mouth. "Are they divorced?"

"No."

"How come you're staying with your dad?"

"School, I guess. I'd hate living in the country anyway."

"Yeah, it's so boring."

They sat quietly for a minute.

"I wonder when they'll get divorced," Liz said, pouring out more punch into both their cups.

"I don't know."

Liz looked at her. "It's not that bad a deal, I mean, you get two different houses to go to."

"Yeah, that would be cool, I guess."

Annie felt more embarrassed than anything. Her mother had been gone almost two months, but it felt like longer. It was getting hard to get a picture in her mind of her parents actually doing anything together: having breakfast, walking to the bus, though she knew that they must have done those things, and that she must have been there, but right now she just couldn't imagine them in the same room.

"Are you going to spend the night? You can sleep in my room, with Sam."

"No, that's O.K., my dad said we were going to go home tonight."

"O.K."

Nick and Tessa dropped out of the marathon and fell onto opposite couches. Sam was left spinning slowly in the middle of the room while everyone else wandered away.

"I won!" she said. "I won!"

By midnight Annie was the only one left on the couch. Justin lay in front of the TV with his eyes shut and his mouth open. He had ignored everyone all night, staring grimly at the television set. Annie finally pulled Janis's afghan around her and slept.

The countdown woke her up. Everyone in the front room was

shouting: "ten . . . nine . . . eight . . ." Annie stepped over Justin's sleeping body and flipped through all the stations until she saw the huge white ball on top of the building in Times Square. The announcer's voice matched the shouts from the dance floor: "four . . . three . . . two . . . one—HAPPY NEW YEAR!"

The ball dropped fast, and Annie couldn't see where it went. Large white numbers filled the screen: 1973. The cameras panned the people in the street, and in the other room she heard the sound of glass breaking as someone put on another record: Frank Sinatra. She wanted to wake up Justin to say Happy New Year, but she knew he'd get mad. She walked over to the glass door and peeked through the crack. Everyone was kissing everyone. She saw her father's back, his head bent into a kiss. There were hands wrapped around him. He started to move in a circle, still kissing, and his hands were holding her buttocks. Annie pulled back from the door before the girl could turn toward her. She was pretty sure she didn't know the girl, but she didn't want to see her face. She looked at Justin lying there in the blue television light. He looked so gentle, with all the fight gone out of him. She got up and went to kneel next to him, her hands on either side of his handsome face. It was New Year's, she thought; she could kiss him. She started to lean down to him, but stopped just before their lips touched. The only way she wanted to kiss him was without waking him, and she didn't know how to do that. She wished she could kiss him in a way that would stop him from waking up mean. She touched his hair gently, lightly brushing the ends without disturbing the hair next to his scalp; his hair felt like cornsilk between her fingers. She held it there for a moment, watching him sleep, and then put her face down into it and breathed him in. His hair smelled like nothingness—like air. She let it go gently without waking him, went back to the couch, and pulled her feet up under the afghan.

Sometime later Annie woke up and heard voices above her. She stayed very still.

"I'll come back first thing in the morning," Luke was saying. Annie felt him looking down at her. She kept her eyes shut tight.

"Sure." That was Janis. "She'll have fun with the kids in the morning. We'll have French toast," she laughed. "Christ, only a few hours from now."

"Tell her when she wakes up that I'll be here by eleven at the latest."

"O.K., go ahead. Have fun. Jesus, Luke, take one night."

"Sure."

Annie heard Janis's hand slap Luke lightly on the back of his blue jeans.

"Have a happy New Year."

"Thanks, Janis."

The toilet flushed down the hall, and Annie heard her father walk toward the sound. She heard a woman's voice whispering to him.

Annie heard the elevator door open and clenched her eyes tighter. She felt Janis putting another blanket over her. Janis turned off the television set and shook Justin awake. He mumbled and went down the hallway with her toward his bedroom. The apartment was quiet, and Annie heard the garbage trucks out on the Bowery grinding their gears.

Part Two

the country   1973–1975

The year that Annie turned fourteen, Janis and Peter decided to hold the game on Memorial Day weekend, instead of the traditional mid-August.

Annie said to her father, "We'll freeze. School will still be going on; nobody will come to the game."

"It's not my decision," he told her. "It has something to do with Janis's work schedule. It'll be fine."

"No it won't," Annie said. "It'll be different."

She hated change. Pizza could be ordered only from the pizza parlor on Ninety-fifth Street and Broadway. She always walked home from the bus stop on the east side of the street, because that was what she had always done. She followed a complicated private code, and it had to do with keeping herself guarded against change. Luke teased Annie that what she called change, he called innovation. But he was the one who had endlessly repeated the same stories and habits of his own life on all of the car rides and long summer days of her childhood. She was reassured by plans, happiest when an expected event actually came to pass. There was a certain comfort in the known landscape.

Annie kept arguing with her father over the weeks leading up to the game. She was sure that Luke could convince Janis and Peter to move the date back to the usual August weekend if she could only get him to see the importance of it. But Luke just sdidn't get it.

"Stop being so rigid," he finally snapped at her one day. She didn't understand what he meant and burst into tears. She had brought it up again while they were discussing summer plans, something that they both enjoyed, since Luke was a great planner, and ever since the divorce, two years ago, he had been free to plot out his time away from the city as compulsively as he liked.

Ellen hated to plan. She told Annie that on an existential level it was pointless, and on a practical level, boring. It had been a relief to everyone when they ceased having to plan anything together beyond what time Luke would pick up and drop off Annie for the weekends she spent with him. Luke would still reiterate his and Annie's plans over the telephone to Ellen when he called to arrange something. He always failed to catch himself in time, and it irritated Ellen into silence almost immediately. Annie also liked to spend an entire dinner telling Ellen yet again of her and Luke's agenda for the weekend, but Ellen was more patient with Annie than she was with Luke. It was one of the ways in which Ellen had changed toward Annie. In fact, by Annie's fourteenth year, everything had changed.

Ellen and Annie had moved as soon as Ellen came back from Vermont, where Annie had never been taken to visit her. It was two years ago that Ellen had come home to the old apartment after an absence of five months. Luke and Annie's routine had been solid, by then, and Annie liked the lack of variation in their life. That winter she had lain in bed beside the window watching the snow whirl down the airshaft and thinking of Vermont. She had never been there, but the maple sugar Ellen had sent her for Christmas tasted like food from another country. She had licked it slowly from the bottom, saving the imprint of the maple leaf for last. The window next to her bed was always open, and the radiator hissed and knocked all night, overheating the room and making Annie dream that an old steam engine was carrying her north to Vermont, where everything she saw was frozen and coated with a layer of snow that tasted like white sugar. The snow never melted in her Vermont, no matter how much she ate, and she never saw her mother in her dreams.

No one said that Ellen was cured when she came home, just that she was "ready." At first she seemed to be doing everything from a distance, as if a gauze curtain separated her from the rest of the world.

Annie had expected Luke to leave, and he had been packing up his books even before Ellen came home. When they finally sat down with her and told her that they were getting divorced, Annie rolled her eyes and asked them to tell her something she didn't know. She didn't care about them not being married anymore, but she didn't want Luke to leave. She had even asked him if she could go with him, instead of staying in the apartment with Ellen. Ellen had spooked her, those first few days, with her distant smile and her overly attentive interest in everything from Annie's hair to her homework. But Luke said he was going to be staying with friends for the next few weeks while he was apartment hunting. How about after he got settled? No, it wasn't possible. She would see him on the weekends, he promised. Where? He'd let her know. When she finally asked him if he just didn't want to live with her, Luke had stopped packing his books and looked at her. They were alone in the apartment.

"Your mother wants you to stay with her," he said. "I think she needs you to stay." Then Annie knew it was partly because Ellen had been sick that she had to stay with her. It must be that Ellen couldn't be left alone, but Luke could. Annie had to make sure Ellen was all right. Annie must have looked a little shaky, because just then Luke had hugged her and said, "I won't be far away. You can call me anytime." But he didn't even have a phone number yet.

Luke had left the apartment for the last time while Annie was at school, and when she came home Ellen had been waiting for her with an understanding look on her face that felt prearranged and false. Annie had thrown down her book bag and gone out to the park all afternoon, making forts and fighting battles in the patchy spring grass with her plastic G.I. Joes.

Ellen's air of not quite participating in anything slowly dropped away after Luke moved out, and her moodiness felt more real to Annie than the person who had come home from Vermont. Annie was glad to have her mother back, and the divorce came through quickly. Her parents had no arguments that Annie knew about; there was hardly any furniture to divide and she would see her father on the weekends. When she stopped to think about it, she realized that she had never seen her parents actually argue about anything.

Ellen moved them into a modern high-rise on Columbus Avenue, where painted cement was the design motif. It was a five-block move, but the territory on the street was completely different from Central Park West. The first month Annie spent at her mother's new apartment, she had to negotiate with the gang of kids who lived in the building. It was a gang of twelve-year-olds led by a Puerto Rican boy named Pablo. All the kids in the gang roller skated, and for the first few weeks they followed Annie around when she was alone and shown her the screwdrivers they carried as weapons, waiting to see if they could make her run. She kept her eyes straight ahead and kept walking, but at the end of the first week, Annie got out her skates and put them on at the bus stop before coming home. She figured it was better to be in the gang than to be beaten up by them, and by the end of the month she was Pablo's girlfriend, which meant she let him kiss her in the basement laundry room. She learned how to use a screwdriver for popping the hubcaps off parked cars, and stole endless packs of gum and candy bars from the Woolworth's on Ninety-seventh Street. Annie got mugged twelve times that first year, always by other kids. Once a boy had come out of the bushes while she was riding her bike in the park and just taken it. He was a teenager and there was no one else around, so she didn't fight back. She stood in the middle of the bridle path that ringed the park and watched him ride away on the bike she had named Silver and pretended was an Appaloosa pony. She didn't want Pablo and the gang to find out what an easy mark she was, so she told them that she had sold the bike to buy firecrackers, the ultimate weapon for the gang.

Sometime around Annie's thirteenth birthday Pablo stopped hanging around the building so much. He was spending more time up on Amsterdam Avenue, with the Puerto Rican gangs, and it wasn't cool to have a white girlfriend. The two of them never talked about it. They just stopped looking for each other after school, and they both knew why. Still, she was safe on the street now because all the kids knew who she was, even though she had stopped skating.

Luke had eventually moved into a ground-floor apartment across the park. Technically, he lived on the Upper East Side, but it was on the edge of Spanish Harlem, right where the trains disappeared underground on their way to Grand Central Station. Neighborhood kids were known to shoot BB guns at the windows of the passing trains, but Annie never heard any gunshots, only the rattle of the apartment windows; and she could smell a faint trace of diesel in the air as the trains descended into the tunnel.

Her mother's new building had an odd smell in the hallways, as if everyone was cooking the same stew in their kitchens, something that smelled vaguely of onions. Annie had understood right away that the divorce had left both of her parents with less money, though she wasn't quite sure why. The apartment was a small two-bedroom, and everything about it was new and cheap. The walls were newly painted white, but they were so thin that she could hear their next door neighbor snoring at night through the wall, and she could smell it when he smoked a joint. There was no wood anywhere in the apartment; even the front door was made of two sheets of metal and was hollow in the middle. It sounded like a one-note steel drum when Annie pounded on it. She knew that Ellen hated the apartment and the big downstairs lobby that was empty and half lit with long, flickering fluorescent bulbs overhead. Ellen always hurried Annie through the lobby as if she was afraid they would get mugged. Annie didn't know how to tell her that she had already taken care of that problem by being Pablo's girlfriend for a year. Across the street was another big building exactly like the one they lived in, and everyone always hurried in and out of that building too, checking behind them as they got out their keys to open the downstairs door.

The only good thing about the apartment was that it had a terrace with an aluminum railing. Every apartment in the building had these tiny concrete porches fenced in metal, suspended high above the street. Some were lined with window boxes of flowers, others seemed to be used solely as an outdoor closet for old furniture and bicycles. Annie used hers to create a campfire in the woods. She hung bamboo screens over the railings and convinced Ellen to buy a hibachi, which she filled with coals to cook hamburgers or roast hot dogs on a stick for the two of them.

Annie also smoked cigarettes out there. She wasn't sure how Ellen would feel about her smoking, but smoking was important for her status, and Annie cared about status. She had begun smoking pot the summer after sixth grade and was surprised when, at the moment of confession to her mother, Ellen had brought an ounce out of the cupboard and confessed that she had begun that summer as well. That had been in the summer of 1973, and Annie and Ellen smoked a bowl together that night at the kitchen table.

Most of her school friends hadn't been allowed to come over to Annie's house since she had moved off Central Park West to an unsavory address. For the first year at the new apartment Annie had left her private school friends as soon as she got off the bus, and once she had quit Pablo's gang, there was no one to be with on the long afternoons after school. She started inviting herself over to the private school kids' apartments on the Upper East Side and often ate dinner with her friends, who usually had meals prepared for them by nannies, and never ate with their parents. By this time Annie had figured out that she had always been a scholarship kid at her school, and her school friends knew that she was different. At first the other girls had actually treated her with a little more respect, as if she must be very smart to be on scholarship. But that faded pretty quickly. She was smart enough, but she wasn't the smartest in the class, and they all knew that, too. No one meant to make her feel bad about being on scholarship, but sometimes the other girls said things as if they had forgotten that she wasn't as rich as they were, and it pissed Annie off. She knew she wasn't poor, not like some of the kids in her building, but, no, she wouldn't be going to Aspen for spring vacation or the Bahamas for Christmas.

In seventh grade, the year Annie turned thirteen, she spent every weekend at Luke's but spent her evenings with her school friends. They were the "fast" crowd at school, which meant they would drink bottles of Southern Comfort on the landscaped islands in the middle of Park Avenue with boys from other private schools and have make-out parties in big empty apartments on the Upper East Side.

Nobody's parents ever seemed to be home at these grand apartments; at Annie's parents' places, on the other hand, it seemed they never left. Ellen spent endless hours drinking coffee, talking, and smoking at the kitchen table with her women friends. But she hadn't had a boyfriend since she and Luke broke up, and as far as Annie could tell she never would. She simply couldn't imagine her mother being romantic with anyone, including her father.

Annie lost her virginity that spring in one of those empty Upper East Side apartments to a boy whom she thought she was in love with. They were both drunk enough not to care where they were, and he had climbed on top of her on a slippery pile of coats and jackets in somebody's parents' bedroom. The experience left Annie feeling that fucking was very overrated. She had already experimented with all of the other possible ways for her and various boys to touch each other, and she thought these were far superior to actual penetration, which was awkward, painful, and held no satisfaction at the end. She was also disappointed when the boy who had initiated her to this next level of experience felt exactly the opposite about it, and soon it was all he wanted to do—without the preliminaries that Annie thought made it worthwhile. She didn't admit this to her friends, however, since more than half of them had lost their virginity before she did and she had been late in beginning her period—halfway through the seventh-grade year.

When Annie began eighth grade in the fall of 1974, Ellen was not strict, never looked into her bedroom, and gave her liberal curfews compared to her friends'. Sometimes Annie thought that since she was two full years past entering her life as a teenager, her mother had pretty much figured that she would act like an adult from here on out. At other times Ellen would react with disbelief at what Annie expected to be able to do, would be furious at the demand for even more late nights, or an increase in her allowance. There were moments when Annie thought she could talk to her mother about anything, even sex. Then there would be days when Annie would wake up and Ellen's bedroom door would remain closed until Annie left for school, and Annie would be afraid to talk to her at all. Days would pass in almost silence between them, Annie staying away until after dinner and then sitting in front of the television until she fell asleep. On the mornings when Ellen's bedroom door was opened, there would be a special breakfast of kippers, eggs, cinnamon toast, and freshly squeezed orange juice from the old metal juicer, and the two of them would be back to the place that Annie never wanted to leave.

It was the winter of eighth grade, after Janis and Peter's New Year's Eve party, the last night of 1974, that Annie had started calling the Shanlick girls on her own. The girls called her back, and pretty soon Annie had permission to go downtown by herself to see them. New Year's Eve had been the night that she and the girls had discovered that they were all smoking pot and seeing boys, though Annie hadn't been able to find out if any of them had lost their virginity yet. It had seemed very important to all of them that they were pot smokers, as if that would bring them together despite any other differences—but there really weren't any big differences, and the four girls had spent most of the party talking and smoking on the fire escape, happily unconscious of the bitterly cold night until it began to rain, as it always does on New Year's Eve in New York.

Justin and Nick had been there too, and Nick had spent some time on the fire escape, flirting and gossiping with the girls, but Justin had been in his old teasing mode, which Annie never knew quite how to respond to. His remarks were usually mean, but then he and the girls would laugh it off as if it didn't really matter. Annie tried to do the same and was half-flattered, half-frightened when he turned his attention to her. Most of the time she was sure that Justin liked her father better than her, and that he simply tolerated her for Luke's sake. Then, Justin would suddenly spend an entire hour talking only to her, and she would fall in love with him all over again. They had never talked about what had happened that time they went out after the flag, and over the past two summers Justin had made sure that they were never sent out alone again.

Nick was gentler and more physical than Justin. He would always sit with his arms around the girls, and Annie was easily included in his gangling embrace. Both of the brothers were wild and distant, and, unlike the girls, they couldn't have been less interested in baring their souls on the fire escape that night. Annie wondered how the Shanlick girls could spend every weekend at their father's loft with those boys and not fall in love with them. But, then, she wasn't sure whether they weren't all half in love with one another anyway. After that night she felt that she was in love with all three of the sisters, and she began to talk on the phone to them every day and go with them to weekend parties in tiny apartments in the Village, where, if the parents were home, they didn't seem to care much about what went on, which was everything.

When she stayed uptown with the private school crowd, she spent the weekends smoking pot, taking downers, and drinking with boys who thought the girls were older than they really were. She and her friends bought bags of pot from a senator's son, and one boy she knew flew cocaine into the country using his father's diplomatic pouch. Cocaine still wasn't as popular as Quaaludes, and Annie was a little scared to do LSD. So far she had managed to avoid tripping without anyone knowing she didn't want to try it. Lots of girls stole pharmaceuticals from their parents' medicine cabinets, and they became adept at dosing themselves with Valium, Darvon, and even Seconal. Nobody's parents ever said anything, so the kids figured that they must all be so doped up themselves that they never noticed. Annie didn't recognize the names of anything in her mother's medicine bottles, so she left them alone.

By the middle of eighth grade she had figured out that if you stayed with one guy for a while you weren't a slut no matter what you did with him—and somehow everyone knew what everyone else did as soon as it happened. If you switched boyfriends a lot, and went all the way with them, then you were a slut and nobody would like you—even the boys. When the boy with whom she had lost her virginity broke up with her she was heartbroken for about two weeks. She had been talking to Liz Shanlick on the phone and said to her, in tears, "I love him so much!"

Liz had answered her—a little bored by it all, Annie knew—"Are you sure?"

That had jolted Annie into realizing that she wasn't really in love with him and never had been. She had thought that she should be in love with him because they had lost their virginity together. When she tried to explain this to her, Liz (who was still a virgin) said, "Well, since you don't like the fucking anyway, I don't think you're missing much."

Annie didn't bring her private school friends downtown with her. She was afraid of what the Shanlick girls would think of them; even though she had some real friends from school, all of the Village kids thought that the uptown kids were snobs. That spring, as the weather warmed up, Annie's school crowd began to spend more and more time in bars where they could get served. Downtown, she and the Shanlick girls could smoke and talk for hours together on the stoop to P.S. 3 on Grove Street, and they almost never went to bars since none of them had any money. "The Upper East Side is only good for doctor's offices," Tessa said, and Annie laughed, knowing for the first time what she meant, and agreeing with her.

But Justin liked it uptown. He was always asking Annie about her friends, and he had even convinced Annie to bring him to an uptown party one weekend. It was going to be at the senator's apartment, and when his son had the run of the place the parties were legendary. But Annie was getting bored with the Quaalude parties, and she was afraid she'd end up sleeping with her old boyfriend again if she went—as if this time was going to be different and he was going to stay interested in her after he fucked her. He had called to invite her, so she knew that he was already assuming that it would happen.

Justin found out about the party and wanted to go. He told her that they should go alone, without Nick or the Shanlick sisters, which made Annie feel guilty and flattered at the same time. How could she not go with the girls? On the other hand, Justin wanted only to be with her. Even if it was a stupid party, with Justin everything would be different.

They did it the way he wanted it. She told the girls that she was going to an uptown party that night, but she didn't tell them that Justin was going, too.

He wanted to meet before the party, and so she told him to meet her at the corner of Park Avenue and Eighty-ninth Street. Justin rode his old three-speed bike everywhere, and when she got to the corner he was leaning against the bike at the bottom of a streetlight. He didn't look like anybody else who was walking by there; in his hooded sweatshirt, loose pants, and high-top sneakers there was nothing preppie about him. She watched him for a minute from behind the corner of a building. He was so restless and different. He wasn't wearing his glasses, and without them his face looked younger than seventeen. He was careless about his looks in a way that made him appear better-looking; and she wished he was her boyfriend, waiting for her on the corner just like that. She tucked in her shirt so that it was tighter across her breasts, reminded herself again that he couldn't be less interested in her, then walked around the corner so that he could see her. He smiled and wheeled the bike over to her.

"I got here ten minutes ago," he said. "I've been watching the building. Shit, these people have a lot of money. I mean, that doorman never stops. Zoom! Here comes one couple ready to go out, gotta get them a cab. Then, zoom! Here comes another cab dropping people off to come to this building. I think I saw some people who were going to Jason's place. Your boyfriend's there already."

"He's not my boyfriend," Annie said. "Me and Thurston broke up a long time ago."

"Good. You should never go out with anyone named Thurston. Who the fuck does he think he is? Thurston's a last name."

Annie shrugged. "Want to go up?" she asked. "You can lock your bike on that side of the street."

Justin looked down and fiddled with the handlebars. "It's kind of early still," he said. "Why don't we go for a ride?"

He's nervous, Annie thought. Justin's scared to go up there. "I haven't got a bike," she said.

"So, ride on the crossbar," he offered. "Come on, I won't let you fall."

"I know," she said, looking at him carefully. She wondered what he was doing, why he was being so nice. "You were the one who wanted to go to this party," she said.

"I do . . . shit, Annie." Justin pulled back on his bike so that the front wheel lifted up. "I just don't want to get there too early, you know what I mean? It's not even ten o'clock. Come on, Annie."

He grinned at her and cocked his head a bit to the side as he straddled his bike, inviting her to get on board.

She got on.

It was like flying. Justin pushed off down Park Avenue with an arm on either side of her to steer, and she sat sidesaddle, holding the handlebars lightly in the middle for balance. Justin was sure of himself, even with Annie's weight in the middle of the bike, and he went easily in and around the flood of taxis that was cruising the Park Avenue apartment buildings. All the lights were on in the big Pan Am building at the faraway end of Park Avenue, and the tulip beds in the middle of the avenue went by in flashes of red and yellow, lit up by headlights. When they got to Seventy-seventh Street, he leaned to the right and they headed over to the park. Annie was a little scared as they crossed Fifth Avenue and sped down the paved hill into the park, toward the model boat pond. It was way past dark now, and she still never went into Central Park at night. But she didn't say anything; Justin's breath was in her ear as he pumped up the little hill toward the pond.

"Ever been here?" he asked.

"Sure. But not at night."

He steered toward the small pond, which was surrounded by a low cement wall. It was pretty in the dark, with the streetlights filtering through the trees above the wall on Fifth, and the small building facing the pond, which Annie supposed was for model boat storage, looked like a cottage from a childrens' book. On weekends the pond was surrounded by model boat fanciers who held regattas by poking their vessels around with long bamboo poles to catch the wind. Justin slowed down and they looped around the pond a few times. She didn't see anyone else there, though she kept looking for muggers. Everything was quiet except for the honking of cars that drifted down from Fifth Avenue. The huge Alice in Wonderland statue sat just to the north of them. It was made of bronze, with Alice sitting on a mushroom that was big enough for children to walk underneath. Annie had always played below the mushroom with the dormouse when her parents took her there. When she got older she would climb up to perch on the bronze top hat of the Mad Hatter, and now she saw the sculpture reflecting the scattered light back darkly, as if the metal made pools of water above the ground.

"Hey, let's go over to Alice," she said.

"No," Justin said. "Check this out."

He pumped hard on the pedals and the bike bumped up the three low steps that led to the other bronze sculpture facing the pond. A man sat with an oversized book open on his lap, while a small duck looked up at him from below. The trees came in closer here than they did near the boat pond, and Annie looked around nervously, afraid of who might come out of them.

Justin stopped the bike next to the sculpture and Annie got off the crossbar. She was sore from the ride and it felt good to be on the ground again.

Annie looked at the sculpture. "Who is this again?" she asked. "I always played more with Alice."

"Hans Christian Andersen," Justin said. "He was the best."

Annie leaned over and saw that the bronze book had real words in it.

"Hey, got a match?" she asked. He threw her a book and she struck a light, holding it close to the words so that she could read them.

Justin started speaking before she did. " 'It was beautiful in the country. It was summer. The wheatfields were golden and the oats were green.' " He stopped.

"You know it," she said. "You know it by heart, I mean."

"That's as much as I can remember," Justin said. He nodded toward the bronze book. "Am I right?"

She lit another match and held it up to the words one by one. "Yeah," she said. "You got it perfectly. 'The Ugly Duckling.' Of course, with the little duck and everything. I forgot."

"I remember sitting on this guy's lap when I was a kid," Justin said. "When my mother would take us on an excursion uptown, to the zoo or something. It didn't happen that much, but I remember it. The zoo always sucked, with those cages that smelled like piss and the monkey house where the animals always looked as if they were either going to kill you or start crying; usually they just beat off. Me and Nick were never allowed to buy anything from the vendors. Not even one fucking hot dog."

"Why?"

"Saving money," he laughed. "Mom always packed a lunch, but that wasn't what we wanted. We were at the zoo, for Christ's sake; we wanted a pretzel or an Italian ice, you know. But then we'd walk up to the boat pond and I remember sitting on this guy's lap. I always thought that Hans Christian Andersen was like, a giant, after that—that he was an actual, real-life giant who had written this huge book, and they had copied the stories out of his book and put them into regular-sized books for us to read. Like some librarian had actually done that. I had it all worked out."

He shrugged and leaned against Andersen's arm. "Got a cig?"

Annie dug out her pack and they both lit up.

"I want to get up there," Annie said.

"What?"

"Up on his lap. Look out."

She clambered up one bronze leg and turned so that she was sitting in his lap. "Oh, yeah," she said. "You're right. I feel really small up here."

"You *are* really small, dipshit," he said.

"Fuck you, Justin. No, you should check it out." She moved over to make room for him next to her. "Come on up."

He looked at her with a trace of a smile, and for a second she thought he was going to do it.

"Nah." He turned away. "Forget it. Let's go."

Annie didn't move. She liked being up there, safe inside Hans Christian Andersen's arms with the streetlights reflecting in the boat pond like dozens of tiny moons. It's like this in the park every night, she thought, and I've never been here.

"What do you think about Capture?" she asked.

He looked at her. "What do you mean?"

"I mean them changing the date. Playing the game on Memorial Day."

"I think it sucks."

"So can't you get them to change it? Dad says it's 'cause of Janis's work."

"Bullshit." He took a long drag on his cigarette and pitched it all the way to the boat pond, where it landed in the water with a soft hiss. "Bullshit. It's not about Mom's work. They said they don't want to be locked into the game in the summertime, or something. I think it's Peter's idea, not Mom's. It's really lame."

"But you'll be up there anyway in August, won't you?"

"Yeah. I mean, we always are. Don't ask me."

"It won't be as good." Annie kicked her feet against the side of the sculpture and it made a hollow ringing sound.

"I know. It's gotta be in August or it isn't the game. But I'm still working on them, Annie. And you've gotta work on your dad."

"You should talk to Dad. I've already tried."

"I hate them fucking up the game like this. As if it doesn't matter when we play. The weather is crucial to any military campaign, even Luke has to admit that. Look at Napoleon."

"What about him?"

"He never would've lost Russia if it wasn't for the winter. That was the beginning of the end for him."

Justin had gotten back on the bike. She looked over at him, suddenly wanting to tell him everything. How she hadn't forgotten that night of Capture the Flag, how she still thought about him all the time. But he rocked back and forth impatiently on his seat, and she took a breath but said nothing. Suddenly, the bushes rustled behind them, up the embankment where the road ran through the park. Annie saw a man walking toward them from up the hill.

"Justin," she breathed, and then she was on the bike without even knowing how she got down. He pushed off and they banged down the steps to where the pavement was smooth. The bike leaned crazily and almost fell, but then Justin put his foot out and balanced them, shoving off again and pedaling as fast as he could for the entrance. Neither of them spoke or looked behind them. Justin was standing up as he pedaled, and Annie crouched down to make herself even smaller so that he could look easily over the handlebars. Justin was breathing hard, and she knew he was going as fast as he could. They got to the bottom of the long hill out of the park and Justin looked behind.

"Do you see him?" she asked.

"No, but—" He started to pedal again, but it was hard and slow uphill.

"I'll get off," Annie said. She slid off the bar and looked behind her. The bushes looked close to the path and the streetlights down into the park cast only small pools of light; at least half of them were burned out. She started to run, and Justin pedaled beside her. Annie was fast, and even without any extra weight on the bike Justin had to work to keep up. Annie ran and ran, feeling as if every step was too slow. She could hear Justin breathing hard behind her, and the skidding of his tires as the bike lost traction up the hill. She went even faster, looking only at the opening in the stone wall that marked the entrance from Fifth Avenue.

They burst out onto the cobblestone sidewalk at almost the same moment, and Annie slowed down only when she got to the corner of Seventy-ninth Street, where there was a lot of crosstown traffic, and the white lights on the Metropolitan Museum shone back the marble reflection of its walls, lighting up the night all around it.

She leaned over, with her hands on her knees, breathing hard. Justin pulled up beside her, and she could hear him panting as well. They looked at each other and burst out laughing.

"You were so scared!" he gasped, leaning on the handlebars.

"You were right behind me!"

He laughed and she laughed too, thinking how they must have looked pounding out of the park.

"Well, no shit," Justin said, looking behind him. "I don't even want to know who he was. Probably some faggot coming back from the Ramble."

"What?" Annie was still catching her breath. "What's the Ramble?"

"It's that wild part of the park, you know, below the castle but above the rowboat pond."

Annie did know, now. She had wandered into that part once when she was alone. The pavement was all broken up, the bushes were untrimmed, and suddenly you couldn't see the city skyline around the park. It had been beautiful in a way, the weeds all spike-topped and multicolored above the tall grass, but it was totally deserted, and Annie had gotten spooked and backtracked out of it after she realized how long it had been since she had seen any other people.

"What happens in the Ramble?"

"Faggots. They go there to get laid. Even during the day they go at it, like a real pickup scene. Totally disgusting."

"You've *seen* them?" Annie didn't know whether to believe him or not. It could all be a setup for making her feel like an idiot.

"Yeah, I've *seen* them, O.K.? Only during the day. By mistake I ended up there once. Two of them were going at it right there in the park. Lucky thing I didn't get raped with this fine, fine ass of mine."

"Oh, please, Justin. Spare me."

"I will," he laughed. "Believe me, I will. It was disgusting!"

He got back on the bike, and Annie climbed onto the crossbar without saying anything. She wondered what boys did together; blow jobs, she guessed, but none of the boys she knew thought those were disgusting—it was the girls who thought that. Justin's probably lying, she thought, and decided not to ask him anything else about it.

They biked past the fountains in front of the museum, a perfect row of white, bubbling jets lit by floodlights. Justin looped around each low oval of water, doing an extended figure eight, then entered Fifth Avenue traffic to head back up to the party. The streets seemed bright and loud after the park; it was a Saturday night and everyone was going somewhere. Yellow taxis traveled in packs and tried to push each other out of the way as the doormen whistled and waved them down. The brass supports in front of the awnings gleamed, and a pair of legs in sheer black stockings was always waiting just inside the door next to suited trousers. Justin hummed happily under his breath as they biked north, and when they got to Eighty-ninth Street he jumped off the bike and dropped her in front of the entrance to the building, helping her down with a mock flourish of his arm.

As Justin locked the bike up, the doorman looked at them scornfully and asked Annie which apartment as if he already knew where she was going. Doormen know everything, she thought. This guy knows the senator is in Washington, Jason's mother is in Amagansett for the weekend, and that Jason's going to trash the apartment and get away with it. Justin was unusually quiet in the elevator on the way up; Annie thought he was a little intimidated by going up to the penthouse floor.

It was one of those apartments that the elevator opened directly into, as it was the only apartment on the whole floor; or, for that matter, the next two floors, because a staircase led upstairs just beyond the main foyer. Annie had been there before, but it always struck her how truly grand it was. The front room was enormous, and each of the walls held one large, unattractive painting. The place was pretty crowded; the large Persian rug had been pushed back to make a dance floor, but nobody was dancing. There was a grand piano in one corner, and some boy was playing classical music on it. In front of the white leather couch was a huge glass-topped coffee table, and placed in the center of it was a big Baggie full of pot. Jason had black Irish good looks and wore ripped jeans and a paint-splattered T-shirt. He had his bare feet tucked under him on the couch and was rolling joints and passing them around the room.

"That's Jason," Annie said to Justin. She knew he wanted to meet Jason because of who he was.

Justin looked surprised. "That guy?"

Annie shrugged. She knew too much about Jason to be impressed by his lineage.

"There's some family pictures on the wall in the upstairs hallway," she said. "If you want to check it out."

They made their way to the bar, which was set up on the kitchen counter. Jason must have just taken his family's liquor cabinet and set it out for everyone. There were bottles of old wine and port as well as plenty of hard liquor. Most people were drinking gin and tonics or screwdrivers because they were easy to make and didn't taste too bad. A couple of the girls were walking around with martini glasses. Annie poured some straight vodka on ice, and Justin started for a beer but then went for a gin and tonic like everybody else.

"This is Justin," Annie said every other minute, as people came over to say hello. She could tell that everyone was wondering if he was her boyfriend, and where he had come from. She kept it vague on purpose, though Justin wasn't acting anything like a boyfriend. Then, after she had gone to the bathroom, she couldn't even find him for a while. She finally saw him sitting on the edge of the couch between Jason and Marcie, a tall, dark-haired girl whom Annie thought was just too beautiful to live. Marcie always got pretty high and ended up doing something unforgettable. Last year she had been carried around the block naked, wrapped only in a sheet. That was during a party at her own place, a town house in the east sixties. She was a grade ahead of Annie and didn't bother to be friendly to her at school, though she was always nice to her at parties like this. Justin was leaning over and talking to Jason as though they were old friends, and Annie wondered how he had managed all that during the five minutes she had been gone.

She started to walk over to them when someone touched her arm. It was Emily Rosenberg and Dina Matthews, who were in her class, and of all the girls in this crowd, she liked them the most. They were always getting into trouble together and didn't seem to care about boyfriends as much as some of the others. They had always liked Annie, even though they wouldn't come to her house.

"Who is that guy you came with?" Emily asked. "He's gorgeous, that's all. Just gorgeous."

"Is he an asshole?" asked Dina, and they all laughed. Annie could tell they were already stoned. She had brought a joint with her, but she hadn't offered to smoke it with Justin in the park because she knew he hated smoking dope.

"He's Justin. The Shanlick girls' brother—well, stepbrother." Dina and Emily had heard about the Shanlick sisters from Annie, though they had never met them.

"And . . ." Emily rattled the ice in her glass and looked at Annie expectantly.

"And he's kind of an asshole, kind of not."

"Ooh, she likes him," Dina said, and Annie blushed.

"Yeah, well. He's not mine, so . . ." she let the sentence trail off.

"So . . . fuck him," Dina said, grinning. "I wouldn't mind."

"Come on, Annie," Emily said. "I want to show you something."

She led the way to a medium-sized room off the dining room, a study belonging to the senator, judging by the law school degree on the wall. There was a big desk opposite a leather armchair and couch. The fireplace looked like it actually worked, which was almost unheard of in the city. Annie could smell the ashes from a real wood fire, and it made her miss the country and the bonfire at Capture the Flag.

Emily closed the door and plopped down on the thick Oriental rug that lay in front of the fireplace.

"I fucked Jason in here once," she said, giggling.

"Really?" Annie was impressed, in spite of herself.

"Yeah, his parents were even home, can you believe that? They were upstairs, asleep. I kept expecting the phone to ring with some White House emergency."

"Where did you do it?" Dina asked.

"On the rug, what do you think?" Emily laughed.

"I don't know." Dina went over and sat in the senator's chair, which was on wheels. She spun around. "You could've done it on this chair."

They giggled.

"Yeah," Emily said. "With Jason on the bottom. He would've liked that."

"Hey . . ." Dina picked up the phone that was sitting on the senator's desk. "Anybody want to make a long-distance call?"

Emily wanted to call every major city they could think of. She wanted to wake people up in Japan and tell them that they had won a lot of money in America. But Annie didn't want to. It was one thing to call someone you knew, but to make calls just for the sake of it seemed pointless.

"It's a golden opportunity," Emily kept saying. "Come on, you guys, there must be someone we know. Even just California. Let's call L.A."

"Forget it, Emily," Annie said. "I don't want to spend the whole party on the phone." She wanted to find Justin.

Back in the other room the party had reached another level. People were dancing now, and couples were leaning against the stairs and making out or pulling each other upstairs to one of the many available bedrooms. The whole place smelled like dope even though the windows were wide open. More people had arrived, and Annie had to push her way through to get to where she could see if Justin was still on the couch. Justin wasn't even in the living room anymore. She wondered if he had gone upstairs.

She stood still a moment, considering whether or not she wanted to go look for him. If he was with Marcie she definitely didn't want to find him. She thought about leaving without saying good-bye. Then someone jostled her from behind and brushed against her hips in a way that didn't feel like a mistake.

It was Thurston.

"Hi," he said, smiling. "You came."

"Yeah." She subtly disengaged her back from his hand, hoping it seemed natural, knowing it probably didn't.

Thurston was smoking a joint, and he passed it to her. They moved over to an open window and smoked together, looking out over Park Avenue. They were facing east, so high up that you could see all the way to the East River.

"You brought Justin," he said. They had met at a party in the Village once, just before Thurston broke up with Annie. The Shanlick girls had decided he was a jerk, though Thurston didn't know that. "Are the girls here?"

"No. Just us." She didn't want to let him know that she had lost track of Justin about an hour ago.

"What've you been doing?"

"Nothing. School. Hanging out downtown."

She stubbed out the remains of the joint on the windowsill and offered the roach to Thurston.

He shook his head. "I don't need it."

Annie put it inside the cellophane wrapper of her cigarette pack and turned to look for Justin. She looked around the room, but the pot made her feel self-conscious and clunky, like she didn't want to go anywhere after all.

"You want another drink?" Thurston asked, and she realized he had been saying something else that she hadn't been paying attention to.

"O.K.," she said, thinking how faraway she felt from everyone around her. "I'm drinking vodka on ice."

"I know," Thurston said, smiling, and took her empty glass. "I'll get you a lemon this time."

Marcie and Jason had disappeared as well. The three of them are probably doing something I'll hear about tomorrow, she thought, wishing she was with them. She felt a little sorry for herself, stupid and slow. It's the dope, she thought, and with that thought the room seemed like a picture of teenagers having a party. Even Dina and Emily, talking together on the other side of the room, looked odd and unnatural. I've got to get out of here, she thought. I'm leaving. Where's Justin?

Then Thurston was at her arm again, and the vodka felt cold and soothing on her raw throat. He lit a cigarette and leaned next to her.

"What are you thinking about?"

"What do you mean?"

"Just now. You looked really faraway."

She smiled at him; he did know her in a way. "I am," she said.

He reached his hand out and held it against her crotch, pressing hard on her blue jeans. His hand was warm, and it covered her completely between her legs. He left it there as he looked her in the eye.

"I want to be right there," he said. "I want to be right there, right now."

"Oh, fuck you, Thurston," she said, but she didn't move.

He pulled her closer against him, cupping her ass with his other hand. Annie didn't pull away. I wish he wasn't so fucking good-looking, she thought.

The party was still going strong when Thurston offered to take her home. Justin was talking with Marcie in the kitchen when Annie came downstairs and told him that she was going home.

"O.K., bye," he said. "See you soon." Then he gave her one of his bad-boy smiles.

Marcie was all over him, and she could tell he was loving it. Everybody's fucked Marcie, she felt like saying, so don't be so proud of yourself. But she smiled at both of them as if it was O.K. and went to find her jacket. She didn't want Justin to see her leaving with Thurston, and she checked behind her when she went to the door; he wasn't even watching.

That was the last time she slept with Thurston, and when Justin asked her about more uptown parties she lied and told him she didn't know of any. Then she found out from her friends that he had become friendly with Jason and had been going to some of the parties himself, without even telling her. They all thought he was so interesting—a scholarship kid like Annie but from downtown—and all Annie could say when the girls in her crowd started to fall for him was, "I don't know him very well," which she realized was true. The party at the senator's apartment had been in early April. Now it was almost the end of May, and the main thing she and Justin talked about when they saw each other was Capture the Flag.

She knew that Justin had called Luke about changing the date back to August, and Luke had told him he didn't see why it mattered *when* the game happened, as long as it happened. Justin retaliated by telling Luke that he didn't have time to get together and plan strategies for the game, as they always had in the past. He didn't even bother with Napoleon. He told him that because of the date change, he would be too busy with school, which both he and Luke knew was a lie. Justin never had to work hard to do well in school. Annie could tell that it really threw Luke; he wanted to have Justin on his side. But to Annie he insisted on putting it off to Justin's adolescent sulks and refused to go into it anymore.

. . .

Of course, everyone went up for the game on Memorial Day. Liz and Tessa and Sam rode in Luke's new Volkswagen with Luke and Annie, and everyone else rode with Peter and Janis in their big station wagon. The two cars drove in caravan up the Saw Mill River Parkway, and when they stopped along the way to gas up, use the bathrooms, and buy snacks, it began to feel the way Capture the Flag weekend was supposed to feel, and Annie cheered up. On the second leg of the journey, she and Luke taught the girls to sing the chorus from Luke's favorite song since the divorce:

"And I think it's going to be all right
Yes, the worst is over now
And the morning sun is shining like a—
RED RUBBER BALL

Her father banged the wheel in time as he sang, and they all hit the dashboard and the backs of the front seats along with him, rocking the little car back and forth.

When they finally arrived late that night, there was frost on the windows. Everything indoors still smelled like wintertime. The windows had swollen shut in the spring damp and needed to be banged open by Peter and Luke. "Wake up!" Peter yelled out of each one as he swung it open. Annie had never visited the summer home except in August, when the house was hardened into a dry smooth husk by all of the sisters and brothers who raced through it, dripping water from the pond and trailing crushed leaves from the soles of their feet.

Summer had never seemed so far away to Annie before. Everyone was cranky and tired, bundled in sweaters and complaining about the cold. Downstairs all of the accumulated leaves and spiders and mouse droppings had to be swept out before anyone could go to bed. The unplugged refrigerator stood in the kitchen with the light burned out and the door swinging open like a broken jaw. Janis walked over, shut the door, and made a joke about it, but Annie saw Liz head for the back door and flip open her pack of cigarettes. Annie saw her chance when Janis bent down behind the refrigerator looking for the plug. The Shanlick girls smoked fairly openly, but it was a nod of politeness to Janis that they stepped outside to do it.

"So fucking cold," Liz said, passing Annie the pack.

"I wish we weren't here," Annie said. "I mean, not now. The game should be in August."

"Janis and Dad said that next year they might not even have a game."

"What?"

"It's just what they said. And Justin says he doesn't want to do it anymore." Liz watched Annie closely, the lit end of her cigarette flared.

"Just because it's happening on the wrong weekend?" Annie was talking loud, not caring who heard her. "Why doesn't he want it to happen anymore? Next year we could do it in August and everything would be back to normal—shit, I knew that this would happen."

"Nobody wants to play the game anymore, Annie," Liz said.

"I do."

"Nobody but you," Liz said. She looked away, pushing her thick brown hair out of her face. Annie bit the inside of her cheek and wondered if this was going to be the first fight she and Liz had ever had.

Liz waited a moment. "Annie . . ." she said, and then she put her head gently down on Annie's shoulder, so that their cheeks were just barely touching. Annie caught her breath but didn't move. Liz kissed her briskly, once on each cheek. "I'm sorry," she said.

Annie didn't reply; she didn't want to cry in front of anyone, even Liz. After a moment Liz looked back toward the house and stubbed her cigarette out on the walk.

"Janis still needs help."

Annie stayed there long after finishing her cigarette. Liz was closer to her than the other sisters. They spent time walking the streets together, or reading, and though Annie liked these times when she looked back on them, while they were happening she was always filled with a kind of anxiety, afraid that she was missing something. But Liz always made Annie feel that if it ended up that the two of them were on their own, it was all right with her. She never seemed to share Annie's disappointment and jealousy when the others paired off: Sam and Justin, Tessa and Nick. Annie knew that she herself would bolt in the direction of the boys if given the chance, just as Sam and Tessa did.

Liz was quiet until you got to know her. Everyone in the family felt they could confide in Liz, and Annie did too, though sometimes she wondered what Liz thought of carrying all of their personal riddles around with her: Sometimes she must have wanted everyone to just shut up.

The back porch light burned out with a sharp pop, shocking Annie, and as her eyes adjusted to the darkness she noticed that the cloud cover had thinned out over the hill in front of the house where the game would be played tomorrow night. The stars were so still and white within the widening circle of clouds that Annie felt they would never move again. She knew that in the end it would all be decided without her—when the game was to be played, what neighborhoods her parents would move into, who they would end up kissing in a bedroom full of coats. More than anything else she felt stuck fast to this piece of earth below the burned-out porch light that she had walked past without thinking for all the summers of Capture the Flag.

Sam stuck her head out of the back door and smiled her big, crooked grin at Annie. That moment of adolescent physical perfection was coalescing in Sam; her skin had a luminescent sheen, and her body practically hummed with new hormonal force.

"Come on, Annie," she said. "We need help making the beds upstairs, and then we're done."

Sam and Tessa both wanted to be in the downstairs bedroom, because it was warmer, so Annie and Liz had the upstairs room next to Justin and Nick's room. The girls had to share a double bed, and they snuggled close together trying to warm the sheets. Liz brought her two new kittens from New York into bed to keep them warm. It made Annie laugh to see them suckle Liz's earlobes like teats; they were still so young. Liz and Annie pretended that the kittens were giving them miniature, matching tattoos on each ear with their teeth, which pierced their skin over and over again like tiny needles.

The last things Annie heard that night were the sounds of the highway, the drone of cars as repetitive and rhythmic as surf, and the kitten sucking at Liz's ear.

The first thing she heard when she woke up was the blender in the kitchen, which meant that Janis was starting to make Bloody Marys. Liz was gone, and it felt so warm inside the room that Annie knew she must be the last one up. From the bed she could see an unyielding blue sky through the window, and she threw off her covers and luxuriated in the warm, still air of the bedroom, lazily wondering when Liz had gotten up. She had woken several times during the night to find Liz's hair drifting onto her face and neck, and their legs intertwined below the knee.

Annie had no close relatives in the city, and as an only child she had always slept alone. Unused to sleeping with another body, Annie had stayed very still, afraid to adjust any part of herself where it lay touching Liz, who slept on with a sensual abandonment of her mouth and limbs. Do I look like that when I'm asleep? she had wondered, as the moonlight etched shadows around Liz's closed eyes and barely opened mouth.

Eventually she got up, went to the window, and saw them all outside on the slate patio, which lay behind the house with a view of the long sloping lawn that led down to the woods and stream. Several years ago Peter and Janis had enlarged the pond into a natural swimming hole, bringing in a backhoe and planting some willow trees on the new banks of raw earth. Now the water was deep enough to swim in, the grass had grown back, and the new trees had taken hold, so Annie could forgive this change and acknowledge that it had been an innovation.

Down on the patio Luke and Peter were behind sections of the *New York Times* with their dark glasses on. Sam lay stretched out on a towel in the grass, reading a magazine and doing her Lolita imitation. She had read the book and seen the movie. Now she was wearing pink, heart-shaped sunglasses, a bikini, and had greased herself up with baby oil. All she needed was to get Luke or Peter to start painting her toes bright red, thought Annie, and she'd have the whole combination.

Annie was trying to get used to seeing Sam lying around almost naked, but her body still stunned Annie. Everything had changed over the last year. It was as if she had gone to sleep one night and woken up looking like a pinup girl. Her figure looked a lot older than thirteen, and she made the most of it. She could get served in any bar in the Village, where they carded Tessa, Liz, and especially Annie, who still looked about twelve.

But it wasn't just Sam's new voluptuousness that made everything different for her. Tessa's good looks kept the phone ringing off the hook. And Annie had no trouble attracting the attention of the boys who had started to loiter each afternoon around the corner of her school. But the major difference between Sam and the rest of the girls was her attitude. "Hi, I'm Sam, and these are my breasts," is what Tessa always said when Sam was doing her number, but the fact was that Sam's breasts had gotten all of them into the movies free, provided rolls of quarters for video games from total strangers, and, of course, plenty of free drinks.

Annie both envied and loathed Sam's absolute lack of morality about using her body to achieve her ends. Sam said that using her tits was like being able to control the weather on a battlefield; men got so confused by watching her that they made only the decisions she wanted them to make. When Sam went out wearing her tiny shirts with no bra underneath, she acted as if she expected the world to kiss her all over just for sharing the sight of them. She had reinvented herself into a force of nature at the age of thirteen. Annie had never seen anything like it.

Annie dressed quickly and went downstairs, grabbing a slice of toast on her way out the door. Luke put down his paper and held out a hand to greet her, pulling her in for a kiss on the cheek. She settled down on the flagstones, leaning back against his knees, and took the bottle of baby oil that Sam silently offered to her. The day was heating up, and she began to slather her legs and arms in hopes of a tan from the spring sun. There was a warm breeze, and the smell of the baby oil, combined with the rustle of the newspapers and the drone of insects, made her feel as if it was late summer after all.

"What time is it?" Luke asked suddenly, putting down his paper as if it had just bitten him. He always sprang from stillness to action with absolutely no warning, and it made people nervous.

"What time is it?" he asked again.

"It's a quarter to twelve, Edwards," Peter said, without moving his newspaper from in front of his face. "She doesn't get in for another hour, and the station is only fifteen minutes away."

At this first mention of Jill, Luke's girlfriend, who was coming up from the city to join them in the game, Annie moved away from Luke and lay down on the towel next to Sam, pretending to be interested in her magazine.

"Twenty minutes, with traffic," Luke said, starting to get up.

"What traffic?" asked Peter.

"Whatever you have up here. Milk trucks, farm vehicles—Volvos."

"Volvos." Peter reached for his Bloody Mary. "You are truly an urban mole, Edwards, come to corrupt us simple country folk."

"Simple country folk. Everyone up here is from New York or Cambridge and you know it—how about your Pulitzer Prize winner down the road? Or the baker who translates Garcia Lorca on the side? Don't give me that crap, Peter." This made Peter laugh, which was exactly what Luke was aiming for. He got up from his deck chair, unconsciously rubbing his hands together in a nervous way. "I'm going to the station."

Luke had been seeing Jill since Christmas, and there was beginning to be talk about them getting married. Annie acted as if it wasn't really going to happen, since Luke still hadn't said anything about it directly to her. She was sure he would tell her himself if it was true. She had held a secret belief since childhood that if she did not speak a thing aloud, she could undermine its chances of ever becoming a reality. Luke hadn't had any serious girlfriends before Jill. Annie had never seen the girl from Peter and Janis's party again, and on the weekends Luke was hers alone.

She loved his apartment in the old carriage house in Spanish Harlem: It was a small studio with one door that led to the street and another door that led to the garage where he kept the car. Luke used to joke that his social life was limited to sleeping with his car, and when Annie was there she slept on a piece of foam he rolled out on the floor. The studio was divided in half by a raised level of flooring, and Luke had made the raised area the living room, putting down a rug and a small couch and a coffee table, though there was no real divider between that area and his bed. Annie and Luke listened to music together and ate popcorn and went to the movies. He played Dylan, the Beatles, and the Rolling Stones as well as Teddy Wilson, Lester Young, and Billie Holiday. Sometimes a friend of hers spent the night, or they had Chinese food with old college friends of Luke's who were like benign, intellectual uncles to Annie. The adults would argue about politics and books, and even though she sometimes didn't understand exactly what they were talking about they never made Annie feel stupid when she asked questions. Luke encouraged her to enter the debate, and she was expected to understand the majority of their cultural references, which, in fact, she did. Though the atmosphere always had an edge of competition, Annie knew that they were testing each other as well as her, and it was part of the game of conversation. Annie didn't understand much of the contemporary political talk, but she could keep up with most of the historical references, and best of all was talking about books with these middle-aged men who felt as passionate about Athos, Porthos, Aramis, and d'Artagnan as she did.

It had felt safe until Jill started hanging around. The idea that Jill might have pretensions to being another mother to Annie seemed absurd to her. That wasn't it—what she hated about Jill was that over the last two years Annie had finally had Luke to herself, and she wanted to keep it that way.

A gun went off three times in rapid succession and then there was silence; even the insect life seemed to pause.

"Justin's giving Tessa and Liz a lesson with the twenty-two down at the pond," Sam said to Annie. "They're shooting at beer cans, or frogs or something."

The gun fired over and over. Peter put his paper down and sighed dramatically. Sam glanced at him quickly, then rolled her eyes at Annie and went back to her magazine. Peter frightened Annie, even though he had always been gentle and funny with her. She had heard him yelling at Janis or one of the children when she stayed over at their loft in New York, and though this had happened only once or twice, in her mind he had grown in size and strength as she listened to him. There was no yelling in Annie's house and never had been; only taut silence followed by disappearances. Peter's yelling terrified Annie when she heard it, and she knew that the girls were frightened too. Only Janis and the boys fought back.

Annie stretched her long, angular body, limb by limb, then got to her feet and picked off a few bits of grass that had stuck to her baby-oiled legs.

"Have I met Jill before?" Sam asked Annie, who shrugged in reply. "And she's real fucking young, huh?"

"I don't know how old she is." Annie wrapped a blade of grass around her index finger so tightly that the tip of her finger turned white. Peter looked hard at Sam, then checked to see if Luke had heard, but he had already gone inside and was talking to Janis in the kitchen.

"You've met her before. I think she's thirty-three." Peter looked over his paper at Sam. Her language didn't surprise him, but something had gotten to him, either the gun or the remark, and Annie was suddenly aware that the three of them were alone on the patio. "She was at the New Year's Eve party this year," he said to Sam, "and she remembers you, so you can pretend to remember her."

Sam said nothing.

"Jill's all right," Peter continued, turning back to his paper. "Nervous."

"Do you think they're going to get married?" Annie asked. Peter looked at her as if he must have misunderstood her. Annie felt the old fear come back, but she kept her eyes on Peter. She wanted one shot at figuring it all out before Jill arrived from the station with Luke.

"I don't know. Of course, it's been three years since . . ." He avoided Annie's gaze and rubbed critically at a smudge of moss growing in between the flagstones. "How is Ellen?" he asked, as if he was changing the subject.

"Fine," Annie said. She and the girls had talked about how neither of their mothers had remained friends with the old crowd, or with each other, after their respective divorces. Ellen was always so polite about Peter and Janis that Annie knew she must have been hurt by them. This was the first time either of them had mentioned her mother to Annie in two years. "They act like she's dead," Annie had complained to the girls. Again the gun fired down at the pond, once, twice, three times.

"She's still teaching at Columbia."

"Yeah."

This was turning into the longest conversation Annie had ever had with Peter. "I don't think she has a boyfriend," she offered. Maybe she could get him to talk more about Jill and her father this way.

"Girlfriend?" Peter grinned at her and Sam from behind his dark glasses and popped his eyebrows up and down. It was one of his favorite tricks to make them laugh, and it had always worked when they were kids.

Fuck you, Peter, Annie thought, smiling at him and knowing that their conversation was over. Sam laughed out loud. "Dad! Stop!"

"O.K., O.K.! I just always thought she would, given half a chance." Peter pushed his glasses back and picked up the paper. Annie waited a moment longer to see if he would speak again, then gave up and flopped back down on the towel next to Sam. She made a silent vow never to ask Peter a real question again.

"Who would what?" Janis asked. She had come out at the tail end of Peter's comment and was standing with a pitcher of Bloody Marys on the back steps leading into the kitchen.

"Ellen—would become a dyke." Peter held out his empty glass without looking up from the paper.

"Don't be ridiculous," Janis said, looking at Annie and laughing a little too loudly. "Here, have a celery stalk." She shoved one into his glass with her free hand. "Why do men always want women to adopt their own sexual fantasies?"

"Don't women want men to adopt theirs?"

Janis said nothing.

"Why aren't women ever interested in men's fantasies?" Peter broke off the top of his celery with a clean snap of his jaw.

"Because your saturnalia is not necessarily our idea of a good time." Janis moved in for a kiss to stop the argument, and Peter adjusted his head slightly so that her lips grazed his cheek. She pretended not to notice, settling into Luke's empty chair and picking up the section of newspaper he had left behind.

The gunfire erupted once more. Janis ignored the sound. Peter took a long sip of his drink, folded the paper into three neat sections, and got up to go into the house.

Janis reached out a hand to him. "You went down and got the gun with him." There was a determined smile on her face.

"It doesn't mean I have to listen to it all day, does it?" He tucked the newspaper under his arm and gently freed himself of her hand. "I'm going in to try to get some work done."

"Peter, come on, the game is tonight. We have to go buy beer and clean up the yard a bit—"

"I have to work."

Janis shut her mouth with a hard little clicking sound and smiled. He went into the house.

Sam watched it all from behind her heart-shaped sunglasses, not moving until her father walked into the kitchen. She then picked up a long piece of grass and examined it very carefully.

"I'm going down to the pond," Sam said. "You coming, Annie?"

"Yeah." Annie got up and stood next to Sam, waiting for her to gather up her baby oil and magazines. Janis stared at the newspaper and stretched her white legs out into the sun with self-conscious nonchalance. Annie noted the varicose veins that Janis couldn't be bothered hiding, and wondered if Janis even saw them anymore.

"O.K., let's go," Sam said. "See you later, Janis."

As she and Sam walked away, Annie trailed her hand along the top of the green hedge that bordered the path down to the pond. She looked back at Janis sitting on the patio, surrounded by sections of the paper, and realized that it was always happening like this—Janis would make all of the drinks, all of the food, and bring all of the towels out to the pond for a family swim. Then something would happen, and she'd be left there holding a big pile of hot dogs, or a pitcher of Bloody Marys. Lucky thing she always brings a book, thought Annie, and forgot about her completely.

Liz was standing behind Justin with her hand on her hip exactly like her stepbrother, her face squinted in utter seriousness at the target, an old beer can. Tessa was sitting a little farther off, smoking a cigarette under the shade of one of the new willows that trailed its branches into the water at the edge of the pond. It was now late morning, the air was humid, and the sky had hazed over. By midsummer the grass would be dried to a yellow-brown crust over the dirt that cracked in a thousand directions underfoot. Justin was holding the gun tight against his shoulder. He held his breath when he aimed and let it out when he pulled the trigger. The gun slammed back against him as the empty can of Budweiser flipped twice in the air and fell behind the stump.

Liz ran to pick it up, shouting, "You got it, Justin! Right in the middle of the 'B.' "

"Put it back up there," he yelled.

Liz balanced the can carefully on top of the target: Justin's relief map of the farmhouse and the fields. Justin had put the map out on the stump by the pond when they arrived the night before. Annie had wondered then why he had hauled it out of the car instead of waiting to set it up with Luke in the living room and plot strategies for the game. She didn't know until she came down to the pond that he had never brought it inside the house. It had rained overnight, and the papier-mâché was beginning to slide off the sides of the wooden base.

"How come you did that?" Annie asked Justin, as they walked up next to him.

"Did what?"

"Put your old map of the game out there."

"I'm sick of looking at it," he said, giving her a harsh look as if she'd better mind her own business.

Annie felt herself start to blush. Even after all these years she kept leaving herself open for the kill. When it came to Justin, she couldn't help it. She always forgot how quickly he could turn against anyone. She looked away, trying to hide her face from him, and he shot the gun again. This time Sam ran to pick up the beer can.

She smiled at Justin. "Can I have a turn?"

Justin handed her the gun. She placed it against her shoulder, the way Peter and Luke had taught her, and closed one eye as she looked down the barrel.

"Remember the kickback," Justin said, reaching around her oily shoulders for the gun to help her aim. "You have to aim a little lower, to make up for the kick."

"O.K., O.K. I got it."

Justin took a step back. She pulled the trigger. The field on the model exploded, bits of colored paper spraying out into the air. The beer can stayed exactly where it was, slumped against a cherry-colored hill. Sam let the gun drift down from her shoulder and turned to Justin, scared.

"I'm sorry, Jus—"

"Fuck it."

"I was trying to aim a little lower."

"Forget it, Sam. That thing will be totally destroyed by the end of the weekend anyway."

He took the gun from her and leveled it directly at the model, firing six shots, fast. The relief map trembled and slouched over, tilting off the edge of the stump. Sam looked as if she was about to cry and wouldn't look at anyone; but Annie did, her eyes widening as she tried to catch the eyes of each of the sisters. Tessa had joined them to watch Sam shoot, and she kept her eyes on the target. Liz shrugged at Annie, then looked away. Justin had built the model in the eighth grade, spending every afternoon that year in the shop class after school. Every other year he had spent hours over it with Luke; they would lock themselves in his room all day before the game so nobody from the other team could get in and see the war games they had set up there.

"Blow you away, motherfucker," Justin said quietly. A lock of long brown hair had fallen in front of his face, and he shoved it back before shooting one more time and sending the map facedown into the grass. No one said anything for a long time. The sun was directly overhead and there were no more shadows now. Then Justin started laughing, hard. Sam joined him, and Tessa and Liz both giggled a little, wanting to be part of it. But the farmhouse lying on its side in the grass spooked Annie; she scuffed her black high-top sneakers in the dirt and didn't laugh at anything.

Justin suddenly spun around in a circle with the gun, firing it into the sky again and again with only one hand, like a cowboy stuntman in the movies. He waved the other arm slowly back and forth, as if he were pushing himself through water instead of air. There was a pure, solid recklessness to Justin that drew all of them to him. As she watched him turn round and round, Annie felt caught, unable to take her eyes from him. The rifle shots were deafening, but no one spoke or took a step away. At the same time she knew that their witnessing this meant nothing to him. Justin was alone with the gun and his own centrifugal force.

Justin reminded Annie of the whirling dervishes she had seen with her mother at the Cathedral of St. John the Divine the past winter. They had come to perform, and Ellen had wanted to see them. Annie had loved the bright costumes, which flew around them in a blur, and the seeming physical impossibility of what they were doing. Annie and Ellen sat together in a back pew, lulled by the music beneath the vaulted roof. To Annie, it had felt as if the dancers were spinning everyone there into a dream fabric, that time had lengthened and changed.

Then one of the dervishes abruptly stopped spinning and crumpled to the floor. Some of the people watching got halfway up and stood still, unsure of what to do. Ellen actually gave a small cry and gripped Annie's arm very hard, but she didn't move. When Annie looked over at Ellen she seemed frozen, staring at the one fallen figure. The other dervishes kept spinning, as if unaware, except for the one closest to the crumpled man, who now looked small and vulnerable, a smudge of brown skin enveloped by red and gold cloth. Ellen's grip on Annie's arm started to hurt, and she tried to pull away, but Ellen wouldn't let her.

"Look," she whispered.

The man whirling beside the fallen dancer did not stop immediately but slowed his dance by degrees until he came to rest, his feet still patterning a circle on the great stone slabs that made up the floor. He stumbled slightly with the effort of becoming still, then looked at the spectators with a reassuring smile and reached down to lift the fallen dervish as if he were carrying nothing more than an armful of air. He carried him off behind the altar and out of sight. Ellen had insisted on leaving immediately, instead of waiting for the end of the performance, and Annie had been unable to talk to her about anything else all afternoon.

"Do you think he was all right?" Ellen asked Annie more than once.

"Of course he is, Mom," Annie had answered. "They must fall all the time. It's hard to dance like that." But Ellen kept bringing it up for weeks afterward, so that Annie didn't ever want to go to the cathedral again.

Justin stumbled also as he tried to stop spinning around and around. He pushed the barrel into the dirt, leaning against the wooden butt of the rifle for balance. They all stood in the sudden quiet and watched the small bits of wood and papier-mâché that were starting to blow off over the pond and settle on top of the water.

Annie waited for Justin's breathing to slow down before she spoke. "Jesus, Justin. I thought you loved that thing."

He looked at her and smiled. "I did."

"Wow," said Sam after a moment. "What a mess."

There were only twelve or thirteen on each team that year. Maybe it was the time of year that kept so many people from coming up from the city. It got very cold just after sundown when Luke and Peter led everyone up the driveway from the house. They were a sparse little band of partisans, Annie thought: Peter and Janis's friends from the country who lived there year-round, and the extended family that included all of the siblings, Luke, Jill, and Annie.

Jill had stayed within arm's reach of Luke since her arrival in the early afternoon. She and Annie kept at a polite distance. She had a nervous habit, which Annie detested, of continually glancing from one person to another. Jill was the physical opposite of Annie's mother. Where Ellen was small, Jill was zaftig, with an apparent indolence that was contradicted only by her dark, glancing eyes.

She looked very "put together" as Ellen would say, in colors that complemented one another and clothing that accentuated her voluptuousness. Annie had almost never seen her without her straight brown hair brushed smoothly back, and her makeup carefully applied. Even after she had begun to spend the nights at Luke's apartment when Annie was there, and they would meet uncomfortably at the bathroom in the early mornings—Annie struggling to maintain a stoney face before she was really awake, and Jill smiling desperately against the girlish scorn directed toward her—even then Annie could tell that Jill didn't like to be seen without her "face" on.

Everyone gathered for Capture the Flag was comparing Jill to Ellen, as Annie and Jill both knew. Luke had never before brought a woman to the game since he and Ellen had split, and though none of the Shanlick sisters said anything to Annie that afternoon, she was aware of their glances and of the ridiculous figure Jill cut when compared to the other adults, whose faces held some traces of age and who cultivated an offhand attitude toward personal appearance. The girls' disapproval was a sign of loyalty to Annie, but it didn't make Luke look good; Annie's Luke, who had always declared that his taste in all matters was impeccable, and she had believed him.

Annie couldn't say that Jill was stupid, or pushy, or even unkind. In the beginning she had tried very hard with Annie, then given up. Now she seemed to settle for an uneasy coexistence. One fault that Annie held against her was her age—she was a decade younger than Luke, so she didn't quite fit in anywhere—but even that would have been forgivable eventually, given her clear alignment with the adults. In Annie's opinion, one of the worst things about Jill was that she was such an obvious lapse in Luke's judgment.

The game felt disjointed right from the start. Tessa was nowhere to be found. Peter decided to start without her after yelling for her and sending Nick to try and find her. Justin's usual high-keyed excitement about the game had been replaced by sardonic remarks under his breath. He and Sam made cracks about trying to end the game as soon as possible, even "throwing" the game by telling each other where the flag was hidden. Annie was determined to play the game for real, just as it had always been. She wanted Luke to see that she wasn't like the rest of them. But her father was distracted by Jill, who clung to him in her white anorak and matching white jeans.

"No one will be able to miss her tonight," Liz said in passing to Annie, knowing how, in past years, Annie had been the sole enforcer of the dark clothing rule established by Justin. It was the only thing anyone had said to her about Jill since she'd arrived. Annie shrugged and scuffed impatiently at the rocks in the driveway. She was wearing all black, right down to her black Converse sneakers, and she was the only one of the teenagers who had smeared black greasepaint on her face, something they had all done last year.

"Looks like they're going to start without Nick and Tessa," Liz said, watching Luke and Peter confer a few yards away.

"Good," said Annie.

She wanted the game to begin. She wanted to infiltrate enemy territory and make her assault on Peter's flag alone. She would run back down the hill gripping it tightly in her fist, ignoring Justin and Sam and all the rest of them until she crossed back over the borderline and won the game for Luke's team. Then they'll see, she thought; then they'll get it.

The two captains stepped apart and held their hands out to each other across the borderline. It was too dark for Annie to see whether they were smiling or not.

"Ready, Edwards?" Peter asked.

"Ready to bust your ass, Shanlick," Luke answered.

They laughed, shook hands, and in that brief pause, before the two teams dispersed into their own fields on either side of the driveway, Annie yelled out, high and strong, as she had every year: "Let the game begin!"

She felt Liz smiling at her, and she turned and smiled back, her breath blowing white in the cold. Then Peter and Luke both ducked back into their respective fields, and everybody scattered. There was the usual chaotic huddle around Luke, but unlike other years, Annie stayed back and waited until everyone had been assigned to a position as a scout or a guard for the prison and the flag. She had told her father last night that she wanted to go for the flag alone, but he hadn't made any promises. He has no idea what's at stake this year, she thought, stunned by his lack of intuition where Justin was concerned. It hadn't occurred to her that even Luke might not care as much about the game as she did.

Once he had sent Jill up to guard the prison, Annie stepped up to her father and Justin, who was pacing impatiently. He just wants it to be over, Annie thought.

"Please, Dad," she said quietly, "I want to go for the flag alone. I know I can get it."

"But what about Justin?" he asked, looking distracted and checking his watch. She saw that it was bothering him a lot, now that the game was actually being played, that he and Justin had made no plans and had in fact no real strategy this year.

"I'll run border patrol," Justin said.

Luke turned. "What do you mean? You're always on offense."

"Not this year." Justin stopped pacing for a moment. "What's the point? We don't have any strategy."

"Well, you wouldn't meet with me in the city, Justin—"

"Oh, come on, Luke, forget it. Just let me run border patrol, O.K.? Annie can go for the flag if she wants to."

"I do," Annie said.

"Good." Justin was sarcastic.

"At least I won't get lost."

"Fuck you, Annie," he said under his breath, so only she could hear him. To Luke, he said, too brightly, "I'll watch the borders this time." Then he was gone, running down the border with what Annie knew was false enthusiasm.

Luke looked at Annie and then back to where Justin had been standing, as if he wasn't quite sure what had just happened. There were only the two of them now.

"He doesn't care anymore," Annie said, and immediately wished she hadn't. Luke looked straight at her. His face was a pale triangle with dark hollows where the eyes were meant to be.

"Yes. I know."

Annie had never heard him sound so tired, as if he had suddenly grown old—she had never thought of her father as old. Don't be tired, she almost said out loud. Don't get old yet. But she said nothing, and he put out his hand and rested it on her shoulder, giving her his weight. She remained rigid and didn't move, willing his weakness away. Beams of light from flashlights on both sides of the playing fields were cutting across the grass, intersecting, then being flicked off one by one as everyone settled into their assigned positions. She knew that there were scouts from Peter's team already heading over to their side. They would be sneaking up the long way around, taking the northern route through the cow pasture, or perhaps just coming up the center of Luke's territory on their bellies—lying still and hidden in the uncut hay as a defensive patrol walked within inches of them.

"I want to go for the flag," Annie said again. "I've got it all figured out."

"All right," said Luke.

He suddenly pulled her against him in a tight embrace and pressed his lips against the top of her head. Then he pushed her away with a rough gesture that shocked her with its force. She stumbled for a brief second, recovered, and when she looked back at him, he had already turned away.

Annie took off, heading south along the edge of the border toward the house and the lower lawn, which they called no-man's-land. Her plan was to sweep up on Peter's territory from the south, circling the house and heading across the meadow and into the woods. She ran down to the edge of the border of no-man's-land with a new recklessness. Peter's team was weak this year (as was their own because of the poor showing), but Annie knew that the other team didn't have anyone who wanted to win as much as she did. She felt strong and sure and took only a quick look before running out into the open space that lay behind the house, dispensing with the rigorous war moves Justin had insisted upon when they did this run together. Nothing can stop me but bad luck, she thought, and spat over her left shoulder as she ran—to ward off the evil eye. It was something she had read about once, something Jim Hawkins would have done, and it made her feel brave.

In the woods beyond no-man's-land was the shed that Peter had built far enough from the house to be his private writing studio. More than a year ago he had given it to the kids, and it was now their private club. Last summer Nick had painted a sign: THE ASYLUM, which hung over the door. Inside he had painted a mural with portraits of each member of the family. In the background was the big house, and sprinkled on the lawn in front of it marked gravestones for all of the dead family pets. The pets had always been buried in the country, even if they died in the city. Annie had been present at more than one of these burials, usually presided over by Justin, who used the Latin he was learning on his own to give it an official air. The Asylum was furnished with a garage-sale couch and a fake Persian rug. There were candles on the floor and posters on the walls, and after Justin put up a dartboard and Tessa found a five-dollar lamp with a red-fringed lampshade, it was perfect.

As Annie approached, she saw a soft yellow light through the windows and went into a crouch, afraid of being seen. Nobody should be in the Asylum during the game; they were all supposed to be playing. She lay flat in the wet grass, inching her way toward the Asylum on her belly. There was a good chance the enemy would be coming down this way, heading for Luke's flag in the opposite direction, but she couldn't go on without knowing if one of them had ditched the game from the start. I hope it's not Justin, she thought, as she crawled closer to the open window near the front door.

She heard a pile of books fall to the floor, a giggle, and the creak of the old sofa springs. She climbed up onto the wooden lean-to that was built over a woodpile at the back and peered in the window. It was Nick and Tessa. They had lit a candle and she could hear them talking quietly as they settled on the couch. She realized it had been a long time since Peter had sent Nick off to find Tessa for the game, and that Nick had never come back. She squatted on top of the lean-to, which gave her a good view of the room and where she thought she couldn't be seen by candlelight. They were lying next to each other on the couch, and though their backs were facing her, from her spot on the lean-to roof Annie could hear every word.

"Nick," Tessa said. Her voice sounded damp and hoarse; she had been crying.

"Yeah?" Nick made a sound as if he was clearing something out of his mouth. She saw him reach up his hand and move a strand of Tessa's hair from his face.

"I don't want to go up there," Tessa said.

For a while, all Annie could hear was Tessa's crying, half-hidden in Nick's shoulder. Then Nick lifted himself up and began to lick the tears from her face. Tessa quieted down and sighed, a sound like a perfect "O" that came out of the open window to where Annie crouched, unable to move away.

"We don't have to go," he said.

Tessa dug her chin into his shoulder, looking past him the way she always did when she wanted to think carefully about what she was going to say. Annie wondered if she was going to say something about her; that would be what she got for spying on them.

"Let's just stay here." Nick's voice sounded thick and unfamiliar to Annie. Tessa giggled, and Annie held her breath as they turned to each other.

Nick lifted Tessa's face toward him and kissed her in a way that Annie had never thought they would kiss. They were kissing over and over, without speaking, and Annie knew it couldn't be the first time they had done this. How long? she wondered. There was a pause as Nick hitched his way up farther onto the couch and Tessa shifted her position. They all began to breathe again.

Annie remembered the night she had lost her virginity in the bedroom at that Upper East Side party, and she waited for what came next, silent and unmoving. The idea that Tessa and Nick might actually be making out, or even making love, had never occurred to her. She knew that Tessa had a crush on Nick—but so did all of them, at one time or another, and she had thought there was an unspoken rule in the family about not taking it any further.

There was no more talking. Nick pulled up her shirt and Tessa took off her bra. Annie watched as he kissed her breasts, which shone with a sudden whiteness in the darkened room. As she watched, she touched her own breasts almost unconsciously, feeling her nipples harden under her cold fingers as Tessa pulled Nick against her. He unbuckled his pants, as Tessa undid hers, both of them moving with frantic awkwardness. The sofa creaked more and more, and at the sight of Nick's white buttocks, Annie had an almost uncontrollable desire to giggle. Then Tessa cried out briefly, and it was over. Annie hadn't allowed herself to make any noise when she lost her virginity, despite the pain, and she wondered if this was the first time for Tessa.

She started to shift her position and then froze. There was no sound inside the room except their combined breathing, and Annie realized that her legs had fallen asleep. She began to slowly shift them beneath her, terrified of her inability to jump down if they came outside. She looked around, afraid that somebody might be watching her, as she was watching them.

"Did it hurt?" Nick asked.

"Not as much this time," Tessa said, between the small kisses she was placing along the top of Nick's ear.

"Your dad sent me down to get you," Nick said. His voice was suddenly loud, jarring in the quiet, and Annie held her breath against the tingling pain of her joints.

Tessa pulled him close against her. "It felt good," she said.

"Come on," he said; and now Annie recognized the old Nick in his voice and realized that what had been missing before was fear. It was back now, covered by a thin gauze of nerves that Annie had always mistaken for his cool.

"I'm really not going." Tessa sounded lazy and proud.

"What are you going to do?"

Their breathing was separate now. Is it always so brief? Annie wondered, stunned at how quickly his desire had left him. She had thought that was only Thurston's way.

"Stay here," Tessa said languorously. "Like you said."

"Someone might come looking."

"You know they've already started without us. It doesn't matter."

There was a long silence. Then Nick got up, gently disentangling himself from her, and below her navel Tessa's curled, darker hair was revealed, looking pressed flat like the nest of an animal. Nick stared at her for a moment, then knelt next to her and put his ear to her belly. His naked chest was white and hairless, and his arms looked very thin. He stood up, smiled at her, and pulled up his pants. Tessa pulled one of Janis's afghans, which lay across the top of the couch, over her naked body, and closed her eyes.

"Come on, Tess." Nick had put on his shirt by now and was lacing up his sneakers. "What if Justin comes down?"

"I'll tell him I've been beating off," Tessa said, her eyes still closed, and Annie grinned.

Nick smiled at her, then shrugged and got up. "All right then, I'll go steal us a couple of beers from the house."

Annie jumped down at the same moment he opened the door, hoping the sound of her landing would be muffled. It worked. Nick went down the steps from the Asylum, slipping a little when he forgot the broken one, and cursing to himself about it before heading up to the house.

Annie crept away from the Asylum, a slight pain still throbbing through the numbness of her legs. She hobbled as quickly as she could to the tree line and leaned back into the shadow of the trees. They're brother and sister, but not by blood, she thought; and I'm not blood either. I'm not really a sister to any of them; it's just what we say to strangers. She remembered what Justin had done to her up in the cow pasture three years ago, before they became blood brothers and swore it to secrecy. Justin had stopped being her friend after that; maybe things would be all right with Nick and Tessa because they hadn't sworn to anything. Actually, even though it was weird, she kind of liked the idea of the two of them being together. It kept everything in the family. If Justin or Nick had brought a girlfriend, it would have been as bad as her father bringing Jill.

The candle still burned inside the Asylum. There were shouts from the field above the house, which rose quickly and then died down. A prisoner, thought Annie. It's not the flag or they would've kept on shouting. She shivered, chilled from squatting for so long. Then she turned away from the Asylum and took off at a run along the tree line, toward enemy territory.

The cloud cover was thinning, and the moon was almost over the ridge behind her as Annie made her way up behind the enemy lines. She had no idea how long she had been outside the Asylum and began to run. She was going in a rough parallel to the back of Peter's field, and she used the trees for cover, ducking in and out of their long shadows. After all the years of complicated strategic failures by Luke and Justin, Annie was betting that Peter might ignore the more obvious attack routes.

Then she heard Jill's voice and froze. What was Jill doing on Peter's side? Annie crept slowly toward the sound and reached the edge of the stone wall that bordered the back of Peter's territory. She was breathing hard from running, and she tried to slow her breath down to a silent pant. There was a group of people on the other side of the wall, and Annie kept her head low.

"You were so easy, Jill!" That was Sam. "You were supposed to be guarding the prison for Luke, not coming with us."

"But when you came and tagged the prisoners, I thought we all had to go." Jill giggled. "*I* didn't know."

So, it was the enemy prison on the other side of the wall, and Jill had been caught somehow.

"What happened, Sam?" Janis was there, too. She must have been guarding Peter's prison, just as Jill had been guarding Luke's. Annie wondered if they had caught any other new prisoners along with Jill, or if they had managed only to liberate their own people.

"I went over to tag free our prisoners after Liz was captured by Justin, and Jill just came right on over with us—so I captured her!"

She and Jill laughed together, and Annie hated Sam for sounding so chummy with her.

"Welcome to the Shanlick Prison, Jill," Janis said. "Have a drink." Annie heard them passing a bottle back and forth.

"Better rations over here," said Jill, and they all laughed. She wondered how many members of Luke's team were in the prison now, and she thought about freeing them all. She could just jump over the back of the wall and tag them—once tagged they were officially liberated and allowed free passage to the other side. If it's only Jill, it's not worth it, she thought, and settled down to see who else was there.

"So, how long is it going to be?" That was Doug; he must be a prisoner as well. Doug was an old friend of Luke's, who always came up to the game. He was older than Luke and Peter, and walked with a limp that Luke said had come from a case of polio when he was a child. He never seemed to have much to say to the kids, though Luke was always talking about how sharp and funny he was, and he worked hard to convince him to come up every summer—that it wouldn't be the game without him.

"You mean, how long till we win?" Sam said.

Doug ignored her. "What time is it, Janis?"

"I don't know. I stopped wearing a watch five years ago. I don't want to know."

"Isn't that about when you married Peter?"

Janis laughed. "Longer."

"It's late, Doug," said Jill. He was a special favorite of hers and often came to dinner at Luke's when Jill was there. "Don't worry about the time."

" 'I have wasted Time, and now doth Time waste me,' " he said in a self-pitying tone.

"Yes, it has," laughed Jill.

In terms of the rules of combat, Annie knew that Justin and Luke would say that she had a certain moral obligation to free the prisoners, given such a perfect opportunity. But it's not worth freeing them, she thought. Those two won't help us win. And if she did free them, she would have to give away her position and start all over again. Going for the flag was more important. If only it were a real prison, she thought. If only the game were never over, and they were imprisoned forever in a stone garrison on some barren island.

The adults were talking New York gossip. Annie could feel Sam's boredom right through the stone wall. She wished that Sam were on her team, just for tonight, and that she could sneak over the wall to Annie and go the rest of the way up to the flag. She leaned her head against the rock, suddenly exhausted, and wanted to stay where she was. Being near anyone was better than being alone for the rest of the way through the woods. She had always been afraid of the dark; even now she couldn't sleep without her door open to the lighted hallway of her mother's apartment. She heard the scraping of a match and smelled cigarette smoke quite close to her. Looking up, she saw Sam settling her elbows onto the wall directly above Annie. Annie didn't breathe. All Sam had to do was look down and she could tag her. Justin would never let me forget being captured practically inside the enemy's prison camp, Annie thought. Sam looked out at the trees beyond the wall and shifted impatiently.

The clouds turned again in the sky, covering the moon completely, and everything became much darker. Just then Sam looked down and saw Annie crouching there. Their eyes locked for an instant, and Annie took off. She ran for the trees. Sam was right behind her, shouting to everyone that she had seen her. Everyone from the prison ran after Sam, including Jill and Doug. Don't they know they're helping to catch someone from their own side? wondered Annie. But she didn't worry about them; they were too slow. What she did worry about was Sam.

Neither of them said a word to each other, though they were close enough to speak. Annie ducked into the trees about twenty yards ahead of Sam and started to run in zigzags. Now she was glad she had worn her camouflage clothing and greasepaint because she knew that she was hard to see in the darkness. She could be heard though as tree branches snapped underneath her and the undergrowth tore at her clothes and hands.

She heard Sam crashing through the woods behind her and took a chance. She ran to the far side of a blackberry patch and threw herself down on the ground, worming her way underneath it, ignoring the wet dirt and the blackberry canes, which scratched at her face. Sam crashed on, then stopped, suddenly aware that she couldn't hear Annie anymore. In the stillness Annie heard Sam's breathing and realized that the others must have given up and gone back. She lay perfectly still.

"Annie?" Sam called out. "Annie, I know you're here. You might as well come out."

Annie did nothing. Sam began to circle the blackberry patch, kicking her feet into the edges of it as she walked. She could kick me in the face, thought Annie. She got closer to where Annie was lying and stopped again.

"Annie! Cut the shit, I know you're here. Just come on out and we'll go back to the prison and hang till it's over. Justin must be way ahead of you by now, anyways."

Annie smiled. Sam doesn't know anything, she thought. Then Sam started moving again. She got to the spot where Annie was lying. She stepped directly on Annie's lower arm, and stopped. The pain made Annie's eyes water, and she held her breath, killing the gasp rising up in her throat. Sam stood there for what felt like a very long time.

"Annie! Come on!" She waited, and Annie silently breathed out the pain, then inhaled, and held it again. Sam raised her head, as if listening very carefully. There was nothing but the sound of distant shouts from the other side of the wall.

"Fuck it," she said, moving at last, and Annie breathed again. "Forget it, Annie. I don't care anyway. You can have the goddamned flag—if Justin's not there already!" She walked back toward the prison, cursing at the stray branches that slapped at her in the dark, while Annie clutched her arm to herself, afraid it was broken, but Sam's sneakers and the soft ground had saved her. It was the closest she had ever come to being captured, and she couldn't wait to tell Luke about it.

She crawled out from under the blackberry patch and began moving slowly and carefully toward the northeast corner of the field, where Peter always hid his flag. The chances of being seen by one of Peter's scouts was much greater now. There were boulders that led in a broken line from the stone wall, and Annie pressed herself against the cold granite and glared at the moon, willing it back behind its ridge.

A dog started barking far away across the valley, and Annie dropped to her hands and knees, crawling over rough tufts of grass. There was nowhere to hide between the line of boulders and the flag; all that she could hope was that no one would notice her crawling or stumble over her before she could see them coming. She had gotten this close only once before, with Justin and a friend he had brought up from the city. It was the last time they had won a game. Justin had told Annie and his friend to stand and sacrifice themselves, a diversionary tactic while he got the flag. And she had done it, running only about a hundred yards before she was caught; but Justin had made it to the flag, and she had watched him run with it trailing white behind him and laughing at everyone who tried to tag him in the dark. She missed Justin with a sudden intensity and shoved a fist into the palm of her other hand, as if she could punch that thought away.

The sharp smell of tobacco made her look up. There were two figures about ten yards ahead of her, the larger one smoking a cigarette. She listened for their voices, hoping that the smoker wasn't Peter. She knew that they had to be standing on the perimeter of the circle that was required to be drawn around the flag and that no one could enter after the start of the game.

Annie crawled backward, working her way around to the far side of where she imagined the flag to be. The two guards were standing facing the west, waiting, Annie knew, for Peter to begin the charge that he always led up the hill. When she had reached the opposite side of the circle from the guards, she stopped and thought of what Justin would do. When would he just stand up and go for it? How close to the flag would he crawl?

She stayed down, moving slowly forward with her belly pressed close to the sharp grass that bit through her clothes. She strained to see the glimpse of white, which she knew was the flag, and wondered for the first time if they had cheated, for she saw nothing. Then she heard Peter's guttural laugh and froze. A glowing cigarette end flew out in a great arc from where he was standing with the smaller guard. If Peter was still there when she went for the flag, her chances were shot. Peter was an ex-jock, and fast.

"What time is it?" Peter asked, but Annie couldn't hear the reply. She wondered how long they had been playing, and how long she had knelt outside the Asylum. It was a grown woman talking with Peter, but she couldn't recognize her in the dark. Janis must still be down at the prison, with Sam. Just then Peter took a few steps toward Annie, and she went up on her haunches, ready to spring away and run for it if he came any closer. He pushed at something on the ground with his boot, and in the sharp white moonlight she saw that it was the flag, barely hidden from her by a small clump of grass. She went down to the ground again and tried not to breathe, pressing her face into the dirt. Peter stopped, as if sensing something.

"Hey, Peter," the woman said, and he turned back toward her.

"Yeah?"

"You'd better get going."

"Yeah, yeah, I know."

He walked back over to her, and Annie opened her eyes just enough to watch him. The thin grass looked like a defoliated forest here at ground level, and Peter's boots were monoliths of rubber and leather.

"I hate to leave you here alone," Peter said, glancing back toward the flag. "But the charge . . ."

"Oh, go on. It's all right."

Now Annie knew the voice. It was the mother of the two girls who were their closest neighbors in the country, the baker of meringue pies whose stiffly constructed tops separated from the filling like oil when you plunged a fork into them. She had always been at the game, with her girls. Annie smiled, remembering that this woman was not much of a runner.

"I'll be fine, Peter," she said again. "I can fend off Justin if he shows up. Give me a kiss, for luck."

Peter made a sound like a snort or cough, leaned down to her, and pulled her against him. They kissed for a long, slow minute. Then they pulled apart and looked at each other.

She laughed. "Get out of here."

Peter turned toward the downhill slope and walked away, his boots disappearing into the tall grass and darkness. Annie wished she could remember this woman's name, so she could ask Liz about her later. She wouldn't tell her that she had seen them kissing. She remembered seeing her father kissing that girl at the New Year's Eve party when she was eleven and her mother had been in Vermont. She wondered if this kiss meant that Peter and Janis were going to get divorced too, and it made her want to hit Peter. What is wrong with Janis? she felt like shouting at him. Janis, with her smile and her ease and her rings that clicked together on her long fingers. Fuck you, Peter, she thought, and suddenly she wanted to get the flag more than ever, to humiliate him in front of this woman who pretended to be Janis's friend.

She decided to count to eleven, her lucky number, before going for the flag. The neighbor woman paced back and forth, slapping her hands against her thighs to keep warm. Annie had stopped feeling the cold.

Now, she thought, and threw herself at the flag. Even though the woman was slow, all she had to do was tag Annie, and she tried, turning as soon as she heard Annie jump up. She reached for her, but Annie had already snatched the flag. She swerved out of the way and ran downhill.

The woman started yelling. "The flag! They've got the flag!"

It was all about speed now, strategy was out the window. Figures appeared in the dark, holding out their arms to stop her, but Annie leapt around all of them. Far away, she thought she heard her father's voice yelling, and she held the flag closer, dashing in zigzags the way Justin had taught her. She threw her body to the side as one more body tried to block her way. It was Peter, she realized, and his football player's body seemed to block every way out. She made one final sharp turn and he fell, crying out in pain. Then she was over the border and onto the dirt driveway, the gravel hard and sure underfoot.

"I got it!" she shouted, whipping the flag up and over her head. "Dad! We won! I got the flag!"

Everyone came up out of the fields. Liz and Sam were there, and even Justin punched her in the arm, grinning. Before she could turn to him, her father was there. He caught her in a hug, but after a quick kiss on the cheek he was looking past her at Peter, who limped up, leaning heavily onto Janis's shoulder as if he was in real pain. He gave Annie the thumbs-up sign.

"We were just about to do the charge, Edwards," he said. "She tricked me!"

"What happened to you?" Luke asked.

"Twisted my ankle trying to catch her. It hurts like fuck." He sucked in his breath and glared at Annie.

Annie didn't know what to say, so she didn't say anything, which Peter took as an apology.

"Oh, come on, Annie. It's all right," he said, smiling and wincing a little. "It's war."

Annie figured she didn't have to say anything to that. It really was war, and all she could think about was winning. She had done it. She had showed them all. She started to laugh, her whole body shaking with it, and even her arm had stopped hurting. There was Liz's gentle grin greeting her through the other faces, and Janis, supporting Peter's weight, but still smiling. Her father wanted to hear all about it, he said.

Even while she was talking to Luke, Annie kept half an eye on Nick, who was lurking about, though there was no sign of Tessa. She was surprised that he seemed exactly the same as always. Maybe he and Tessa had been doing it for a while, she thought. She couldn't imagine having sex and then coming out and chatting to her parents as if nothing had happened; sex was too complicated for that.

Annie held the flag up as high as she could: "Another year for the Edwards!" she cried, and everyone laughed.

Jill stepped in next to Luke, smiling as if she were a presidential candidate's wife. A look of relief crossed Luke's face, and he put his arm around her, squeezing her tight. Annie looked over at him and he smiled at her in a slightly absent way. It was an unfamiliar look, and Annie suddenly felt the cold again. She wrapped the flag around her neck like a scarf. It had been two years since their team had won the flag. It was impossible that Luke didn't care.

The three of them walked down to the house together, and Annie wanted to tell him everything about her journey: what route she had taken, how Sam had almost captured her, and how long she had lain still in the grass near the flag. But with Jill there, Annie didn't know how to begin. Her arm started to throb, but she kept quiet, and when she didn't launch into her story, Luke began to talk to Jill about things that had nothing to do with the game. Annie pulled the flag closer and kept silent.

It started to rain. A thunderstorm was moving up the valley, and the first fat drops splattered on the trail of people walking down the driveway. Everyone started to jog as they pulled their jackets over their heads. The rain started coming down hard, and Janis yelled instructions as she tried to hustle Peter, who was limping badly but wouldn't let anyone help him but his wife.

"No bonfire!" she called. "Everybody into the house!"

Peter threw his head back and howled like a dog. Annie wished she had the courage to join him; it would be so simple just to howl all night in the rain, but maybe I have to get drunk first, she thought. Then she looked at Janis's face and saw that she hated it when Peter was like this, and she remembered the kiss. The neighbor woman must have already gone into the house.

As she walked into the kitchen, Justin was heading out through the pantry with something under his sweatshirt, a six-pack probably. Annie knew he was heading down to the Asylum, and she paused, wondering where Liz and Sam had gone; somehow she didn't want to go down there alone. Her father cracked the seal on a gallon bottle of scotch; Janis smashed an ice tray against the green linoleum counter and threw the cubes into a plastic bag for Peter—to ice his foot. He had exchanged Janis's shoulder for Jill's and limped into the living room, where Annie could hear him directing someone to set up his chair with a footstool for his ankle. Luke had begun his usual lecture on the benefits of cheap scotch mixed with soda versus the single malt, neat, that Janis preferred. He poured Jill and himself identical drinks and started for the living room. He paused once to look back at Annie, as if to see if she wanted to come with them, but it was too much of an afterthought, and she shook her head, kicking open the back door and listening for the girls. Someone had put a Coltrane album on in the house, and she strained to identify the song. Dad would know, she thought. It was a game they played, identifying the song and the artist in the first few bars. She immediately hated herself for wanting to play that game with him. She could see the lights from the Asylum through the trees, so she shrugged to herself once, for bravery, and walked down the hill.

"Hail! Hail, the conquering hero!" Justin sang to her as she walked in the door, holding up an open beer in tribute and taking a long swallow.

"Shut up," Annie said automatically. "Where's the beer?"

They were all there, Tessa and Nick in conspicuously opposite corners. The Stones were playing on the old blue and white vinyl turntable, which folded up like a suitcase for travel. It had been a gift to one of the girls many years ago. Liz and Sam were sprawled on the couch, an ashtray balanced on their outstretched legs. Nick circled the room restlessly, smoking an enormous joint, which the others occasionally reached out for; he was looking up at his half-completed mural on the ceiling and didn't seem to be in the same room as the rest of them. Tessa was slowly working a pile of candle wax off of the floor with the edge of a key. She smiled at Annie. "Hey, I heard you got the flag. That's great, Annie." Tessa was smiling her same old smile, but Annie felt as if she were being humored and didn't say anything. It *is* great, she thought to herself, fuck you. She took extra time with her cigarette, fumbling with the match and letting her hair fall forward.

"And I almost caught you," Sam said. "Where were you, Annie? You just disappeared."

"I was right there. You stepped on my arm, see?" She held up the arm, bruised and swollen.

"You're kidding! I did that?" Sam said. "Jesus, Annie, I'm sorry. And you didn't say anything?"

"I didn't want to get caught." Annie snuck a look at Justin and was glad to see that he looked impressed with her at last. She shrugged at Sam and smiled.

"You're crazy, Annie," Justin said, but she knew what he meant.

"Come here," Liz said. "Let me see your arm, is it bad?" At fourteen she looked like a slightly more voluptuous version of Tessa, with the same dark hair but stronger features. Annie was always looking at Liz when she thought she wouldn't notice. Lately she felt a new nervousness around her, as if she was sure that Liz did know she was always watching her, and she wasn't quite sure why. Annie sat down at the opposite end of the couch from Liz, pushing Sam into the middle, but Liz got up and walked around so that she could see Annie's arm.

"And after this, you got the flag all by yourself?" Liz asked. "I guess it's not that bad." She gently turned Annie's forearm toward her and quickly kissed her wrist. Annie looked up, startled by the lightest touch of Liz's tongue in the center of the kiss. A circle of pure heat traveled up her arm from her wrist. Liz gave her a small, secret smile and turned away. "Where were *you,* Justin?"

"Minding the farm."

"What do you mean, didn't you go up?" Tessa asked and looked over at Justin, pretending that it didn't matter to her either way.

"No . . ." Justin got up and sauntered over to her. "It was you who didn't make it to the game."

Annie wondered if he knew about Nick and Tessa.

"I wasn't up for it," Tessa said.

"Tell Dad that one!" Sam laughed at her own joke until she collapsed into a coughing fit. Just like Peter would, Annie thought.

"Does Dad know?" Tessa asked, looking at Liz.

"I don't know," she said. "He twisted his ankle going after Annie, so he's probably forgotten everything else."

Nick whirled around and focused in for the first time. "You tripped up Peter?"

"Not on purpose," Annie said. Nick exploded in laughter, high, wild Nick laughter that pulled everyone, even Justin out of his hole.

"You're the best, Annie—the best!" Nick said, still laughing, and Annie didn't care what he said, but was glad that everyone was getting it at last. Liz reached over and tugged on Annie's hair until it hurt. Annie leapt up to wrestle her, knocking over the ashtray and making Sam groan as a knee poked into her stomach. Now Sam always pretended to be too old to wrestle, unless she started it first. Tessa was the only one who really was too old; when she said she hated wrestling with her sisters, Annie believed her. Sam left the couch, and Liz pinned Annie down easily onto her back, counted slowly to ten, leaning closer and closer in until her long hair covered both of their faces and Annie could feel Liz's heart pounding hard against her own rib cage. Annie looked into her eyes, surprised by Liz's intensity, and tried to hide how aware she was of Liz's breasts pressing against her. She knew that everyone must be watching. When Liz got to ten, she laughed and let Annie go.

Annie sat up, panting, and smiled at her. "Fuck you," she said. Liz smiled back.

"Come on, Nick—how about a game?" Justin threw a dart at the board on the wall.

"Maybe, baby." This was Nick's standard response to everyone these days. "Nah, I don't think so." He settled down next to Tessa, and she smiled at him.

"I'll play," said Sam.

"All right," Justin said. "A real game, at last."

"Oh, come on, Justin," Annie said. She was feeling good now, and she pressed the soles of her feet against Liz's for a feet-fight, the way they always did when Annie slept over in the city.

"Nobody gives a shit about the game anymore," Justin said to Annie, throwing a dart with perfect precision toward the dartboard. "It's just another reason for them to come up here and get shit-faced. Couldn't we all do that in the city? Separately?"

"My dad does, my dad gives a shit," Annie said, staring at him. I'm going to watch him until he looks back at me, she thought.

"Your dad." He still wasn't looking. "One of these days, Annie, you're going to realize that Luke Edwards is not God, no matter how much he says he is."

"You're a real asshole, Justin." Annie said it so quietly that it took Justin by surprise, and he did turn and look right at her, finally, but it was too late for him to stop throwing the dart, which went wild and landed quivering in the wall behind Annie, just missing her face.

"There—you ruined my shot!" he yelled, turning on her. Annie flinched, expecting a blow, but he threw the other darts on the floor instead. I won't move, she thought to herself, until he does.

"Oh, shut up, Justin," Tessa said. "Give it up before you hurt somebody." She sounded scared. It had been close.

"Yeah, sure. Have another downer, Tessa," he muttered, but then he looked up at Annie. "Are you O.K.? I didn't mean to—"

"I'm O.K." But then she started crying. She didn't want to cry. She wanted to tell Justin that he was wrong about Luke, and he could just go fuck himself for all she cared. But she couldn't say anything, and everybody got very quiet. Annie pushed her sleeve angrily across her eyes and started for the door.

"Hey, Annie, wait!" Tessa said, but she didn't get up to follow her.

"Come on, you guys," Nick moaned, "Justin, sit down, have a beer—"

The door slammed behind Annie.

Liz found Annie in the kitchen. A watermelon lay hacked open on the counter, and the light from the pantry made everything look very stark. There was a Buck Clayton record playing in the living room, and the sound of adult voices. Annie automatically tracked the artist and the song. All of the cars were still parked in front of the low stone wall that ran along the front lawn. No one had gone home yet. Annie had the big bread knife in her hand, and she was methodically cutting the watermelon into smaller and smaller squares of bright pink flesh. She turned to Liz, smiled shakily, and set down the knife, gesturing at her little project with a shrug.

"Why is he such an asshole to me?" she asked. "You know, Justin used to like me," she added, knowing right away how lame that sounded.

"He's pissed at Luke, not you."

"But what did Dad do?"

"I don't know." Liz moved next to her and stared out the kitchen window. The rain was getting heavier. "He let Dad and Janis change the date of the game. He invited Jill along."

"Yeah, but that's not it. He just hates me, that's all."

Liz didn't say anything but picked up one of the squares of watermelon. "Open up," she said, and popped it into Annie's mouth.

Annie looked at Liz, surprised, then laughed. "He's not worth it," she said, looking sideways at Liz and spitting the slippery black seeds into the sink in front of them.

"He's worth it," Liz said, after a minute. "But it's not your fault." She picked up another square of watermelon. "Here. Eat."

"Why don't you have some?" Annie asked, picking up a chunk for her.

"Oh, please. I couldn't eat anything. I'm strictly into this for texture and color. I took a Quaalude before the game."

Neither of them said anything about Tessa and Sam staying down there with the boys, but Annie knew that they were both thinking about it. In the old days, all the girls would have come after Annie. Liz placed piece after piece of watermelon in Annie's mouth, and neither of them said anything. Annie reached up and held Liz's hand still for a moment, licking Liz's index finger and tasting the mixture of fruit and fingertip. Liz shuddered involuntarily, then closed her eyes and giggled.

Annie giggled too. "I like you on Quaaludes," she said. "Got any more?"

The sound of shattering glass suddenly cut through the noise from the living room, and they broke apart. The voices from the party suspended for a moment, then Peter yelled something, and they heard everybody laugh as Janis walked into the kitchen.

"What broke?" Liz asked her.

"An ashtray." Janis was distracted. "Liz, what did we do with the whisk pan and broom?"

"I'll get it," Liz said, reaching down under the sink, where it was always kept.

"Will you, honey? Thanks." Janis leaned against the counter. "I need to take a little break, here." She looked over at them. "Are you kids hungry? There's watermelon."

"No thanks," Annie said. "We're not hungry."

She and Liz looked at each other and started to laugh. Janis smiled at them and shrugged without asking them anything, and for some reason their laughter died as quickly as it had begun. The three of them stood at the kitchen counter, looking out the window for a minute. The rain on the window made everything outdoors blend together, as if a clear plastic curtain had come down between the three of them and the rest of the world.

"I'll go clean up," Liz said. Janis didn't move. Annie gave Liz a funny look. This was how Ellen acted sometimes with her, at home. Not drunk but somehow absent. Liz gave Janis the imitation of a smile and motioned Annie to follow her into the party.

Peter was sitting in the far corner of the living room, near the fire, his ankle propped up with pillows on another chair. Jill was laughing uncontrollably about something, and everyone else in the room seemed to be looking anywhere but at her. Doug was leaning on his cane and flipping through the record collection. The neighbor woman whom Annie had escaped from was applying bright red lipstick over and over again, with her compact held out in front of her like a shield. Luke watched Jill with grim intensity. She must be smashed, Annie thought, and kept her eyes on the ground as she lingered by the doorway. Jill's laughter was even louder than the music, and every time she took a breath it would come out again at a higher pitch.

Peter noticed them standing in the doorway before Luke did and threw out his arms, as if for an embrace, to Liz. "Did Janis send you in to clean up after us?"

"Yeah, I guess." Liz rubbed the broom against the whisk pan in her hand and stayed pressed against the doorway with Annie. Jill had finally slowed her laughter down, and when Annie looked over at her, there were tears washing her mascara down her cheeks. She was still smiling as she wiped the back of her hand across her face.

Peter slowly let his arms drift back down to his sides and kept staring at Liz, as if he were daring her not to come in for the embrace now. She moved toward him. There were bits of glass and scattered ash and cigarette butts on the floor all around him, and Annie saw a gouge in the wall above his head. She wondered who had thrown the ashtray and looked over to Luke. He had seen her by now, and he patted the arm of the couch next to him as a place for her to sit. She went over, carefully avoiding Jill, who was now in a new conversation across the room and acting quite normally.

"How's your ankle, Dad?" Liz asked, as she bent over and began to sweep up the mess.

Peter smiled and wagged his foot underneath the half-melted bag of ice. "Fine. But Jill here just about killed me with the ashtray." He gestured down at the floor. "Here, Liz—look, she almost got me!"

"It was your fault," Jill said over her shoulder. "You dared me to. You said I didn't have the guts to—"

"To what!" Peter roared at her with what Annie thought was supposed to be a joking laugh but sounded more like a growl. "To attack the cripple?"

Jill looked embarrassed and turned to Luke, who said nothing and raised his eyebrows.

"It's all right," Peter said, draining the glass that sat next to him on the armchair, sweating a cold circle onto the upholstery. He held the empty glass toward Jill in a toast: "Now you're really one of the family."

Annie watched as Jill smoothed her hair back and smiled in response to Peter. She gave Luke another look that was more proud than embarrassed. If she looked over at Annie as well, Annie never knew—she kept her eyes on the ground as Luke put his arm around her, pulling her up next to him without saying anything. Jill walked over to Peter and took a drag from his cigarette with a new familiarity that Peter clearly enjoyed. They look like they've just had sex, Annie thought, watching them from under her half-closed eyes. Liz was just about finished sweeping up, and she squatted back on her heels, glancing around her for anything she had missed.

"Annie!" Jill said, too brightly, as if she had just noticed that she was there. "Did you have fun during the game?"

"Uh huh." Annie kept her eyes down and moved closer to Luke.

"I loved it," Jill said. "And I'm so glad that we won on my first try. Luke says that this is one of your favorite times of year."

"August is my favorite time of year," Annie said.

Jill smiled blankly at her.

"We wouldn't have won if it wasn't for you, Annie," Luke said. "You're the best. You're an Edwards."

This was one of the little routines Luke had perfected over the years, and Annie knew it like a meaningless poem she had memorized for school: "No, Dad—you're the best."

"You never would have won if I hadn't twisted my goddamned ankle trying to catch you," Peter said.

"Ha!" shouted Luke, smacking his glass down hard on the coffee table. "You've always been a sore loser, Shanlick—and a rotten winner."

"We just have so much more practice at winning," Peter said, winking at Liz. "We're never quite sure how to behave when we lose."

"With grace, and politesse," said Luke, squeezing Annie's shoulder hard.

"Shanlicks are gonna win next year," Peter said, winking at Liz. "You Edwards can't hold the flag for long."

Annie looked over at him. "Wanna bet?"

Peter grinned. "I'll bet you a quarter."

Annie stood up, holding out her hand to shake. "No, no—gentleman's bet."

Luke laughed. "That's right, Annie. Get him where it hurts!"

Peter held out his hand. "All right, Annie, a gentleman's bet. We'll whip your asses next year!"

Annie grinned at him, and they shook. The other adults in the room broke out in simultaneous applause, and Annie shrugged, embarrassed. Liz got up from the floor, holding the whisk pan in her hand, and Annie noticed how thick the pieces of glass were. Jill must be stronger than she looks, she thought, to be able to shatter that old ashtray. Peter reached for his glass and handed it to Liz.

"Make me another drink."

"Lots of ice?"

"You got it," Peter said, "thanks."

She took the glass and started for the kitchen. Annie followed her out. The kitchen was empty. As soon as they were alone, the girls rolled their eyes and started laughing together.

Tessa came in the back door, shaking the rain off her hair. "Hi," she said. "What's so funny?"

"Nothing, really," Liz said, opening the freezer and cracking the ice tray against the counter where a gallon of bourbon sat open. "Jill threw an ashtray at Dad."

"Did it hit him?" Tessa looked toward the living room. "How come?"

Annie laughed even harder. "It didn't hit him. She's a weirdo."

"It sounds like she fits right in," Tessa said.

Annie stopped laughing suddenly and looked at her. "That's right," she said. "That's exactly why she did it."

"What?" Tessa looked blankly at Annie.

"Forget it. You had to be there." Annie was still a little pissed that Tessa hadn't followed her up to the house.

Tessa looked at her, then Liz. "I guess so. To tell the truth, I just can't give much of a shit about Jill." She started to make herself a drink identical to the one Liz was making for their father. Annie and Liz gave each other a look, surprised that she was being so blatant about getting herself a drink. Usually they did their drinking down at the Asylum.

"Sam says that Jill and Dad are on the make for each other," Tessa said, looking at Annie. "Maybe that's why she threw the ashtray."

"Sam just says things, you know, to get an effect," Liz said, as she poured two shots of bourbon, neat, into a glass, and handed it to Annie.

Annie took a sip, breathed hard, and gave it back to Liz. "No, it was more like—now she can be in the Boys' Club."

Tessa jumped up to sit on the counter. "Jill will never get into that club no matter what she does. Look at Janis. Look at our moms."

"Don't tell *her* that," Annie laughed.

"Liz!" Peter yelled from the living room, and she jumped. "Oh, shit, his drink. I hope he doesn't smell my breath." She wiped her mouth with her hand.

"He won't even notice, are you kidding?" Tessa leaned back and took another sip of her own drink.

"Yeah." Liz shrugged and walked back into the living room.

"Where is everyone?" Annie asked Tessa. "Still down at the Asylum?"

"Nick is, I guess. Sam and Justin went out for a cruise in the Deathmobile." Deathmobile was the name Justin had given to the old Dodge Dart he had bought last summer.

"In the rain?"

Tessa smiled. "I don't think Janis is too crazy about him driving at night either."

Peter's voice came suddenly from the other room. "Tessa! Come in here for a minute!"

They looked at each other. "Shit," Tessa said and walked toward the living room as Liz walked out, rolling her eyes at her sister. Tessa composed herself with a perfect smile and headed into the room. Annie joined Liz at the doorway, wanting to watch. Tessa had always been her father's favorite.

Peter threw out his arms as she walked over to him. "Come say hello to your old man," he said. "Look—a cripple at forty!"

Tessa looked down at his ankle. "Does it hurt?"

"Not really, no. The game wasn't so bad, after all, was it, Tess? You're glad you came?"

So, he doesn't know, thought Annie.

"Yeah, sure." Tessa wanted out of there.

Peter smiled and held up his right hand. "Scout's honor?"

He and Luke had always done that with the girls, ever since they were little. Tessa held up her hand and pressed her palm against his. "Scout's honor."

She put her hand down first, and he reached out and touched her shoulder, tentatively. It struck Annie, then, how seldom she saw Peter and Tessa together these days. Janis came in the front door from the outside, the door that nobody ever used, with an armful of wood. She looked bedraggled but triumphant, and she tossed her hair out of her eyes with a smile.

"Who wants a fire?" she asked, and Luke got up to take the logs over to the fireplace. Peter looked up at her and smiled briefly, then turned back to Tessa.

"O.K.," he said, looking down at the drink Liz had handed to him. "O.K. So, where have you kids been all night?"

"Just down at the Asylum," Tessa said. "I'm really tired, Dad. I think I'm going to go upstairs."

Peter looked past her as if he was thinking about something else. "You've all got enough pillows? Blankets?"

"Of course, Dad."

"O.K."

Tessa leaned down to kiss him. "Good night."

He turned his complete attention to her then and gave her one of his famous smiles. Tessa looked warm and happy for exactly as long as the smile lasted, as if he had his finger on a light switch, and then it was over; Tessa looked around politely, said her good nights, and went upstairs to wash up. Grace and politesse, Annie thought, as she and Liz watched her go.

"Do you think she's actually going to bed?" Liz said, as they wandered back to the kitchen. It was past midnight now, but the idea of going to bed before the adults seemed ridiculous.

Annie thought for a minute about telling Liz everything about Tessa and Nick down at the Asylum during the game. "She said that she wanted to sleep in her old room tonight. I guess she's tired," she said instead, and drained the glass of bourbon that Tessa had left behind.

Annie refilled Tessa's glass almost to the rim and topped off Liz's drink. They both knew that Peter and Janis didn't keep track of how much bourbon was drunk on a night like this.

"Come on," Liz said, pulling her by the hand, and they went out to sit on the back porch and smoke. The grown-ups wouldn't be going anywhere for a long time, they knew, and the bourbon was getting easier and easier to drink. The rain was really coming down now, and the sound of it drumming on the small porch roof over their heads blocked out all other sounds and surrounded them on three sides with a curtain of water.

"It's like being behind a waterfall," said Liz.

"It's like we're somewhere else. I love being up here when it rains," Annie said.

"Lucky thing it held off for the game," Liz said, sticking her hand into the stream from the gutter, making it spray in all directions.

"I don't think it mattered."

"The rain? It would've sucked out there."

"No. I mean, my getting the flag and everything."

"Winning?"

"Yeah, winning."

Liz looked at her for a moment. " 'Cause of Justin?"

Annie wouldn't look at her. "Justin . . . and everybody. It just didn't make any difference who won, did it?"

"No, not really."

Liz moved closer to her. Annie stared dry-eyed at the night beyond the halo of the porch light.

"You worry too much," Liz said. "It's going to be all right."

Annie turned and looked right at her. "What is?"

Liz took Annie's face in both of her hands and kissed her. Her mouth tasted like Annie's own, sweet with bourbon and sharp with the taste of too many cigarettes. Annie pulled back, shocked by the suddenness of Liz's mouth against hers. Then, without speaking, she pulled Liz back against her, so that she was pressed hard against the wall and Liz had to lean into her more and more as they kissed. They broke apart slightly and Annie leaned her head back. Liz kissed her neck over and over. Annie let her kiss her almost to her ears, then she couldn't take it anymore and pulled her up for a long kiss. The girls had been friends for so long that the kiss was both comforting and arousing to Annie. But then their hunger for each other was pushing them so fast through those boundaries that Annie watched herself going over the edge of desire until she stopped thinking at last.

"Come on," Liz said, and she led Annie into the house.

Annie winced at the sudden, indoor light as they walked through the kitchen and upstairs to their bedroom, unnoticed by the adults, who had at last cranked up the record player and begun to dance. Once in their room they both tore off their clothes, giggling at the cold sheets and their feet and hands, which were like frozen outposts under the covers. Annie had never been so frightened and so unable to speak. Then Liz became hushed as well, as their hands found each other's warm places, and Annie traveled half-reeling over the landscape of Liz's body, which was simultaneously foreign and familiar. She felt as if she had wanted this for years without knowing it. The smell of Liz's hair was like wood smoke, and on her tongue was the salty taste of her own sex. Annie wanted to stay cleaved to her body forever, their hips and breasts in perfect parallel.

Liz fell asleep first. The house had gone quiet without their noticing it; everyone must have finally gone home. Annie got out of bed, disentangling her limbs from Liz's, and wrapped herself in the bedspread that had fallen to the floor. She went to the window and looked out over the fields, which were still and dark, as if every living creature but herself had finally fallen asleep. The rain had ended, and the sound of Liz's soft, even breathing seemed to fill the room, the translucent blue curtains shifting just slightly with each inhalation. Everything had changed since she had watched Liz sleeping last night, and she didn't know what would happen tomorrow. The curve of Liz's hip rose up against the white sheet, and Annie wanted to make love to her again, but she was too afraid to wake her. She was almost too afraid to get back in bed with her at all, but she knew that she would. Annie felt something inevitable was happening, and she allowed herself to think that just maybe everything would be all right. Maybe it was just one night. Maybe sex was just one more thing to do together. And Liz would never stop talking to her; she was sure of that.

There was the groan of a truck downshifting on the damp highway three miles away, and as she looked up the hill she saw Justin's car parked at the top of the driveway with the headlights still on. She could just see the dark outline of his body sitting on the hood, leaning back against the windshield, and in his hands, darker still, the shape of the twenty-two, leaning up against his legs, pointed toward the sky. She wondered if he was going to shoot.

Part Three

the city 1975

It was the end of June, and Annie hadn't seen the girls since the game. Over the last four weeks there had been final exams, end-of-the-year athletics, and then suddenly it was Last Day. Annie's graduation from the "middle school" to the "upper school" meant that high school was to begin next year. A lot of the girls were going off to boarding schools, and the rest would be moving to new classrooms on appropriately higher floors of the old building. This was the last year that the class Annie had grown up with would be intact. She had considered applying to boarding school; Luke thought it was worth trying for a scholarship if she really wanted to go. She had gone to visit one of the more popular ones, St. John's Academy, earlier that spring and was impressed by the largeness of the place, and with the lane of giant elms that lined the long vista from the library. She was told by healthy looking preppies about cross-country skiing on the school's private trails in the winter and running on them in the spring and fall. Then at night she was brought out to the woods by the druggies and given a hash pipe and beer from a keg. The most interesting people seemed to be the most depressed, but then that was also true in New York.

Luke was uncharacteristically indifferent to her going away to school, but Ellen didn't want Annie to go. She told Annie that she had hated all of her boarding schools, and that she didn't want Annie to be living away from home. Annie responded that they hardly saw each other anyway, which was true, since Annie left early while Ellen slept late; and most nights Annie stayed at friends' houses long past dinnertime. But Ellen said that wasn't the point, it was where you slept at night that mattered. Annie didn't know about that. The truth was that as long as Annie called her to let her know where she was going, Ellen pretty much let her do what she wanted. And after spending that one weekend at St. John's, where the proctor of the girls' dormitory explained to her about the "four legs on the floor with the door open" policy that applied to male visiting privileges, Annie realized that she had a lot more freedom from her own parents than she would ever get at a boarding school.

Luke and Ellen both came to Annie's eighth grade graduation. In fact, they sat next to each other, which made Annie's stomach jump when she saw them sitting together in the balcony. She had known that both of them were going to attend, but it somehow never occurred to her that they would sit together. She kept sneaking looks at them throughout the assembly, which went on with traditional predictability. Her parents looked unreal from where she was sitting, as if they were propped up cutouts from a photo of someone else's life. It felt wrong to her that they should look comfortable together, and once, when Annie saw her father lean over and say something to Ellen with a smile, she thought she wouldn't make it through the rest of the assembly without bolting from her seat. Don't pretend to be friends, she thought. You're never going to be friends. I don't want you to be friends. Her knees began to jig up and down without stopping.

"What is it?" Emily Rosenberg whispered. She was sitting next to Annie wearing a long denim skirt with embroidered flowers around the pockets.

"My parents," Annie whispered back. "They're here."

"So?"

"So. They're sitting together."

Emily glanced up. "So?"

"*So,* it makes me sick!" Annie hissed.

She couldn't remember the last time she had seen her parents together. Luke never came upstairs when he picked Annie up or dropped her off on the weekends. They talked on the phone sometimes, when they had to, but as far as Annie knew those conversations were always brief.

Annie was wearing lace-up Frye boots outside her patchiest jeans, and she pulled nervously on the laces. The girls were supposed to wear dresses to Last Day, though they were allowed to pick any dress they wanted. But no one had said anything to Annie that morning about her refusal to comply with the dress code, and she figured that the teachers wanted summer vacation to arrive just as much as she did. It had been a little disappointing to have no response at all to her outfit, but now she thought of Luke and Ellen sitting above her and realized that it might make them feel a little embarrassed to have the only daughter in ripped jeans. That thought made her smile, and she worked at one of the big holes in the knee of her jeans with a ballpoint pen, making a design on her skin.

The headmistress was giving a speech as Annie broke the skin with the point of her pen. She watched the bright red blood ooze out and mix with the black ink. It didn't hurt much, and she dug at it a little more, enjoying the sensation. She led the blood in a line with her pen, following the triangle design she had been doodling. She wondered if it would make a real tattoo. Then she stopped the game as she became aware that Emily was staring at her. She quickly wiped the pen on the side of her pants and pulled the blue jean material over the cut to wipe it up.

"It doesn't hurt," she said to Emily, but it was beginning to throb a little, and Annie wondered if it would keep bleeding through her jeans. She looked up to see if her parents were watching her and she caught Ellen's eye. Ellen smiled and gave her a little wave. Annie turned away quickly, without smiling back, and pressed her hand hard against her knee until the material stuck to the bloodied skin.

Then the headmistress was saying, "The eighth grade becomes . . . the ninth grade!" and her entire class jumped to their feet, shouting and twirling in their Last Day dresses. They weren't supposed to jump and shout like that, of course, and the teachers who sat with them gave disapproving looks. But they were the eighth-grade teachers, who were no longer officially in charge of them, and in fact everyone knew it would happen and indulged them because this was the final assembly. Annie looked up to see if her parents were upset by her outfit, and she gave one of her loudest street whistles when everyone was shouting, using her two index fingers to blow against. She couldn't see her parents though, because everyone in the balcony was standing for the school song and the girls' exit. They walked class by class out into the hallway where the parents were coming to meet them with hugs and flowers.

Luke and Ellen found her where she stood with a group of her friends. They each took a turn hugging her, and then Luke gave her a single red rose.

"Thanks, Dad." She dug her hands into the back pockets of her jeans, hitching them even lower so that her belly button showed.

"So, what would you like to do?" Ellen asked brightly—so brightly that Annie looked at her suspiciously.

"What do you mean?"

"Do you want to go have lunch somewhere? We were thinking, maybe you'd like to have a treat."

"All of us?" Annie was sure she couldn't mean that.

"Sure," Luke said, smiling at Ellen. "The three of us could go to—what's that place called—you know, Ellen, the Italian place."

"Oh, right. No, I can't remember what it's called—but it has great cannoli."

"That's it." Now Luke was laughing in a way that felt falsely intimate to Annie. She wanted to hit him, to hit them both and scream at them to stop being so phony. "What do you think, Annie? Still love cannoli?"

He smiled at her as if nothing could possibly be wrong, and she felt her throat close up until she could hardly breathe.

"No," she whispered.

"What?" She could tell he really hadn't heard her, and now Luke was getting irritated. Other parents and family groups were jostling against them in the hall, and she could tell he wanted to get going. "Go get your stuff and we'll meet you in front," he ordered.

She looked at them both, but suddenly it seemed as if they were completely separate from her. Already another parent had come up and they were talking and joking with her, talking about how proud they all were. Bullshit, Annie thought. Bullshit you're proud. She headed toward the stairway with the rest of the students.

"We'll meet you outside!" she heard Ellen call after her, and when she turned to her Ellen smiled a little shakily, as if she wasn't quite sure this was going to work either. Annie glared back at her, but the look was lost as another parent moved between them to hug a daughter dressed in white. Annie turned and pounded up the six flights to her classroom to get her jacket and her book bag. She didn't talk to anyone else as she emptied her locker, and after one look at her face her friends kept their distance, and she was glad they did. She ran back down the stairs, unable to imagine standing shoulder to shoulder with the other students in the elevator.

She found Luke and Ellen outside. Ellen was leaning against a parked car, smoking, while Luke paced back and forth in front of her, talking nonstop. In her white blouse and tailored trousers, with sandals on her bare feet, Annie thought that Ellen looked both more casual and more glamorous than the other mothers and teachers in their midlength skirts and somber blouses with one piece of jewelry tastefully displayed. She walked over to her parents, who both turned to greet her with a sudden silence that made Annie know that they had just been talking about her.

"All set?" Ellen asked.

"I guess." Annie felt trapped.

"Good," said Luke, and he took her book bag from her. "Here, let me take this. God, it's heavy."

"My skates are in there," Annie said.

The three of them walked in silence to the end of the block. The school overlooked the East River, just south of the mayor's residence, Gracie Mansion. As they walked away from the river all of the smells and sounds of the city seemed magnified to Annie. Little rivulets of dog urine crossed their path as they walked along the sidewalk, and a garbage truck slammed metal against metal as the men raised and emptied the cans lined up on the curb. Ellen's sandals slapped against the pavement, and even her father's leather soles seemed to make a sharp sound as he walked. When the striped yellow awning of the restaurant came into sight, Annie stopped.

"Mom," she said. Ellen and Luke looked at her.

"I can't have lunch. I'm sorry. I told the girls I'd meet them downtown right after school."

"But Annie," Ellen said. "We wanted to celebrate with you. It's a big day, and—"

"Well, but, we didn't make a plan." She turned to her father. "Right, Dad? I mean, there wasn't any plan for lunch."

"No," said Luke, with a patronizing laugh that was for Ellen's benefit. "No, we didn't talk about it before, but—"

"And I had this other thing," Annie said desperately. "I promised the girls. It's really important."

"Can't you call them?" Ellen asked.

"No," she said quickly. "We're meeting at the park in like fifteen minutes. I'm supposed to be there."

"Annie . . ." Luke was trying to catch her eye, and Annie would only look at him for a brief second. Then he stopped talking and just kept looking at her. Annie knew then how much she missed him. The old Luke. How long it had been since they had been alone at his apartment all day on a Saturday, eating popcorn and listening to Billie Holiday. It's all Jill's fault, she thought. Now Jill was always around. Annie almost looked back up at Luke, wanting him to know everything, but she forced herself to keep her eyes on the sidewalk.

"Is it all right?" she asked her mother, since she wasn't supposed to be with Luke until the weekend. "I told the Shanlicks . . ."

"Well, all right." Ellen sounded bewildered. She shrugged and looked at Luke. "It isn't a school night, after all."

As if that ever mattered before, Annie thought, but she didn't say anything in front of Luke.

"Dad?"

He swung her knapsack angrily off of his shoulder and left it on the sidewalk between them. "It's up to your mother," he muttered. "It's her night with you."

Annie stood still for a moment, pinned into place by his disapproval. Then she shrugged insincerely, bravely, and threw her knapsack over one shoulder. "O.K., I'll see you later, Mom. See you this weekend, Dad."

She looked quickly at both of them, forcing a smile.

"All right, Annie," Luke said quietly. Now the fight was gone from him in a way that frightened Annie even more than his anger. He didn't bother looking at Annie but looked out at the traffic coming up Third Avenue. Ellen nodded to her but didn't try to smile this time. Annie knew that if she stayed one more second they wouldn't be able to stop themselves from wanting to talk to her, so she turned and headed down the block away from them, back over to the East River and the paved walkway that could take her wherever she wanted to go.

As soon as she was around the corner, she ran full out until she got to the walkway. At the river she slowed down, running her fingers along the curved wrought-iron fence that ran along the top of the guard wall. She supposed it was there to prevent people from jumping, but they would have to be pretty undecided to let that little fence stop them, Annie thought. She breathed the cool river air deeply into her lungs again and again. She felt as if she hadn't taken a good breath since the beginning of the school assembly. Across the water was an island Annie didn't know the name of, where an abandoned hospital for the insane sat staring at the city. There had been a fire there long ago, and the brick shell that remained had always frightened Annie. She stopped and leaned against the edge of the wall and pulled out a cigarette, taking her time to smoke it. She watched the gulls wheel and dive at a garbage scow being towed downriver toward the Atlantic.

After she left the walkway and headed back into the numbered streets, Annie stopped at a phone booth and called the Shanlick girls' number. It had been a lie that they were expecting her to come downtown that afternoon. She hadn't been calling them as much as usual since the game, and she knew that Liz thought it was because of what had happened that night. Annie was determined that nothing would change between her and Liz, but that didn't stop her from feeling that everything *had* changed. That first morning in the country everything had seemed just right, but then the weeks had gone by without them seeing one another, and now, leaning against the glass and metal walls of the phone booth, she felt a tightness in her body that hadn't been there before while she waited to see who would answer the phone.

It was Liz. Annie caught her breath at the sound of her voice, then quickly covered it up by launching into her day. The final assembly, her outfit, how they had all whooped and whistled at the crucial moment. Her escape from a long, horrible lunch with Luke and Ellen. When she stopped for a breath, Liz said, "Dad and Janis are getting divorced."

Annie giggled. She didn't want to giggle, but she did.

"What's so fucking funny?"

"Nothing. I'm sorry. It's just—" she giggled some more. "It's not funny, Liz. Jesus, I'm sorry."

"Well, who's surprised?"

"I am, I guess." Annie wasn't giggling anymore.

"I'm not."

There was a pause. Annie knew that her dime was going to run out.

"Liz, can I come over? My mom will let me spend the night. No more school."

"Us too. We got out on Wednesday."

"When did you find out?"

"Today. They told us this morning."

"Shit. It's the shits."

Liz didn't say anything. Annie heard a rattling noise in the phone.

"Can I come over?"

"Yeah. Come on down, we'll be—"

The phone cut off. A mechanized female voice came over the wire demanding more money for the overtime. Fuck you, thought Annie, as she hung up the phone. Stupid goddamned phone company. She kicked the base of the phone booth, jamming the toes inside her boot so hard that tears came to her eyes. Leaning back against the glass wall of the booth, she cradled her foot for a moment in her hands. Her foot throbbed and she squeezed her eyes tight. What would happen with the game now? she wondered. Would Janis let them come up and play after the divorce? They couldn't play without Peter; unless Justin— She felt someone watching her. A woman in a business suit was waiting for the phone, and Annie saw her look change from impatience to concern as she watched Annie. Annie glared at her, then swung open the hinged glass door, and limped out onto the street.

"Are you all right?" the woman asked. I could be lying here dead and she'd say the same thing in the same tone of voice, Annie thought.

"Yeah, fine," she muttered to the woman, then walked over to the nearest stoop and pulled her skates out of her knapsack for the long walk from the river to the East Side IRT. Even though her foot still hurt, she wanted to skate to the train. She didn't want to see any of her friends who might be riding the bus home with their parents.

By now Annie knew the subway lines of the city perfectly, though once the trains left Manhattan for the boroughs, she had to admit that she wasn't so sure anymore. But she could navigate her way to the Village from anywhere in Manhattan, a skill the other girls in her class respected. Most of the parents at her school insisted that their daughters remain aboveground when they visited each other and were liberal with money for cab fare as their sophisticated, half-grown children traveled and retraveled the four square miles that encompassed the Upper East Side.

It was one of those perfect New York days, not too hot for June, and the breeze from the river blew through the holes in Annie's jeans. Eighth grade was over at last, and as she skated down the broad sidewalk, it began to dawn on Annie that whatever else happened, she would never have to be in middle school again. She started to pick up speed, ignoring the pain in her foot. Her knapsack made a flapping sound against her back in the quiet side streets, and the slow-moving old ladies and uniformed maids who were walking people's dogs turned to stare, but she kept going. "Real Life—Real Life," she began to chant inside her head, in the same rhythm as her skates were hitting the pavement. Real Life was downtown with the Shanlicks in Washington Square Park, or hanging out all night on the stoop of P.S. 3 on Grove Street. If Janis and Peter were breaking up, then they would have to pull together: Justin and Nick, the sisters and Annie. Next year's game was a whole year away; anything could happen. "Real Life." "Real Life." She reached Lexington Avenue and jumped down the stairs on her skates into the subway station, then ducked under the turnstile, skipping out on the fare to celebrate the beginning of summer.

The Shanlick girls lived with their mother, Marie, during the week, and stayed with Peter and Janis on the weekends. Marie had lived in the same apartment on Cornelia Street for ten years, ever since she and Peter Shanlick had divorced, and Annie thought that she would stay there her whole life. It was a dark, first-floor apartment, with only two bedrooms for herself and her three girls, but the location was perfect and the rent was so low that Marie could afford it with the income from her various business schemes. Marie was always working on big ideas: renovating an old theater on Broadway, opening a classy nightclub for the top jazz musicians to frequent. Ellen and Marie had been friends in the old days but had lost touch since Marie's divorce from Peter. Annie knew that the dislike between Marie and Luke was mutual, and this time Annie knew that Luke was wrong again, because she loved Marie. Marie treated her like an equal.

When she got to Astor Place, Annie got off the subway, and as soon as she hit the pavement she slung her pack onto her back again and skated across town. Everyone was out in Washington Square Park that day. There were three or four street performers inside the fountain area, the fountain having been turned off and transformed into a natural amphitheater. In a wider circle around them were teenagers with guitars and dope dealers who walked quietly from group to group calling softly, "Sens? Sens?" the code name for Sensamilian marijuana. You could buy a nickel bag for five dollars, and Annie and the girls had done so several times, but they knew that it was anything but Sensamilian; most of the time it would barely get them high. Annie circled the fountain a couple of times, looking for the girls, or even Nick or Justin, but there was nobody she knew, so she headed for their block on Cornelia Street between Bleecker and West Fourth.

The girls were on their stoop when she got there. Tessa and Sam were sitting with their backs against either side of the stoop, and Liz lay between them, resting on her elbows and squinting into the sun. Annie pulled her feet together and jumped the curb onto the sidewalk in front of them, digging in her toes for a perfect landing.

"Hey, Annie." Nobody moved. The sun reflected her own face back at her in Sam's and Tessa's sunglasses, and Liz cupped a hand to her forehead.

"You got here pretty fast."

"Yeah. I forgot I had my skates in my bag from school." Annie balanced back and forth from the tip of her skates to the heel. "What are you guys doing out here?"

"Mom was driving us crazy," said Sam. "She thinks it's great news about Janis and Peter."

"Why? I thought she liked Janis."

"She likes her even more now that her marriage to Dad is over," Tessa laughed. "Typical."

"What happened?" Annie asked, holding onto the stone pillar at the edge of the stoop and carefully lowering herself down.

"What do you mean 'what happened?' Jesus!" Sam looked at Annie, her lips pouted and scornful. Annie couldn't see her eyes behind the dark glasses.

"They didn't love each other anymore, they fucked around, they lied, they decided they hated each other. Voilà." Sam reached for a cigarette from the pack that lay on the stoop next to Tessa.

"I meant what happened this morning," Annie said. She wondered if Sam really liked her at all; it seemed as if she was always telling Annie that what she said was stupid, and she never wanted to spend time alone with her. Annie looked out at the street and started to work at one of the nicks in her leather skate. It was a new thought, that one of the sisters might not want her around. Then she realized that Liz had already been talking to her for a while.

". . . so we had all spent the night," she was saying. "Which is kind of weird, 'cause it's not a weekend, but Dad made up some excuse, like the boys having the last day of school today—"

"Like that matters," said Tessa. She got up and started pacing back and forth in front of the stoop.

"Right. But we didn't think about it too much—"

"I wanted to see the boys anyway," Tessa said quickly.

"Yeah, me too." Sam frowned and put her cigarette out halfway.

"So, the boys were there . . . ," Annie said to Liz, watching Tessa, who was scuffing her sneakers as she walked and seemed to be only half listening.

"We were all there this morning, that's when they told us. Everyone sat together on the couch, and Dad and Janis faced us in their chairs. It was weird, like being in a TV movie." Liz's voice trailed off, and Annie leaned back against her knees, not saying anything.

"It's not like they were fighting all the time or anything," Sam said.

"They didn't fight at all this morning," said Tessa. She was the closest to Janis.

"How about the boys?" Annie asked her.

"Justin was really upset about the apartment. They're going to move out. I think that's what got him the most."

"What about the game?" asked Annie.

"I don't know. Justin didn't say anything about the game. Nobody did." Tessa shrugged. "Nick's going to boarding school next year, and he told me he's never going to live at home again anyway." Tessa laughed and looked at Annie out of the corner of her eyes.

"Where's he going?" Annie asked.

"St. John's."

"Really? God, I thought he hated that place. He said he'd never leave the city."

"He wants to leave now," Tessa said.

"He got a full scholarship. I think that's why he's going," Liz said.

"He's going because he's a fucking liar," Tessa said violently. "Him and Dad and Janis—they're all fucking liars."

"So how does Justin rate?" Sam asked without missing a beat.

Tessa punched her. Hard. In the face. Then Sam started crying, and Tessa was furiously shaking her by the shoulders so that Sam's sunglasses flew off and landed in the street just in time to be shattered by a taxi. The driver tried to veer, but gave them all the finger instead.

"Yeah, fuck you too!" Tessa yelled, whirling back toward the street and starting off at a run after the cab. Annie jumped into the street after her, but she forgot that she was still wearing her skates and fell over her own feet, landing hard in the gutter.

"Tessa!" Liz shouted, in a voice Annie had never heard before, strange and deep, as if someone else was yelling right through her body. The whole street stopped for just a moment. Then Tessa slowly turned back to them, looking only at Sam. She leaned down and picked up Sam's glasses; one lens was broken and the frame was flattened and skewed.

"Let me see," Liz said to Sam. She was holding her, trying to get a look at her face, the red mark of Tessa's closed fist on her cheek. Sam was sobbing hard. Annie unlaced her skates and pulled them off angrily. "Jesus. Oh, Jesus," was all she could say.

Tessa came back to the stoop and sat next to Sam. She put an arm around her while still holding the crushed glasses with the other hand.

Sam shook her off. "Don't!" she yelled, still crying. "Don't you touch me!"

Tessa flinched, but took her arm off and looked at her. "I'm sorry, Sam. I really am." Her voice broke a little but she was dry-eyed. "I just didn't want you putting Justin and Nick in the same—I'm really sorry, it just happened . . ." Tessa looked up at Liz.

"I'm pregnant, Liz." Tessa said to her, as if there were only the two of them there.

"Oh, no. Oh, fuck. Fuck, fuck, fuck," Liz said.

Annie looked up and wondered if everybody else already knew about Nick and Tessa; then Liz looked at her, and Annie felt herself blushing, remembering Tessa and Nick making love in the Asylum.

"Who is it?" Liz asked, and Annie knew that Liz and Sam really didn't know. Sam had stopped crying and was holding her cheek. She leaned back against Liz's knees and stared silently at Tessa.

"Nick," Tessa said.

Sam sucked in her breath through her teeth, and Tessa shot her a look, daring her to disapprove.

"Nick?" Now it was Liz's turn. "When did you guys?"

"At Capture, and before."

"Before?" Annie asked. She wondered how long they had been doing it and why Tessa hadn't gotten pregnant sooner. "Weren't you using anything?"

"Only once we didn't use anything—at Capture," Tessa said.

"Oh, my God," Sam said at last. She looked embarrassed. She was almost never embarrassed. "Does anyone else know? Have you told Nick?"

"No." She looked out at the street. "Only you guys know. And if you open your little trap, Sam, I'll never trust you again."

Sam glared at her. "Hey, look, I won't tell anybody. Who would I want to tell? I mean, he's practically our brother. How could you do it? I think it's really weird. You guys are sick."

"Shut up, Sam," Liz said. "They're not our real brothers."

"Now, they're our ex-stepbrothers." Tessa laughed. "What are we going to call them?"

"You're gonna tell Nick, aren't you, Tess?" Annie asked.

"I just found out yesterday," Tessa said. "I went to Planned Parenthood."

"Oh, Tess. I'm sorry," Annie said.

"Why? I'm not." Tessa grinned and pushed her dark glasses up higher on her face.

"What do you mean?"

"I'm going to have the baby." Tessa looked at them and smiled. "It'll be all right."

Sam sat up. "You're going to have the baby? Even though it's going to be a little incest freak?"

"He's *not* our real brother, and it's not going to be a freak, you little shit." Tessa jumped up, but this time Sam jumped up too. Suddenly Tessa started laughing.

"Don't you get it, Sam? It's going to be ours, all of ours."

Sam just looked at her. Tessa touched her own belly in a way Annie had never seen before: protective and sensual. "This baby's gonna have three moms," she said; then, looking at Annie, she grinned and added, "Four. It's gonna have four moms."

No one said anything.

"I don't want a baby," Sam said, getting up and going into the house. "I'm gonna get some ice for my face."

The heavy metal and glass door slammed behind her. Tessa lit a cigarette. "She hates me," she said, taking a long drag and leaning back against the stoop.

"You've got to have an abortion, Tess," Annie said quietly. "Nick won't want it. You know that. I can get you the money too; I've got a savings account my grandfather set up, and nobody ever checks it. I even know where the Planned Parenthood abortion clinic is. I went there to get on the pill last winter, and—"

"How do you know?" Tessa interrupted.

"What? I told you, I was there last—"

"How the fuck do you know that Nick won't want it?" Tessa yelled at Annie, furious, then stopped and looked around as if she was afraid he would turn the corner and hear her. She turned back to Annie and spoke more quietly. "I don't want an abortion, Annie. I want the baby." She paused. "Nick . . . he'll be O.K. about it once the baby's here. I hope it's a girl."

Liz and Annie exchanged looks. Annie felt an almost audible click as she realized that this was something she could do. She could organize the abortion for Tessa; she could even find the money for it. All she and Liz had to do was convince Tessa. Looking at Liz now, she wished she could reach for her and hold her. They could plan how to pull it off. Liz gave Annie a slight smile, as if she knew everything Annie was thinking, which somehow didn't surprise her at all. She waited, still and strangely happy.

"Let's see what Nick says," Liz said to Tessa, and Tessa looked up at her, smiling.

"Yeah. Don't worry, Liz. It's gonna be O.K."

"I know."

The late afternoon was finally breaking into early evening, and a cooler breeze came in off the Hudson, blowing sections of newspaper down the street. They lifted and curved and hit the asphalt, only to be swept up again with the momentum of a passing car. Three large pieces started flying up simultaneously, and they looked like a flock of birds scuttling and swooping toward Sixth Avenue.

"Hey, look at that," Annie said, and then they all burst out laughing as the newspapers stuck fast against the leg of a card table that some old men had set up on the sidewalk. The men always sat in front of the same stoop, about four buildings down from the Shanlicks' place. They wore light, slippery shirts and sandals and listened to a transistor radio as they played cards each night. Old women leaned out on the windowsills above them in garish housedresses and rested on their elbows, observing the game and commenting to each other from window to window. The men below always seemed to ignore them, staying serious and fixed on the cards, while the women laughed and gossiped overhead.

"Now it really feels like summer," Liz said, watching them.

"Let's go to the beach," Tessa said suddenly. "Come on, let's go to Coney."

"You want to go to Coney? Tess—" Liz started, but Tessa jumped up and turned to Annie.

"Annie?"

Annie grinned. Tessa knew she would never say no to Coney Island.

"Come on, Liz," she said, pushing against Liz's knee with the edge of her foot. "Tessa's right. School's out. Everything's fucked. Let's go."

"But what about Sam? And Mom?"

"If Sam wants to come, great—if not, fuck her. Mom won't mind, you know that." Tessa shifted impatiently.

"Sam will come," Annie said.

"Sam's pissed," Liz said, looking at Tessa.

"I know. I said I'm sorry to her. Maybe if we go to Coney she'll get over it."

"Maybe."

"Is she gonna tell Marie you hit her?" Annie asked. She shouldn't have said it, just as things were getting better; but there was the red mark on Sam's cheek and her broken glasses on the stoop.

"No," said both of the girls at the same time. "Jinx!" Liz said, then both of them together as fast as they could: "One-two-three-four"—racing up to ten—"You owe me a Coke!" they both yelled. They did this every time anyone spoke the same word at the same time; they had been doing it since second grade. Whoever finished last had to buy for the winner. This time Liz was there a second sooner. Tessa slapped her outstretched palm in acknowledgment of her defeat, and Annie felt all of them ease up.

"C'mon," said Liz, getting up and pulling open the door to the building. "You can buy me a soda when we get to Coney."

As soon as they walked into the apartment, Annie knew that Marie was in a good mood, because she was playing early selections of Billie Holiday; "Miss Brown to You" was spinning on the turntable. The girls could always gauge her mood by which era of Billie Holiday was playing. The final concert at Carnegie Hall, when there was almost nothing left but her phrasing, meant it was going to be a rough night.

Marie had married Peter Shanlick and gotten pregnant with Tessa when she was only eighteen, and the other two girls had been born within the next five years, so she was younger than Annie's parents, and it showed. She was pretty, tall, and coltish with her straight black hair cut in a page-boy cut that framed her pale face. Marie treated Annie like another daughter, partly because they both loved jazz. Luke had turned her into a devotee; the fact that Luke and Marie both loved Billie Holiday and had extensive, rare collections of her recordings was an irony that Annie kept to herself.

The apartment was high-ceilinged but dark. The walls were covered with homemade bookshelves that reached the ceiling and gave the living room the feel of an old library. One of the two bedrooms had a three-decker bunk bed for the girls, who slept in order of age, with Tessa on the top bunk, Liz in the middle, and Sam on the bottom. There were piles of books and papers everywhere, some serving as end tables to the furniture and topped with overflowing ashtrays. The kitchen was the only spot of color, for the girls had painted it bright orange last summer, and black-bottomed pots hung on nails from the walls like black-eyed Susans.

"What's for dinner?" Tessa called, as they came in.

"I'm not hungry," Marie called back from the living room. She was putting a new record on the turntable. She smiled at Annie. "Annie! Good."

Annie went and sat on the couch, taking the cigarette that Marie offered automatically. "Who's on piano?" This was a game they often played; Marie testing on the sidemen and accompanists for Billie. But Luke had trained Annie well.

"Teddy Wilson."

Marie smiled. "Good, but that was easy. Drums?"

"Jo Jones?" This was a guess, but a good one.

"Very good," said Marie, and she smiled at her.

"What year?"

This was the hardest, and they both knew it.

"Nineteen thirty-nine?"

"No."

"Thirty-seven?"

"No, no! She's young, but not that young. It's after 'Miss Brown.' Nineteen forty-six; things were looking up in forty-six and this song was a hit." She tapped her hand along with the song on the arm of the couch, and they both started singing.

"Hey, Annie. Want some spaghetti?" Tessa stood at the doorway. Annie could hear Liz's and Sam's voices from the bedroom, even though the door was closed. Steam billowed out from the kitchen.

"Sure," Annie said. "Want some help?"

"O.K." Tessa tapped a long metal spoon against the doorframe.

"We're gonna go to Coney, tonight," she told her mother. "Annie got out of school today."

"Congratulations," Marie said to Annie; then looking at Tessa she added, "Don't forget your keys when you go, because I'll be out."

"Don't worry, Mom," Tessa said over her shoulder as she went back into the kitchen. "Come on, Annie."

Annie helped her set the table and mixed up some frozen orange juice, which they always had on hand, no matter how broke Marie was. Dinner was going to be a Shanlick staple: spaghetti with ketchup mixed in as tomato sauce. Annie had eaten a lot of dinners like this with the girls. Annie had cooked for herself from time to time, but her mother had almost always left her precise instructions as to what to do. It was different with the Shanlick girls. She admired the girls' ability to walk into the kitchen and figure it out for themselves, though all they usually cooked was spaghetti with ketchup and occasionally instant pancakes or cornmeal mush drowned in maple syrup and butter. Liz came out of the bedroom to eat with them, but Sam refused to.

"You should talk to her, Tess," Liz said as she sat down at the kitchen table.

"After we eat," Tessa said, ignoring the look that Liz gave her as she stabbed open the bright green container of Parmesan cheese with her knife. Liz didn't say anything, and Marie put on another record in the living room. The Teddy Wilson Orchestra, Annie thought automatically, 1944. She stirred the spaghetti, ketchup, and Parmesan together into a goopy mixture on her plate; it actually tasted pretty good, and they all had second helpings. Since they couldn't talk about it, the pregnancy was all Annie could think about. She wondered what would happen if Tessa really did keep the baby, and when she would have to tell Marie and Peter and everyone else.

Marie came in and leaned over Tessa's chair, taking an occasional noodle from her plate.

"Are you hungry, Mom?" Tessa asked, without looking up.

"No." Marie took a long drag on her cigarette. "I'll just have some of yours."

She then sucked a long strand from Tessa's plate into her mouth; it made a kind of slurping noise at the finish. Annie tried not to smile, but Tessa suddenly pushed back her chair, all the color gone from her face, and ran for the bathroom. They heard her throw the toilet seat back with a bang, and then the sound of vomiting. Marie ran into the bathroom; Liz and Annie stayed where they were, staring at each other.

"Honey, Tessa, are you all right?" Marie was saying. Tell her, thought Annie, tell her now. If she were my mother I'd tell her. Marie was cool; she'd help them get the abortion and everything would be O.K.

"I'm fine, Mom." She heard Tessa pant softly.

"Here, honey—take a washcloth." Marie was fussing over her now, getting a cold cloth. "I hope you're not coming down with something. Come lie down."

Liz looked at Annie. "Oh, good. An opportunity for her to be our mother," she said under her breath.

Marie brought Tessa back out to the living room. "Get her a glass of water," she ordered. She set up some pillows and a blanket, making room for Tessa to lie down on the couch. Tessa kept her eyes averted from Annie and Liz and followed her mother's instructions, lying back and covering her eyes with the washcloth.

"Can you turn down the music, Mom?" she asked quietly.

"Of course," Marie jumped up and turned off the record player. In the sudden silence Annie could hear Tessa's breathing was still a little rapid, and Marie perched next to her, stroking the hair back from her forehead. Liz brought her a glass of water, and Annie went to sit down on the other side of her.

"Can we get you anything, Tess?" she asked.

"No, no." Tessa smiled, clearly feeling well enough now to enjoy the attention.

"Is there any spaghetti left?" That was Sam, banging open the door of their bedroom. She walked to the entry of the living room and looked at Tessa. "What's wrong with you?"

"She's sick," Marie said, in a dramatic voice. "If you're going to eat, do it in the kitchen."

"You threw up, right," said Sam, more as a statement than a question.

"Sam!" Marie turned to her angrily. "It's not her fault."

Her words hung there for just a moment too long.

"I feel a little funny too," said Liz, looking at Tessa. "Maybe it was those falafels we got on MacDougal Street."

"Yeah," said Sam flatly. "We shouldn't have gone there. That place sucks."

"Mom," said Tessa. "Will you read me one of those Edgar Allan Poe stories? Like you used to when we were sick?"

Marie smiled and patted her hand. "You girls always liked that, didn't you?"

She got up and went over to the bookshelf. "Why don't I keep these in alphabetical order?" she murmured.

"The Poe is in the other room, Mom," Liz said.

"Can you get it, Liz? And get me a drink," Marie said, settling down into an old blue armchair opposite the couch. Liz got up and Annie heard her cracking open the ice tray in the kitchen.

"How about 'The Cask of Amontillado'?" Annie suggested. She loved Poe. Her mother used to read his stories aloud in the car when they took road trips together, before the divorce. She would lie curled up in the backseat covered by a blanket and listen, terrified, as the trees whipped by them on the road. Luke would try to frighten her with a deep laugh at crucial moments in the story, or reach back and grab her leg to make her scream.

"No, no, we've heard that one too many times," Tessa said. "Pick a new one, Mom."

"All right," Marie took the book and the bourbon offered to her by Liz. "Let's see . . . Here's one we've never read before: 'William Wilson.' " She began to read: " 'Let me call myself, for the present, William Wilson.' "

"There's a guy in my class named William Wilson," Sam interrupted.

"Sam—shut up," said Tessa with her eyes closed.

"Well, there *is,*" she said sulkily, but Marie kept reading.

" '. . . This has been already too much an object for the scorn—for the horror—for the detestation of my race . . .' "

They all settled back. Marie's voice was punctuated only by the scuffling of stray cats fighting at the bottom of the air shaft and her frequent sips of bourbon. Even Sam seemed lulled by the story, which Annie didn't like quite as much as "The Cask of Amontillado," but it was comforting to have someone read aloud. She wished that her mother still did that, and thought that she probably would if Annie asked her to, but it seemed as if they were hardly ever home together: Then she remembered that she still hadn't called Ellen to let her know that she was spending the night downtown.

She saw Tessa's hand resting on her belly again, almost absently, and Annie wished that she could tell Marie, right now, while they were all close together. But I won't let Tessa have the baby, she thought, drifting away from the story; Liz and Sam and I, she thought, we won't let her screw everything up.

" '. . . All is gray shadow—a weak and irregular remembrance—an indistinct regathering of feeble pleasures and phantasmagoric pains—' Oh, my God, what time is it?" Marie suddenly broke off, looking at Annie as if she must know. Annie jumped up; she didn't wear a watch, but there was a clock in the kitchen. She left the room, feeling disoriented and guilty that she hadn't really been listening to the story.

"It's almost seven," she called back.

"I've got to go." Marie got up suddenly, putting the book on top of another stack next to her chair. She looked at Tessa. "Sorry, sweetheart. I've got to meet Allen at the White Horse. We're having a business meeting. Will you be all right?"

"Of course," Tessa said. She bit savagely at a cuticle, then sucked at it as it started to bleed.

"Maybe Sam or Liz . . ." Marie looked at them, then at Annie leaning in the doorway. "Or Annie!" There was relief in her voice. "Annie can read the rest."

"It's O.K., Mom," Tessa said. "I'm not that sick."

"I know, I know," said Marie, patting Tessa's arm as though her sickness was already an event placed behind her. "Otherwise, I wouldn't go out."

Nobody said anything. Marie took her drink and went to the bedroom to change clothes. "Shit, I'm going to be late, shit, shit, shit," she was saying to herself.

"I don't mind reading the rest," Annie said to Tessa, though she really hadn't been following it at all.

"No, thanks," Tessa said, sinking down further into the couch. "I feel O.K. now. Actually, I'm hungry again."

"Wow," said Sam. "Is this all because of—" she waited.

"I guess so," shrugged Tessa. "I've heard of it."

"Wow," said Sam again, and for the first time Annie thought that maybe Tessa really would have the baby.

"Let's go to Coney Isand," Annie said. "You can get something to eat there, a knish or something. Maybe you shouldn't eat any more spaghetti."

"I'm never eating spaghetti again," Tessa announced. Marie slammed the bathroom door as she went in; they heard the sound of her makeup scattering on the tiles and more swearing.

"She's leaving soon," Annie said under her breath.

"Yeah," Tessa smiled. "And she won't be back until the White Horse closes."

"Coney Island? Are you kidding?" Sam stared at them.

"Come on, Sam," said Annie. "It's a nice night. It'll be great out there. The beach."

"I like to go to the beach in the daytime, so I can get a tan," Sam said.

"I think we should go," Liz said, looking at Sam. "We haven't been to Coney yet this summer. Mom's going out, let's go."

Sam leaned into them and spoke in a whisper so that Marie wouldn't hear. "You guys are always telling me to shut up, but I'm the only one with any sense of reality in this family. Jesus, Tessa, you and Nick? I mean, it's so gross I can't believe it. 'Hey, I'm pregnant, let's go to Coney Island—Dad and Janis are getting divorced, let's go to Coney Island'—I've got a brain tumor, let's go to Coney Island!"

Tessa started to whistle between her teeth, staring Sam down. It sounded like "Someone's in the kitchen with Dinah."

"Well, what are we supposed to do, Sam? We just found out." Liz was trying to keep her voice level, Annie could tell.

"But why go to Coney Island?"

Tessa sat up so that she and Sam were only inches apart. "Because I want to. Because I don't give a shit what you think, Sam."

"How do I look?" Marie was standing at the door. She had changed her T-shirt for a dark silk button-down and had put on some lipstick.

"You look great, Marie," Annie said, when none of the girls said anything. Marie looked disappointed.

"Thanks, Annie," she said edgily. "Girls, leave me a note if you go anywhere. Though you shouldn't, Tessa, since you're sick." She walked over to the couch and felt Tessa's forehead, then gave her a hug and a businesslike kiss on the top of her head. She paused and pouted slightly at Tessa.

"I'm feeling better," Tessa said, giving her mother an indeterminate smile.

Marie lit up. "That's wonderful," she said. "I'll bring home a bottle of ginger ale for you. Have a good night." They heard the lock in the heavy apartment door turn behind her as she rattled her keys, then the clicking sound of Marie's shoes down the hall and the second, more muffled slam of the street door.

Marie left a trail of perfume behind her; not my mother's scent, Annie thought, a stronger mixture, possibly jasmine. It reminded Annie of the sweet-smelling blossoms on a tobacco farm Ellen had stayed at when Annie was seven years old. It was called a farm, but Annie never saw any farmers there. Only doctors and nurses and some very large orange house cats. The farm had been in South Carolina, and now Annie was old enough to know that her mother had gone there because she had had a breakdown. Breakdown seemed the perfect description to Annie; sometimes everything broke down inside her mother, like a car, and she just couldn't go any farther. Annie had liked the farm, with its plowed-up red earth that she had used as pretend rouge on her cheeks, mixing it with spit and rubbing hard for effect. At night the scent of the white tobacco blossoms had risen over the fields and blanketed everything with ease. She had wanted to stay longer at the farm, stay all summer, but her father had picked her up after only a week and brought her back to the city. She never went back again to visit while Ellen was there. Even though Luke had said she could, Annie had said no; she had seen the relief on her mother's face as she waved good-bye to her through the back window of the car, through the red dust that rose up behind the wheels of the VW. Ellen had remained standing in the middle of the driveway until the car was out of sight, dressed in a pale yellow dress with no sun hat and flat white tennis shoes.

"Let's go," said Tessa, throwing off the blanket. "I really feel all right now."

"I'm not going," Sam said. "Forget it."

"Liz?" Tessa was already pulling on a jacket.

"Yeah, O.K. Come on, Annie." Liz followed Tessa into the kitchen and shoved the remains of a box of saltines, wrapped in wax paper, into her pocket. They started for the door.

Annie got up and threw the rest of her cigarettes to Sam, who sat unmoving in an armchair. "Sam—please come—we should all be together."

Sam caught the pack without looking up. "Not tonight, Annie."

"But tonight—"

"Fuck off, Annie," Sam said quietly. "I don't want to go."

Annie held her breath, then waited for Sam to look up at her, but she never did.

"Annie! Come on!" Liz yelled from the hallway. She was holding the door open.

"All right, Sam," Annie said at last. "Fuck you too."

Sam smiled tightly, and Annie headed for the door.

"She hates me," Tessa said when they were all outside, heading down toward Sixth Avenue and the F train.

Annie laughed. "Yeah, well, she hates me too."

"Bullshit, you guys, bullshit," Liz said. "She just doesn't know what to think."

"Who does?" said Annie, giving her a look. "We should be together, anyway."

Liz took her hand and squeezed it hard. Annie was so surprised by the sudden tenderness she felt that she glanced at Tessa to see if she had noticed, but Tessa was striding quickly, looking straight ahead.

"Maybe we shouldn't all be together," Tessa said shortly. "I don't know, Annie. Maybe not."

Annie held Liz's hand harder and decided not to let go, even if Tessa turned around.

The subway to Coney Island came out from underground somewhere in Brooklyn, and the three girls turned to face Manhattan, which gleamed like a silver dime on the sidewalk. There was a stretch of pavement on her way home from the bus stop that was filled with mica, and whenever Annie walked there she half shut her eyes and willed the shiny bits to become airborne in her altered vision. She did that now to the distant skyline.

The sun had finally set, and the lights left on in the buildings were bright metallic squares against the sky that went from azure to green to red. The subway swayed back and forth, and the car was filled with people going home from work. Their heads drooped and swung with the car, and Annie watched a woman whose ankles seemed ready to burst from her tight shoes as she held two bags of groceries between her legs and another on her lap. Her chin kept hitting the jagged paper edge of the shopping bag and jerking up quickly; she grimaced, closed her eyes, then drifted down again.

The long stretch between the two islands of Coney and Manhattan was a foreign country to the girls. They didn't know anybody who lived in Brooklyn, and as the train passed through stations identified by names instead of numbers, they watched each ethnic group get off the train. The blacks, the Latinos, and the Hassidic Jews all had their own areas, and though they shared the same subway car, they almost never shared the same station stop. The Russians and the Asians seemed to wait until almost the end of the line, and then it was back to the Jews, non-Hassids this time, who, along with the girls and a few assorted strays Annie couldn't identify, rode the train into Coney Island itself. The train rattled high above a street filled with hawkers selling candy, newspapers, and fresh produce all jumbled together with the smell of knishes and "Coney Island Foot-Longs"—the giant hot dogs that turned on stacks of rotating metal tubes inside the window of Nedick's. Everything tasted better at Coney Island, and even with the exhaust and the garbage and grease in the air, there was still the smell of the sea coming off the beach. It was a different smell from the harbor in lower Manhattan, and in the summertime the scent was mixed with suntan lotion and cotton candy.

On the way down through the station Annie stopped to call her mother and tell her she was staying over at the Shanlicks' house. Ellen answered the phone with an urgency that made Annie think she had been expecting someone else to call, and she wondered who it was. She told Ellen that they were out at Coney Island, and her mother sounded amazed that her own daughter knew how to navigate her way there by herself.

"How did you get there?" she asked.

"Just took the F train, Mom. It's easy."

"Oh. The F train." Ellen never took the subway; she hated it when the subway stopped between stations. She was panicked by the thought that she might never get off. She would leave extra time in order to take the bus around the Upper West Side and certainly never went as far as Brooklyn.

"Well, have a good time. Will I see you tomorrow?"

"I'll come home in the morning."

"O.K." There was a pause and Annie shifted impatiently. She could hardly hear Ellen, there was so much static in the line. "What, Mom?"

"I said, how are you doing?"

"I'm fine. Good."

"The eighth grade becomes the ninth grade—congratulations, honey."

Annie laughed. "Yeah, thanks. I don't ever have to be in eighth grade again."

"What?" There was more static on the line.

"Nothing. I gotta go. Bye, Mom."

Annie joined Liz and Tessa, who were flipping through magazines at a newsstand. The man who ran the stand glared at them, knowing they weren't going to buy.

"O.K.?" Liz asked.

"Yeah, let's go."

They didn't have to talk about where they were going. Tessa led them through the midway, past the miniature golf, the rifle ranges, and the Skee Ball alleys, all overhung with enormous pink and white stuffed animals who stared out with plastic eyes permanently shocked open. They stopped to buy three potato knishes under the shadow of the Wonder Wheel, the enormous Ferris wheel that dominated Coney Island and could be seen from the train as they came in from Manhattan. Out beyond the Ferris wheel lay the horizon stretching as far away as Europe and the Canary Islands Annie had always colored bright blue and yellow in geography class. She thought of the sailors and immigrants whose first sight of America might be this lit-up neon wheel, stopping and starting and spinning at the edge of the sea.

The knishes were hot, and they blew on them between bites, holding them by wax paper wrappers. They watched the Wonder Wheel for a while, the couples getting on and off, the Puerto Rican boys who worked the wheel and their friends who lounged nearby, calling out to pretty girls who walked by in platform heels and short dresses, their lips painted dark red. The girls would never turn their heads, but the boys knew they heard, and after they passed by the boys would laugh to themselves and hit each other, embarrassed and proud. Annie and her friends didn't wear makeup and they dressed in jeans and T-shirts; the Puerto Rican boys didn't even notice them. If Sam were here *she* would be noticed, Annie thought, no matter what she was wearing.

"Should we go up?" Liz asked.

Normally she would never ask. They always went on the Ferris wheel first, but without Sam there it was an odd number, and being faced with the series of two-seaters, her absence made the three of them feel off balance.

"Of course." Tessa was defiant. "I'll ride alone. You guys go together."

"No, Tessa," Annie said. "You shouldn't be alone."

"Why not?" Tessa narrowed her eyes as if she was going to get angry again, but then she smiled instead. "I want to go alone."

"Anyway, we'll just be right behind you in the next car," Liz said. They bought their tickets from a boy who was their age but looked older. He looked right past them as he collected the soft dollar bills that had been warmed in Annie's back pocket; she was treating them tonight since she had some money left from her allowance. The Shanlicks didn't get an allowance, but they got paid for cleaning a friend of Marie's apartment once a week. A friend who kept pot in her freezer and so much Valium in her bathroom cabinet that the girls stole supplies of both as a matter of course. It was understood that whoever had money shared it equally with the other three.

The seats swung back and forth as they got in. Tessa got into the car ahead of Annie and Liz, and the wheel jerked her forward as soon as the boy swung the metal bar across the front of the gondola and yelled something in Spanish over his shoulder to the operator. Annie noticed that the person who actually operated the wheel was older, and he never looked up, just listened to the boy's shouts with his back bent over against the weight of the motor lever. A white T-shirt was stretched tight over the taut curve of his back.

When they had finally loaded everyone on board, the wheel began to rise up and up. Annie leaned back against Liz and smiled. As they went over the top, Tessa was below, in front of them, and there were only strangers behind. Annie took Liz's hand and kissed the palm; the center of her hand was hot and salty. Liz looked at her as if she was surprised, and Annie shrugged.

"It doesn't have to mean anything, does it?" she asked.

"I don't know." Liz let Annie keep her hand.

"I mean we're not lesbians, or anything."

"Maybe we are."

Annie laughed. "Maybe. What would Sam say?"

" 'Gross me out!' " Liz laughed too now. Then they stopped talking and Annie put her hand on Liz's thigh, close enough to mean something or nothing.

"I love you," Liz said, not looking at Annie but out over the boardwalk, where the fires lit in garbage cans by the bums glowed like small watchfires from far away.

"I loved you before," Annie said.

"Yeah." Liz turned to her. "But it's different now."

"It's not that different. Just more," Annie said.

"More," Liz repeated in a flat voice. Then the wheel stopped in its second revolution at the top, and they rocked their gondola back and forth together like they always did, leaning way out over the edge of the gondola and daring Tessa to swing more. Tessa was sitting in the middle of her seat. If Sam had been there she would have swung it more and more until Tessa screamed at her and made her stop. But tonight Tessa was swinging it surprisingly high, with apparent fearlessness, and Annie suddenly thought to herself that it might not be good for the baby—then stopped and realized that she shouldn't be thinking of it as a baby anyway, but as an abortion.

"I hope she doesn't go through with it," Liz said.

"Having it?"

"Uh huh." The wheel had started down again, and Tessa was leaning out over the edge of the car, her long black hair whipping back against her. "I hope she doesn't throw up again either."

"I'll find out everything," Annie said. "The doctor, the money, everything."

"O.K.," Liz said. "O.K., but she's gotta go get it done, you know."

"She will." Their car paused as someone was let out at the bottom. "What does she think Nick's gonna say anyway?"

"I don't know," Liz said. " 'Marry me'?"

"I'm never getting married," Annie said.

Liz looked at her. "No, I bet you will," she said. "But not me, I really won't, you'll see."

"Ah, fuck you," Annie said, and squeezed her leg. Then they arrived at the bottom where Tessa was waiting, and the boy unhooked the bar across them and released it, still speaking an unending stream of Spanish and never looking at them.

They walked to the boardwalk. In the dark the beach looked clean, and the waves broke along the shore the same way they broke along beaches everywhere else in the world. This still surprised Annie whenever she came here; she never expected anything to happen in

New York the way it happened elsewhere. It was a warm night, and the old people from the neighborhood had taken over the benches that lined the boardwalk, their walkers and canes set to the side or clamped between their rigid hands as their owners argued and gestured to each other, their eyes always returning to the sea and the lights of the tankers that passed slowly along the horizon, too far out and too numerous to count.

As soon as they hit the beach, Annie started to run.

"Hey!" Tessa called.

"Come on!" Annie yelled back, and they followed, their jackets flapping behind them, scaring the gulls who were picking over the day's garbage and greasy wrappers. The fires that burned in the metal trash barrels were surrounded by small groups of men who dressed in overcoats despite the summer heat. They were people who always had to wear their possessions or have them stolen from them. They looked up as the girls ran by but didn't yell as the young boys had; they kept to themselves. The girls ran until their breath came painfully, and at last Annie leaned over, her hands on her knees, facing the ocean. Tessa and Liz came up behind her, and Tessa knocked her down, catching her off guard. The two of them rolled in the sand, one on top of the other as Liz watched, laughing. Tessa pinned Annie at last and sat on top of her, wrestling her wrists into the sand.

"Forget it, Edwards," she said, grinning. "Shanlicks always end up on top."

Annie laughed. She couldn't see anything but Tessa's teeth in the dark, smiling down in victory, and for once she didn't care who won. Tessa hadn't wrestled her in years. She rolled off Annie and they both lay on their backs, panting in the sand. Liz came over and sat next to them, digging her sneakers in until she found the wet sand.

"Want to get high?" she said. They all knew she had brought a joint from home; she was in charge of that end of things. Annie looked at both of them, then sat up suddenly.

"Not here," she said. "Let's go under the boardwalk."

"Nobody'll see it here," Tessa said. "Nobody cares."

"That's not why," Annie said impatiently. "We always go to the boardwalk. Come on, Tess."

She got up and started away from the water, and after a moment she heard the other two heaving themselves up to follow her. It was true, they always went to the boardwalk to smoke. The boardwalk was high enough so that they could stand underneath it, and this far down the beach there was almost nobody on it. The streetlights cast white bars onto the sand through the wooden planks overhead, and as they sat down their bodies became striped with light. It was like being in a cave, and Annie felt as if no one could see them under there. When they went to Coney Island during the day they eavesdropped on conversations above them, and at night they could watch the beach and the ocean as if they were inside a bunker. Liz pulled out the joint, lit it, and passed it around.

"Where'd you get it?" Annie asked.

"Nick gave it to me at Capture," Liz said. "I've been saving it."

As soon as Liz mentioned Nick, Tessa stiffened and reached for the joint, took a hit, and passed it to Annie, who took a deep drag and held her breath; if it was from Nick it was better than the stuff they usually got in Washington Square Park.

The only difference being high made was that it was harder not to talk about the baby. Annie wished she had thought of that before she smoked; she often regretted getting high after she was high—but always forgot that she was going to feel that way while the joint was being passed around. None of them spoke for a while after the joint was finished, and Annie fidgeted, throwing rocks out onto the sand in front of them. She wasn't going to be the first to bring it up.

"What do you think Mom's going to say?" Liz said finally.

"I don't know." Tessa sounded scared for the first time since she had told them the news. "She had us when she was pretty young."

"Not this young."

"And she was married," said Annie.

"Not till she was pregnant with Tessa," Liz said.

"Really? God."

"But Dad loved her anyway," Liz said.

"I wonder how long," Tessa laughed.

"Oh, shut up, Tess." Liz looked at her.

"No, I mean exactly how long were they in love do you think. One year? Five?"

"Well, they had Liz and Sam too," Annie said. "So . . ."

"So what." Tessa lit a cigarette. "So they kept having sex."

"I still think Dad loved her," Liz said.

There was a pause, and all of them listened to the irregular constancy of the breakers.

"Maybe she'll help," said Tessa.

"She'd help you get an abortion," Annie said. They all knew that was true; having a baby as a teenager would not fit in with Marie's idea of them as feminists. She had raised them to have abortions, not babies.

"She's a snob," said Liz. "Teenage motherhood is for other people. People she can demonstrate for, lobby for. Uneducated people."

"You mean poor people," Tessa said. "Black girls, Puerto Rican girls."

"She's not prejudiced!" Annie said.

"She is in a way," Liz said. "It's not so much because we're white, but because we're supposed to be higher class—even though we don't have money."

"You go to good schools," Annie said.

Tessa laughed. "Yeah, they're good for public school, even though it's not like uptown private schools or anything." Annie didn't say anything, and after a beat Tessa went on. "And if we do it the way we're supposed to we'll get scholarships to good colleges. I guess that's why we're not supposed to end up pregnant."

Tessa laughed again, then rolled onto her stomach and began throwing rocks with Annie. There was a sharp, clacking sound when they hit other rocks, and a soft thunk like a punch landing in a punching bag when they hit just sand.

"Nick goes to a good school too, so fuck that noise," Liz said.

"Shit, he's going to St. John's next year. Why does it just have to be *your* problem? You should tell him so that he has to deal with it too."

"I will," Tessa said, and she took a breath as if she was going to go on, but then didn't.

Liz was quiet too, and Annie knew she was pissed off. Annie threw five rocks in rapid succession, pretending she had a machine gun; they were in a bunker during World War II, and German submarines were cruising off New York Harbor. She started to make small piles of stones next to herself in the sand, trying to change the game; the dope was making her watch herself do all of these things as if she was standing outside herself, smiling ironically. She forced herself to stop playing with the rocks, leaned her head down against her arm, and looked at Tessa, who was twisting her hair into a thick black rope.

"What do you think he's gonna say, Tess?" Annie's voice sounded loud to her, even though they were outside.

"I don't know." Tessa threw a small rock far out, as if she wanted to throw it all the way into the ocean. Tessa brushed the sand off and sat up, holding her knees and looking out. "I want him to stay in the city—not go away to school."

"He's going to want you to have an abortion." There. Liz said it. Annie took another rock and held it tightly in her fist, not throwing, looking at the two sisters.

"He is, isn't he?" Tessa said, in a small, dry voice, as if she were stopped in wonder at this idea but knew it to be a fact as surely as she knew the tenderness in her breasts and her own vomit.

There wasn't anything else to say, so nobody did. Good, Annie thought, good, now she'll get the abortion.

When they came home late that night all of the lights in the living room were out except for the television. The blue dotted light spread out over Marie, who was asleep, lying on her side on the couch. She had pulled bits of the unfolded clean laundry over her, and there was a fan set up in the window that led to the shaftway, sucking in the night air and spinning it around the room. Tessa turned down the sound on the television, but left it on, afraid of waking her mother. In the bedroom, Sam was already asleep and they pulled out the foam pad that Annie always slept on. They found a fitted sheet that was too small for the pad, and there was nothing to put over her but a bathrobe of Tessa's. It was a hot night, so she didn't care about what was on top of her, but her feet kept getting tangled in the elastic corners of the sheet, and long after Tessa and Liz had fallen asleep, Annie lay there listening to the drone of the fan and the occasional skittering sounds from the shaftway: pigeons, rats, and cats. Eventually she climbed up into Liz's bunk, kissing her along the neck instead of speaking. Liz smiled, remaining only half conscious and moved over so that their hips would fit together. It soothed Annie to lie in a room filled with the sound of sisters sleeping. She felt surrounded and protected by them, and tried to match her breathing with theirs. She held onto Liz's body and felt herself beginning to join the other girls, their limbs loosening them out into the unshared sanctum of sleep.

Peter and Janis had to be out of the loft by the fifth of July, and it was unimaginable that they would leave without a final blowout on the Fourth. Independence Day parties on the roof of Great Jones Street were a tradition, or had been during the years they had stayed in the city through July. This time they called it a "divorce party," and as the invitations went out Peter told everyone it was a theme party: "Bring Your Ex." The kids were told they could invite as many of their own friends as they wanted, partly as a concession to Justin, who was angrier than anyone else about having to move out of the loft, clearly blaming Peter, whom he now referred to as "your father" to the girls. Peter had pulled out all of his country music 45's about divorce, broken homes, and being untrue. He thought it would be funny to have him and Janis slow dancing to "D-I-V-O-R-C-E" as the first guests arrived. Janis admitted that she thought it was funny, but she didn't say if she would do it or not.

The weeks before the party had been spent packing and sorting and trying to throw out ten years of history. There were all the usual fights about everything: whom the books belonged to; whom the television belonged to; who had bought the blender seven years ago. Annie had gone over to help one day, and she had been surprised by how bitter all the siblings were being to each other. Even Nick and Tessa weren't getting along, and among the five of them nothing was being thrown away. Janis would go through the whole house with a garbage bag at the end of the day and make executive decisions about what was going to go anyway, so things were hidden under shirts or inside books if they looked like shit but still mattered. At the loft that day Peter had been silent and determined, while Janis regularly bawled everyone out for fighting. Annie hadn't gone a second time to help out, and she wasn't asked.

Annie went to Planned Parenthood and found out where Tessa could get an abortion and how much it would cost. She told Liz that the important thing was that it happen quickly. The office she went to was on Seventeenth Street and Ninth Avenue; the waiting room was small and smelled of rubbing alcohol and cigarettes, with folding chairs lined against the walls. There were girls there who looked younger than she was with huge pregnant bellies; and others who sat together in nervous duos, probably waiting for the results of a pregnancy test or to get contraception. The walls were covered with posters depicting the female reproductive system, warnings against drinking and smoking while pregnant, and how easy it was to get diseases. She was glad there weren't any pictures of the fetus in development. She didn't see any men, young or old, in the waiting room and there were never any men pictured on the posters. By the time her name was called, Annie had pretty much decided never to have sex with a man again, considering all of the awful things that could happen to her as a result.

She hadn't been able to tell the woman who was counseling her exactly how long it had been since Tessa's last period, and she knew that the woman thought she was finding out for herself, that Annie's "friend" was fictional. Tessa would have to be counseled before getting the abortion, and this worried Annie too. The woman told her that the abortion had to be done in the first three months if they were going to be able to keep it secret from their parents; after that time she would have to go into the hospital overnight to have it done.

"And after too long," the woman had warned, looking Annie over, sure that she was the girl who needed it, "no one will do the abortion. It can't be more than twelve weeks if you want to do it through us. Of course, there's always adoption." Annie had said nothing to that. She just gathered up a lot of leaflets with more information and left. No one would be putting this baby up for adoption, she was sure of that much. She brought the leaflets down to Cornelia Street and left them in the bedroom, but Tessa never discussed them with her, and Annie didn't even know if she had read them.

The night of the party Annie rode downtown in a taxi with Luke and Jill. They had moved into a new apartment and started living together at the beginning of the summer, and Annie had seen less of her father since then. She didn't want to stay at the apartment with Jill there, though Luke kept a room for her. She had told him that she was spending her weekends down at the Shanlicks' apartment, which was true—she was there most weeknights as well; but she wanted him to notice, to take her out to lunch or to a movie alone. But he hadn't asked her to, and she felt as if she wouldn't know what to say if he suggested that Jill come along. So there were no suggestions and no invitations, and she told herself that it didn't matter because she would outlast Jill even if they did get married. She's not blood, Annie said to herself sometimes, hardening herself against both of them.

As she settled into the taxi, Luke gave her a tight hug and a searching look, which she answered with a blank face. She knew he wasn't fooled and felt a small jolt of success as he tried to hide his disappointment. Jill was dressed in a long skirt and simple T-shirt, the kind of clothing that Annie knew Luke liked best. She's learning to please him, she thought, as she watched the familiar blocks of Central Park West (including their old apartment building) rush by on their way south to Columbus Circle, and she wished that Jill would just shut up, but it was her babbling that made Annie stop short.

"—and then after the baby comes, of course, we may have to get a new apartment."

Annie turned back into the cab and stared at them.

"Oh, sorry—" Jill looked helplessly at Luke and covered her mouth with an inadvertent gesture that was both clichéd and genuinely Jill. "You had wanted to tell her first. I'm sorry, honey."

"You're having a baby?" Annie couldn't quite get her mind around the words even as they were coming out of her mouth.

"Yes," Luke said, reaching for Annie's hand and holding it. "You might as well know it wasn't planned, but we're welcoming it. We're going to get married."

"Because of the baby?" Annie didn't care that Jill was there anymore.

"Sooner, because of the baby," Luke said. "We had discussed marriage—"

Jill didn't know enough to stay quiet.

"You'll still have a room with us, don't worry," she said. "We'll have to move into a bigger apartment anyway."

"I was going to tell you tonight, after the party," Luke said, still holding Annie's hand. She looked out the window. They were at Times Square by now, which was surprisingly quiet for the Fourth, more cops than people.

"Congratulations," she said, turning to look Luke right in the eyes.

"Annie, cut the shit," he said, and she could feel Jill stiffening on the other side of him. "Things happen."

"What about birth control?" she said angrily, thinking of all the leaflets she had given to Tessa. "Haven't you ever heard of the Pill? I got on the Pill last year, remember? As soon as I got my period off we went for birth control. I was still a virgin, but who cared? You and Mom said—"

"That's enough, Annie," Luke said, his hand squeezing hers so hard that she almost cried out, but she breathed through it, refusing to give in on anything to do with this. Jill put a hand on Luke's arm, her eyes wide, and he relaxed his grip and looked away. Stupid fuck, Annie thought, watching Jill, who was astonished that Luke could be so harsh. You stupid, pregnant fuck.

"Annie," Jill said gently, "we wanted to have a baby. We want him now."

"Him?"

Jill giggled self-consciously. "We're hoping it will be a boy. You'll have a brother."

"Half-brother," Annie said, and then she started laughing, watching the skin on her hand go from white to red as the blood rushed back in. They don't know anything, she thought triumphantly, looking away from Luke and Jill at the litter flying up in small tornadoes from the streets and at the overheated tourists struggling with enormous shopping bags through the garment district. The Fourth was a big sale day at Macy's; Ellen had gone down with a friend to buy sheets and towels. Annie looked back at Luke and Jill, who sat holding hands and staring straight ahead, her father unconsciously chewing at the inside of his lip in the way that used to drive Ellen crazy. No, Annie thought, her laughter slowing down and ending; they don't know anything at all.

As soon as they arrived at the party, Annie bolted, heading down to the other end of the loft as Peter Shanlick walked over to greet them with a look on his face that made her think he was going to embrace all three of them in a bear hug, and she didn't want to be in physical contact with Jill. There were a lot of kids she didn't know hanging around the kitchen, and Annie could tell that Janis really didn't care how trashed the place got tonight. The paintings were off the walls, and much of the furniture had already been moved out. The stripped feeling of the place gave it a kind of freedom, and as Annie walked toward the girls, who were sitting together on the back windowsill, smoking, she saw Nick on his knees with his oil paints spread out next to him, painting directly onto the wall.

"Hey, Nick," she said, stopping and looking over his shoulder. It had been a couple of weeks since she had seen him, and he looked bigger, and though he was still pale and thin for the middle of the summer, there was a new broadness in his back that made him look older.

He turned to her and smiled. "Yo, Annie, whas' up?" he teased, and she shrugged. His bright blue eyes were surrounded by pink where there should have been just white, and she knew he had probably been smoking all day.

"What is it?" she asked, looking at the painting, which was more like a mural, spreading across the wall in big, sloppy strokes.

"Nothing. Just the story of my life," he laughed, and pushed back a lock of fine, brown hair that fell over his face, streaking it with blue paint from his hands.

"Careful, you've got paint on your hands."

Nick just looked at her, then took both hands and ran them right through his hair, red, blue, black, and yellow. He smiled at her without saying anything, and Annie smiled back, then pretty soon she giggled, seeing him there so handsome but with hair stuck together and smeared with paint. Then he was giggling too, and they both just squatted there, laughing. She looked at the painting again, and it was true, Nick was painting his history on the wall. Stick figures of a man and a woman, the woman painted with breasts like circles stuck on her torso and a billowing triangle for a skirt, represented his various parents. First there was a painting of a man and a woman with two small children, one was a baby in the woman's arms.

"That's me," Nick said, following her eyes.

The woman was walking toward an open door, and on the other side of the door another stick figure man was waiting, arms outstretched, with three small stick figure children around him, also with triangle skirts to show that they were girls.

"That's Peter."

The next panel showed the man and the woman holding hands, with a house on a green hill in the background, and the five children, their arms and legs at right angles from their bodies, playing in the field behind them. There were long streaks of blue reaching up from the sky onto the white wall, and the green field overlapped the panels before it. He had begun the next panel, which showed the woman heading for an open door again, but this time there was no man on the other side, and the stick figure boys were as tall as she was, all three of them were looking back at the man, who was sitting in a chair, facing away from them.

"It's a little obvious, isn't it?" said Annie.

Nick laughed. "It's supposed to be obvious—it's like, you know, the walls of the pyramids with the story of a person's life on their tomb."

"Where are the girls?" Annie asked.

"I haven't done them yet. You know, it's hard to do them now, they're grown up."

"Just make them taller," Annie said, "with tits."

Nick cracked up. "Yeah, that's just it. Taller—with tits."

He quickly painted in a girl standing next to Peter, her legs much longer than her body, and on top of the shortened torso Nick painted two huge circles with a dot in the middle of each one.

"There," he said. "That's Sam."

They both cracked up, and Nick rolled on the floor, laughing hard. Annie looked up and there was Tessa, looking down at both of them with a mixture of tenderness and disgust. Nick saw her and sat up slowly, still laughing. He pulled her down next to him and tried to explain, pointing at the picture. Tessa couldn't understand a word he was saying, but it didn't really matter. Annie would have fallen in love with him too if he was holding her tight against him like that and looking the way he looked right at that moment, flushed and full of his own joke.

"I can't believe Janis is letting you do this," Tessa said, looking at the painting. "Has she seen it?"

"She said she didn't care if I painted on the walls, and she's seen me doing it."

"Has she seen *what* you're painting?"

"Ah . . . noooo." He elongated the "o" and put on a look of sweet innocence. "But it's a divorce party, right?"

"Yeah, no shit," Tessa said. "D-I-V-O-R-C-E" was playing for the twentieth time on the turntable, and it was still early.

"Who's here?" Annie asked, looking at all of the people she didn't know.

"Lots of Justin's friends from school; I don't know them either," Tessa said.

"Yeah, leave it to my brother to invite all the girls in the eleventh grade." Nick laughed. "He just wants to up the chances that he gets laid."

"We didn't invite anyone but you," Tessa said, smiling at Annie. "Sam still thinks a divorce party is the stupidest thing she's ever heard of."

"She's just embarrassed," Annie said.

"Nah." Nick turned back to his painting. "Sam's never embarrassed; she's just losing her sense of humor. Might as well have a party. We're losing the loft."

"See that?" Tessa said suddenly.

"What?"

"That was Kate Dover, she writes for the *New Yorker.* See how she looked at us?"

"Come on, Tessa. Kate's all right; she's been around forever," Nick said, watching Kate go down the hall toward the music.

"No, I like her, it's not that. It's the way she looked at us, like 'Oh, those poor kids.' Fuck her."

"She was probably really thinking 'Oh, shit, Peter and Janis are already out of gin,'" Nick said, painting in the other two girls.

Tessa looked at him and shrugged. "All of their friends are either acting sorry for us or like nothing is going on. Luke even pulled me aside."

"What do you mean?" Annie said quickly.

"He gave me one of those meaningful Luke Edwards looks and asked how I was doing."

"Well . . ." Annie was embarrassed, and started to look away. She wanted to find Liz and get a drink.

"It wasn't that bad, Annie," Tessa said. "It was just—it's weird having everyone in your life who's known you since you were a baby, all so *concerned*, you know?"

"I don't remember that happening when my parents broke up." Annie looked at the two of them. Tessa was leaning against an unpainted section of the wall; her blue-jeaned hip resting casually against Nick's. "Well, I'm gonna get a drink," Annie said, then, looking directly at Tessa, "and anyways, you guys probably have to talk."

Nick stopped painting and turned to Annie, completely confused, and Tessa gave Annie a disbelieving look as she started to blush. Annie just stared back at her, deadpan, and walked away.

Fuck it, she thought. If Tessa never has the guts to tell him, I'm going to make her tell him. And if she still won't tell him, I will. She went to the counter where all of the bottles were and poured herself half a glass of cranberry juice, then, with a quick glance to see if Luke was anywhere around, she filled the rest of it with vodka.

"Caught you." Liz was standing next to her, grinning at how quickly Annie put down the vodka bottle. Liz put her arm around Annie's waist and pulled her in slightly. Her black pupils were almost obliterating her irises, and Annie wondered what she had taken. Probably a combination of purloined Valium and whiskey, knowing Liz. Annie turned into her and maneuvered her drink between them. They hadn't acted like a couple in front of anybody yet, though it was starting to feel more and more like they were one. Every night Annie spent at the Shanlicks' house she had started out on the floor and ended up in Liz's bed. Tessa and Sam hadn't said anything about it, and Annie wondered how much they knew.

"You won't believe what I just did," Annie said, taking a big sip of her drink.

"What?"

"I set up Tessa to tell Nick—I mean, I almost forced her to."

Liz looked scared. "What do you mean?"

"I mean, that I was sitting with them both, you know, and I said that I thought they needed to talk and I left."

"You're kidding."

"No. I'm sick of it, you know? Tessa's just going along like everything's going to be all right, and—"

Liz cut her off and moved her over to the window. "Come on, let's go out on the fire escape," she said, climbing out and onto the narrow metal landing just outside the window. "People are gonna hear you."

Annie followed her but kept talking the whole way, not bothering to lower her voice. "I don't care anymore. People should know. They think this divorce is such a big deal. It's nothing. She's just being chicken shit, and she's going to run out of time. I told her. I told all of you guys—"

"Yeah, but what are we supposed to do? It's up to her to tell him."

"No, it's not."

"What? Bullshit, Annie. Tessa's going to kill you."

"I just think we should protect each other, don't you?"

"Up to a point. I mean, maybe. Sometimes . . ."

"I don't care if she gets mad at me. We can't just sit here and let her fuck everything up."

"Hey, Annie, you're really on a roll, you know that?"

Annie stopped and looked at Liz, who was sitting on one of the metal steps that led to the roof. Annie started pacing back and forth, the metal shaking under her. She thought about telling Liz that Jill was having a baby, but she didn't even want to form the words in her mouth. She leaned on the railing; to the north was the Chrysler Building, which looked like a child's toy rocket stuck into the top of the skyline.

"Let's go up to the roof," Liz said. Annie followed her up the stairs, and they walked out to the edge of the building. Music and voices from the party floated up, mixing with the sounds of the city. The honking of the cars along the Bowery sounded like an off-kilter orchestra blaring out at undetermined intervals. The fireworks wouldn't start until later.

Liz reached for her and they kissed. Annie tried not to care anymore who saw them, and she pulled Liz down until they were lying together on the tar roof, still warm from the heat of the day.

The sound of Justin's voice pulled them apart. He was yelling something, and they heard the fire escape clanging under his feet.

"He's coming up here," Annie said, pulling away quickly. Liz giggled and rolled onto her back. Annie was already standing up, stuffing her shirt back into her jeans and looking for Justin. He came onto the roof with a bottle in one hand and about ten people behind him.

"Come on!" he was shouting. "Let's go swimming!" He led the way to the water tower that sat on top of the roof, a big wooden barrel on metal legs that supplied the building with some of its water.

"He didn't even see us," Liz said. "Don't worry."

"I don't care if he sees us," Annie lied. She didn't want to think about what Justin would say if he knew. This thing with Liz was just something they were doing right now, that's all. Liz got to her feet and stood beside her as Annie watched the others climbing up to the roof. "What are they doing?"

"Going swimming in the water tower, I guess." Liz shrugged.

"Really? God."

"We've done it before."

"Is it gross?"

"No, not really. It's cool."

Justin was stripping down to his boxer shorts, and there were people in various stages of undress circling around the bottom of the small metal ladder, watching him climb up to the roof of the tower and open the hatch that led inside.

"Aren't there rats inside? Or water bugs?"

"Maybe, but we've never seen any."

"Look at Sam."

Sam was already down to her bra and panties, and Justin's older friends were circling around her as well.

"Any excuse," Liz said, and they both laughed.

"Come on, let's go over there."

"O.K." Liz looked at Annie for a minute. "Is this the last I'm gonna see of you tonight?"

"What do you mean?" Annie smiled at her. "I'm spending the night, aren't I?"

"I just don't want you to disappear on me."

Annie laughed and pulled her toward the others. Sam was leaning against the bottom of the ladder, acting as if there was nothing unusual about being the only girl there who was already down to her underwear. There were a few of the girls that Justin had invited, and they were hanging back a little, waiting to see if everyone went in or not. Nick was there, but Tessa wasn't, and Annie felt a coldness creeping into her throat and wondered what Tessa would say to her when she did come up. Nick paid no attention to Annie. He was smoking a joint and passing it into the circle of spectators. Justin sat up at the opening to the tower and then, when he had everyone's attention, gave a military salute, leaned backwards, and landed inside the tower with a splash and a yell. A shout went up from everyone on the roof.

"Look out for the rats!" Nick shouted, and people laughed nervously. Justin stuck his head out of the top of the tower again; he was dripping wet.

"It's great!" he said. "Who's coming in?"

"What about the rats?" Sam asked.

"And the roaches!" someone else shouted.

"Nothing in here but me—and a lot of nice, cold water." He reached his hand inside the hatch and splashed the crowd. The water felt good in the close, humid air.

"All right—fuck the rats!" Sam yelled suddenly as she climbed up the ladder and through the hatch. There was a splash and then a shriek as she hit the cold water. Sam and Justin's laughter echoed wildly back and forth inside the tower. Pretty soon everyone was either inside the water tower or in line to go up. Annie and Liz went in wearing their T-shirts and underwear, which gave the pretty girls from Justin's school an excuse to do the same. Annie climbed up the ladder right behind Liz and hoisted herself into the darkness where her feet touched nothing but water and a jumble of bare legs and bobbing bodies. She couldn't see anything for a few minutes, so she groped her way along the circular wall. People could see her, however, since they had been in for a while, and before her eyes could adjust she heard Justin's voice.

"So, Annie, you finally made it to the wet T-shirt contest, congratulations."

"Fuck you, Justin." Annie ducked lower in the water and looked around the circle, wondering who else was in there. Sam, Nick, and Liz were squeezed together around the edges, and since there was nowhere to sit, everyone was holding on with their hands, or balancing on the back of their elbows as their legs floated free in the middle. Two of Justin's friends were on the other side of him, and now that Annie had come in everyone was crammed in shoulder to shoulder. The water reflected off the ceiling from the light that came in through the hatch, and Annie was surprised that it smelled strangely familiar inside, like a covered bridge or an old fashioned boathouse. After a while the splashing slowed down and Annie let her body float up and across the middle, closing her eyes and letting the water come in and stop up her ears. She listened to underwater sounds, the voices recognizable but farther away; there was a burst of laughter and she popped up.

"What? What is it?"

"I asked if I could pee in the water," Sam said, laughing. "Since Justin says they only use this water to flush toilets anyway."

"Go for it, Sam." Justin's look was a dare. "We're moving out anyway."

Nick reached out and ducked Sam's head underwater, yelling,

"You gonna pee?! You gonna pee?!" Then he let her up again as she spluttered and punched ineffectually at both of her stepbrothers. Her elbow did knock one of Justin's friends in the eye, however, and he headed for the hatch as Sam apologized over and over again, trying to convince him to stay. Annie had to get out for him to be able to climb down past her, and as soon as she came out onto the little conical roof of the water tower, she saw Tessa waiting at the bottom of the ladder, half undressed and ready to go in.

She climbed down to her, but instead of going up the ladder, Tessa turned and walked away from her, heading back toward the fire escape and the loft.

"Tessa!" Annie kept her voice down but ran after her. Tessa stopped and looked at her, her eyes deadened with anger.

"What, Annie? Anything else you've gotta tell me to do?"

Annie took a breath, "Tessa, come on—"

Tessa came at her so fast that Annie took three quick steps back; she wanted to look behind her, to see how close she was to the edge of the roof, but she was afraid to take her eyes off Tessa.

"You little dyke. Who are you to talk about the 'right thing to do?' Who's doing it every night in the same room with me and Sam, huh? Pretty fucking disgusting. Pretty fucking selfish. Maybe you should tell everybody about that, huh? Do you want me to tell them?"

"I didn't know you knew." Annie's voice was dry and harsh. She felt as if there were no saliva left in her mouth.

"I don't really give a shit about you and Liz," Tessa said. "Just don't tell *me* what to do, Annie."

"I didn't mean to. I'm sorry, Tess—it's just—look, *I'm* not pregnant but—"

"No—*I* am, *I* am!" Tessa was practically shouting. "So keep your fucking leaflets and schedules and reminders! Just stay out of my face."

Tessa brought her hand up and Annie flinched, but the blow never landed. There was the sound of an explosion high above their heads. It turned them both around, and the sky behind them was filled with fireworks. The display was beginning over the East River, and windows were being thrown open all over the neighborhood with people leaning out on their sills and calling to each other. Tessa turned and walked back to the water tower, climbing the ladder as fast as she could and joining the others who had climbed out of the water and sat perched on the roof of the tower to watch.

Annie went around to the other side of the roof and sat down in the lee of a small hutch that rose up from the building's stairwell, out of sight of the water tower and the fireworks. She leaned back against the brick that was blackened with soot and tar and breathed hard, determined not to cry. But there were no tears, just a numbness that she hadn't known before. For once she couldn't see any way around the future, and Tessa would do what she wanted. They would all go on in their own ways, and she couldn't do anything about it. At least nobody knows, she thought, nobody saw or heard me and Tessa. She wanted to get away and thought about leaving, but that meant navigating her way through the party, and if Luke saw her he'd know something was wrong.

She could still hear the fireworks going off, and there was a colored glare in the sky, but she never turned to watch the display. Instead, she stared out over lower Manhattan unblinking, until the streets became like water and the lit-up city blocks became ocean liners filled with people streaming toward a different destination with absolute certainty of purpose. Each set of blocks formed a distinctive liner, and on each boat she placed swimming pools, ballrooms, and black-and-white film stars at the bar. She thought how other people could look at Peter and Janis's building and think it was part of some larger ship going somewhere too, but they would be wrong. Not this rooftop. Not tonight.

Part Four

Dean 1975–1976

Peter and Janis's loft was left abandoned after that Fourth of July party, empty of everything but bags of garbage and Nick's mural on the wall. Nobody ever went back, but Annie always looked up at the windows from the street when she walked by; there were never any lights on. At first Justin and Nick came by Marie's apartment a couple of nights a week and went down to the P.S. 3 stoop with Annie and the girls to smoke and talk. But after a while they stopped showing up. They were going up to the country as usual that summer, and the girls weren't. It made the fact that the country house belonged to Janis, not Peter, very clear to all of them, and nothing would ever be the same among the siblings. Annie and Luke wouldn't be going up to visit either, and of course there wasn't going to be another game that summer. Halfway through August, Justin came down for a weekend and told them that Nick wanted to stay up there because he had a girlfriend in the country, and after that Tessa mostly ate and slept.

"He doesn't give a shit about me," she said when they asked her about it. "He wouldn't do anything to help anyway. He'll figure it out when it's born."

Tessa was bigger by the end of the summer, but she still didn't exactly look pregnant, and she wore clothes that didn't show it at all. Most people would have thought she was just gaining weight. Marie worried about Tessa's weight and was always trying to get her to eat less. But Tessa just helped herself to another plate of spaghetti while Marie stayed thin on cigarettes and one meal a day. Annie knew that the first three months of pregnancy would be over by the end of August, and she watched the days go by—too scared to talk about it with Tessa after what had happened on the Fourth. There had been an uneasy peace between them since that night, as long as Annie didn't mention the pregnancy. Tessa knew what she thought. An abortion was something Annie could get a handle on, but she didn't know how to help with a baby.

Of course, she and Liz talked about it all the time, trying to think of ways to get Tessa to change her mind. But Tessa refused to talk about it with anyone. Sam was the only one who believed all along that Tessa was going to go through with having the baby, and she liked to predict how dead Tessa would be when Peter and Marie found out.

"And what's she gonna say when they ask her who the father is?" Sam asked. "The immaculate conception?"

"Could work," Liz said. "Dad still thinks she's a virgin."

"Yeah, well, she's pregnant and you're a dyke. Thank God I'm normal."

Sam started to make pronouncements about lesbians as a type, and at first she had made a big deal out of not undressing in front of Liz or Annie, as if she hadn't done it hundreds of times before. Annie still didn't think of herself or Liz as dykes, and she did her best to ignore Sam.

Tessa had pretty much gotten over it, but she wanted Annie and Liz to sleep separately when Annie came downtown.

"It's O.K. and everything," she said. "But in the same room, it's kind of gross, you know?"

Annie and Liz figured that was as good as it was going to get, and at least Tessa was nicer about it than Sam. Liz started spending the night uptown a few times a week. Annie wished it didn't have to be that way; it separated them from the other sisters. She hadn't thought that after sleeping with Liz the others would pull away; and now she knew that things were irrevocably changed among them. But she didn't want to give up sleeping with Liz. She was the first person who had ever made Annie feel safe. She hadn't known that sex could ever be relaxed, or that she could actually get what she wanted again and again. It didn't stop them both from feeling guilty about everything, especially their pleasure.

Annie and Liz took turns worrying about the others. It didn't feel right to go uptown to sleep. But Liz pointed out that Sam was spending more and more time with her own friends anyway, and Tessa would hardly leave the apartment. Annie was a little afraid of both of them right now, and she didn't want Marie to find out. Ellen seemed glad that Annie was spending more nights at home, and after a few conversations with her, Annie was sure that Ellen was completely unaware of what was really going on. If she ever looked into Annie's room in the morning and found them asleep together, their long hair covering their faces, mouths half open in sleep, pressed against the back of an arm or neck, she never said anything. So Liz stayed with Annie, never leaving the city that whole hot summer. They arrived at the apartment long after Ellen had gone to bed and stayed up until dawn rubbing ice cubes on each other's skin and pretending that nothing else was going on. Then one day the summer was over, and Tessa still hadn't told Nick she was pregnant.

When Annie walked out of school after the first day of ninth grade, she saw Justin's car waiting on the street. Tessa and Liz and Justin were in the car, and Justin honked the horn—as if she wouldn't have noticed his pale green Dodge Dart among all of the black Mercedeses and Jaguars parked on the block. At last, was the first thing she thought. At last something is happening.

She knew that everyone from school was watching her as she ran to the car and jumped in the backseat next to Liz. She was tempted to turn and wave to them, but she felt cooler, more triumphant, pretending she didn't even notice them.

"What's up?" she asked. "Where's Sam?"

"She didn't want to come," Tessa said.

"Where are we going?" Annie asked as Justin pulled out onto East End Avenue.

"To the country," Tessa said. Annie was surprised that she sounded so happy. A beat later she added, "Justin knows."

Annie looked at Liz but didn't say anything. Justin reached up and adjusted his rearview mirror so that he could look at Annie.

"Tessa told me," he said. "Just 'cause Nick's an asshole doesn't mean I have to be."

"No," said Annie, smiling at him in the mirror. "You guys usually take turns."

Justin laughed. "Fuck you, Annie," he said. He sounded happy too.

"Anyway, Nick doesn't even know yet, right?" Liz asked. "I mean, how do you know he'd be an asshole?"

"He's already an asshole," Tessa said, throwing her cigarette out the window.

"You're both assholes," said Justin. "For what it's worth."

"Justin—" Tessa said.

He looked at her. "I know, I know. I'm helping, aren't I?"

"I still think you should tell Nick," Liz said. "He can't help it if he doesn't know."

Annie knew what Liz was thinking; they had both wondered if Tessa had been waiting to tell him until it was too late for an abortion.

"I'm gonna tell him. I will. As soon as we're up in the country."

They pulled out onto the FDR Drive and headed north, following the Harlem River, which was lined with cement piers, abandoned cars, and fishermen. It was a warm day for September, and all of the car windows were down. They drove by a bread factory, and the comforting smell filled the car just long enough for Annie to feel hopeful again.

"I went to school today," Tessa said. "And it was horrible. I mean, all those same people, and of course they just think I've gotten fat."

"Assholes," Liz said, shaking her head. "So what if you *had* gotten fat?"

"So, I just said 'fuck it.' At my first break I went out into the hallway and started emptying my locker. Everyone was looking at me, too—like I was crazy or something—but, you know, it felt so good. Later for that shithole." Tessa laughed and lit a cigarette, passing the pack back to Liz and Annie.

"So, what happened?" Annie asked.

"I got Liz after her next class and told her I was leaving. And she said she'd come with me."

"I wasn't going to let you move up to the country alone," said Liz. "Forget it."

"You're dropping out?" Annie asked. "I mean, completely?"

"No . . ." Tessa looked at Justin. "It was Justin's idea, when we talked last night. I mean, I hadn't decided—but we talked about it."

"She's gonna go to school up in the country," he said. "I guess both of them are."

"You and Tessa? You are?" Annie asked Liz. Liz nodded her head. "But, I mean, how can you? School's already started."

"It doesn't matter," Justin said. "It's only been one day, and it's a public high school. If you've got a local address they're required to take you. This way, Tessa can be pregnant and nobody will know the difference. She can hide it, 'cause nobody will know what she really looks like."

"What do you mean? She can't hide being pregnant," Annie said. "What about gym?"

"We'll figure it out," said Liz.

"Anyway, I can hide it from Mom and Dad," said Tessa. "Justin's already asked Janis if we could stay there this fall, and he said we—"

"You and Liz are really 'troubled' by the divorce." Justin laughed. "You hate school and you never see your dad anymore. I laid it on her 'cause she feels so guilty about not having you girls up this summer."

"She should," said Liz.

Justin ignored her and kept talking to Annie. "So she said that Tessa and Liz could stay at the house if they don't burn it down or use it as a party pad. She also got Elise to agree to come by every week and make sure they are eating and stuff." Annie remembered Elise, the neighbor who had been kissing Peter at the game in May. "She said she'd let them try it for a month," Justin continued. "If Elise says they're not fucking up, and it's O.K. with Peter and Marie, they can stay. She also said you'd better not mind the cold. It's not really winterized, you know."

"That's all right," said Liz. "We'll build fires and live downstairs."

"Well, shit . . ." Annie said slowly. "What about—I don't know—everything?"

"We tried to get Sam to come, went by her school at lunchtime, but no way," Liz said.

"Even with you there, Justin?"

"Even with me." He grinned at Annie; he just wasn't going to fight today. "I'm not dropping out. I'm just the driver. And the mastermind, of course."

Annie laughed. "Of course."

"Mom knows we're going, but not why," said Tessa. "I haven't talked to Dad yet. She said we're supposed to call him tonight."

"What did Marie say?"

"She told us we shouldn't do it, but we told her we were going. So, what could she do? Call the cops?"

"Of course she could," Justin said. "But it's not worth it. They might fuck with her rent control situation."

"That is so stupid, Justin." Liz giggled. "The cops don't care about rent control."

"Listen, your Mom does not want cops coming over, am I right? And everybody knows everybody in the neighborhood. Everybody's on the take."

"O.K., Al Capone," Liz said.

"Oh, my God." Annie leaned her head against the top of the backseat. "Oh, my God."

"She didn't call the cops, she called Dad," Tessa said. "They already talked. She said that Dad's O.K. about it." Tessa laughed. "He's been worried about me being depressed. Like, who *isn't* depressed? I think Mom told him I was getting fat and not leaving the house. I'll tell him it's school. The divorce. That'll shut him up."

"My dad would never let me," Annie said. "He'd come get me or something, I don't know."

"Well, what about now? You're coming aren't you?" Justin challenged her.

"Yeah, I'm coming," Annie said. "But when are you heading back to the city?"

"Tonight."

"Tonight?"

"Yeah. I told Mom I'm taking you guys up there, but I gotta be at school tomorrow."

"O.K., I'll come back with you. I'll call my mom too." Annie sat forward and held Tessa by the shoulders. "You're really gonna do it, aren't you?"

"Hey, Annie, like I've been telling you—we're having a baby." Tessa smiled. "And none of those assholes at school have to know."

"Till we get back," Liz said, but Tessa ignored her. She was rooting around in her book bag, which she had thrown on the floor of the car near her feet. She picked up a light blue binder with loose-leaf notebook paper in it and snapped open the metal rings; then she held it out the window. The papers fluttered out and up over the car like confetti.

"Hey!" Justin yelled. "Cut it out. I don't want to get in a fucking wreck, Tessa!"

But she just laughed and held the notebook out farther, shaking it until it emptied itself into the air. Annie turned around in the backseat and looked out the window. Trails of paper skittered along the highway behind them and looped airborne into the sky over the garbage and the piers and the fast gray water. Annie and Liz started laughing. It seemed unbelievable that they had actually just walked out of school and nothing really bad had happened to them.

Justin looked in the rearview mirror and stepped on the gas. "Yeah, well. Let's get the fuck out of Harlem," he said, and turned right onto the bridge that led north toward the Bronx, the Saw Mill River Parkway, and home.

It was already night by the time they arrived; none of them had ever been up at the house without the grown-ups before. At first it was fine, because everyone was busy bringing the house to life again after it had been shut down for the winter. Janis had decided not to go up for weekends this year; it was too long a drive and she was doing everything differently without Peter around. But Justin knew how to turn the water back on and how to light the pilot lights for the heat and the oven. Liz and Tessa got the downstairs bedroom set up for them to share. Annie was cleaning the kitchen and seeing what food was left. She found some popcorn and made a big batch, which pulled everyone into the kitchen.

"There's your dad's old car," Justin said to the girls. "But neither of you has a license."

"Yeah, but I know how to drive," Tessa said. "I'll get a license. I'm old enough."

"What about until then?"

"Until then, I'll drive without a license."

Justin grinned. "Let's go out in it once together, to make sure it's working O.K. Get some gas."

He and Tessa went out to the car and started it up. Tessa was behind the wheel as they drove out to the road. Annie and Liz watched from the kitchen window, scraping their fingers around the bottom of the popcorn bowl and licking them off.

"Justin's being pretty great," Liz said.

"Yeah. It's like the old Justin."

"I can't believe Tessa told him. Maybe it was the closest thing to telling Nick, without having to tell Nick." Liz looked at Annie.

"Justin's good at rescuing when he feels like it," Annie said bluntly. "What about Sam?"

"I don't know." Liz wiped her hands on a dishtowel, and then flicked it idly at the counter. "I feel like she wishes she lived somewhere else."

"Well, now she does." Annie didn't feel too sympathetic about Sam. As far as Annie was concerned, Sam just wasn't coming through. "You and Tessa are gonna live up here, and she'll be in the city."

"So will you."

"I can't live up here, Liz. My dad . . ."

"Yeah. I know. He'd freak if you ever went to a—God forbid—public high school."

"That's the part that makes me really want to do it," Annie said. "I hate school, you know that. I'd rather be up here with you guys, but he'd come up here, you know. And he'd figure it out."

"Everyone's gonna figure it out someday."

"I guess so."

There was a pause.

"Your dad was pretty O.K. about you staying up here," Annie said. Janis hadn't turned off the phone service for the winter, and Tessa and Liz had called him almost as soon as they'd arrived.

"Yeah. It went better than we thought. As long as we stay in school, he'll send us food money. When I talked to Sam, she said that Mom and Dad are afraid we're really gonna run away—so they figured this was better."

"It doesn't feel like you're running away. Being here."

"I know. It feels—I don't know—it feels safer here than in the city. Justin was right. I'm glad he called Janis."

"You haven't talked to her since the Fourth?"

"A couple of times. On the phone. It was weird."

Neither of them said anything. Annie wondered if she would ever see Janis again. The house looked the same, and the girls told Annie that their father hadn't wanted any of his things from the country house. The girls' own books and summer clothes were still undisturbed in their rooms, and they were glad. It was as if Janis hadn't wanted to sweep us away so quickly, Tessa had said when they first arrived.

Annie saw Tessa and Justin coming back along the road above the house, and as they turned the car into the top of the long driveway, she quickly walked behind Liz, putting her arms around her waist and kissing her. Liz picked up her thick hair and arched her neck back. Annie inhaled her warm, clean smell.

"I'll miss you," Liz said.

"I'll come up," Annie said. "I will. I'll take the bus every weekend."

"No, you won't."

"Bullshit." Annie turned Liz around to face her, and she saw that she was smiling.

Annie smiled back. "You know I will."

"Maybe not *every* weekend."

"A lot. I'll come up a lot."

There was the sound of tires on the gravel in front of the house, and they pulled away from each other. They didn't have to talk about it. Neither of them wanted Justin to know.

"If you drink Mom's liquor, she'll kill you," he said as he walked in the kitchen door and laid a six-pack on the counter.

It was great being up there without anybody else. It made Annie realize for the first time how much pressure there was on everyone when they were there for the game. There had always been so much organizing to do before and after the big night. Even during the best years, they had never gotten through the whole weekend without one of the grown-ups getting angry. It wasn't so much that the grown-ups were always telling them what to do, but that it was nice not to have to share the house with them. Now they shouted from one room to another, and Justin helped Liz tack an old blanket over the stairway so that the heat wouldn't escape upstairs. Annie brought in extra wood and Tessa figured out what food they would need. Liz made more popcorn for dinner, and it felt as if the four of them were playing house, like when they were little and brought all of the pots and pans under the kitchen table. Tessa seemed like herself again, and Annie realized how long it had been since she'd seen her happy. After everything was set up, and they were sitting in front of the fire, Tessa joked about what kind of impression she and Liz would make at the local high school the next day. Justin coached them on what to say to the school administration, and they practiced their story: They had just moved back because they wanted to try a year in the country. It was fine with their parents; they could call and check. Tessa was confident, but Liz was sure that the school was going to tell them to get lost, and then what?

"They *have* to take you if you live here," Justin told her. "Just don't get caught smoking or something stupid like that." He paused and looked at Tessa. "Or you could just tell them you fucked your step-brother, got pregnant, and had to get out of town for a while." He shrugged, smiling.

"Fuck you!" Tessa yelled, but she was laughing. She threw one of the pillows from the couch at him.

"Well, it's true!" he said, catching the pillow and throwing it back at her.

They both laughed a little too hard, and then in the quiet afterward Justin said, "Why do you want to keep it, Tess? Nick isn't exactly—"

"You don't know what Nick will be like when he finds out," Tessa said. "We talked about this already."

"Yeah, and I told you what I think. He's gonna be pissed you never told him."

Nobody said anything. Tessa looked at them. "Oh, come on. It's not like this is news to anybody, right?"

"Right," Annie said when nobody else said anything. "But I didn't believe it till today."

"Well, it's too late now to do anything but what we're doing, right?" Tessa looked at Annie. "I mean, that's what it said in your pamphlets."

"You read them?"

"I couldn't do that, Annie. Just kill it. I mean it always felt like an alive thing, right from the beginning." She looked at Justin. "Not very liberated, am I?"

"You were born in nineteen sixty," Justin said. "You're automatically liberated."

"What about putting it up for adoption?" Annie said, looking at Liz. That had been Liz's idea.

"Give it away?" Tessa looked around at the other three. "Look, help me if you want—or don't—I don't care."

"All right, Tessa, forget it," Annie said quickly. "I'm sorry."

"Tess, we *are* helping you," Liz said, "aren't we? Shit, I dropped out of school today."

"I'm having the baby," Tessa said in a low voice. "And I don't want to talk about it anymore."

Justin leaned forward, getting right into her face. "Well, O.K., we won't talk about it," he said slowly, "but it's not the kind of thing that nobody's gonna notice."

"No shit," Tessa said sharply, and Justin shrugged and got up from the couch.

"One more beer," he said. "Then we go back."

They didn't talk about the baby anymore, but the mood had shifted. While Justin finished his beer, they made coffee and toast for the road. Annie filled a thermos and Liz wrapped almost an entire loaf of toasted bread layered with margarine in paper towels. Tessa had fallen asleep in front of the fire, and before they left Justin tried to wake her up to say good-bye. Tessa just rolled away from him and pulled a blanket tighter around herself. Annie thought she was faking being asleep, but she didn't say anything.

Justin shrugged at Annie and Liz, then looked back at Tessa.

"She doesn't look that pregnant," he said. "I mean, if you didn't know her."

"We'll hide it as long as we can," Liz said. "But don't let Janis come up for a visit."

"She won't," he said shortly. "Don't worry."

"What do you mean?" asked Liz.

"Just that . . . I know she won't come up. That's partly why she said O.K. about the house."

"She doesn't want to see us?" Liz asked.

"I don't know." Justin dented the empty beer can between his fingers.

"Why?" Liz was getting that set look on her face. "What did *we* do?"

"Nothing. I don't know. I just know she won't come up, so be happy, O.K.?"

"Oh, O.K., Justin. Now I'm happy," Liz said, showing her teeth in an expression that was not a smile.

"Come on, you guys," said Annie. She was so tired that her eyes felt raw. She didn't want them to fight now, when everything was done.

Liz handed off the bundle of toast to Annie and wiped her hands on the back of her jeans.

"Did Tessa make you promise?" she asked Justin.

"What?"

"Not to tell Nick?"

"Yeah." He kicked gently at the bottom door of a kitchen cabinet and there was a scurrying inside. "Mice," he said. Then, "Yeah, she did."

"We can't, Justin. It's up to her."

"What if she doesn't ever tell?"

Liz shrugged, but her eyes never left his face.

"O.K., O.K," he said. "I won't."

"She'd fucking kill you."

"I know, I know. Listen, we gotta go, Liz. It's three-thirty in the morning, already."

She walked them out to the car.

"O.K.," she said in a tight voice. "Have a good trip back."

"Hey, come on," said Justin, jangling his keys against his hip and hesitating in front of his open car door. "Liz—I came up, didn't I?"

"Yeah," she muttered. "You'll probably never come back. I mean, while we're here."

"No. I will." But Justin didn't sound sure.

Annie hugged Liz and kissed her on the ear. "I love you," she whispered. "I'll call tomorrow night."

"O.K.," Liz said. She wouldn't look at Annie.

"I wish I could stay," Annie said.

"No. It's O.K." Liz looked up and smiled a little. "We'll be O.K. You know we will."

"Or you'll come back down to the city."

"Right."

Annie glanced at Justin. He had gotten in and was leaning back in the driver's seat with his eyes closed.

"I better go," she said.

"Yeah." Liz took a step back toward the house. "Don't let him fall asleep at the wheel. You know you don't get to die before me."

They smiled at each other in the dark, and Annie got into the car. Liz turned and walked back into the house, her outline disappearing quickly into blackness.

As the car reached the top of the driveway, the moon was just going down behind the ridge in front of them, silhouetting the big maples. Justin swung the car onto the road. A low-lying mist blurred the beams of the headlights, but above them the sky was clear. Annie realized that she hadn't looked up at the stars once while she was at the house. Justin moved uncomfortably in his seat, and she looked over at him.

"Tired?" she asked.

"Yeah." He laughed a little. "I can't believe we came all the way up here today and now we're going back."

"Thanks for doing it, Justin. For driving."

"I guess she's not my sister now, anymore than you are, but still . . . it was kind of fun, actually. But don't get me wrong. I think Tessa's crazy. It's never gonna work."

"You mean, not telling the school? Not telling Marie and Peter?"

"And Nick. None of it. Sam's right, you know. She's crazy."

Annie felt too tired to think about it anymore and said nothing.

"I've got Patsy Cline, Bruce Springsteen, and Buddy Holly," Justin said, shoving a tape box across the seat to her. "What do you want? There won't be anything but Christian crap on the radio right now."

"Patsy Cline," she said. She reached down on the floor for the portable tape player Justin had brought along. The music sounded just right for how she was feeling, and she and Justin both started singing along with the standards.

"Patsy Cline was meant to be played out of one speaker," Justin said. His fingers drummed the top of the dashboard and he slowed the car down as they drove through countless sleeping towns with their one gas station/general store and houses with children's playsets in the front yard. The plastic slides and sandboxes glowed weirdly in the headlights as they went by. There were roofs covered by green tarpaulins tacked down with strips of wood along the edges. Old cars stood partially dismantled in almost everyone's driveway, and dogs chained to porch steps barked and lunged at the car as they drove past.

"So, come on, Annie," Justin said. "Tell me your life story."

Annie laughed. "You already know it."

"Yeah, but that's what people do on long drives to stay awake. Tell me what I don't know."

So Annie talked. She talked them through the state routes and onto the interstate. She talked as they headed south toward the city and began seeing the first mileage signs for New York. She told him about school and about Luke and Jill; how they were preparing for the baby "as if it was the Christ child." She told him about how Luke had changed and Ellen hadn't, really, even though she had been to the funny farm and back. They ate all the toast, drank the coffee, and stopped to pee by the side of the road. Annie crouched close to the car while Justin politely turned his back and peed into the trees. Then after they got back in, Justin told her about this past summer and how strange it had been to be up in the country without the girls. He said that he was glad school had started again and that he didn't miss living with Peter Shanlick—but he did miss the loft. "When I get rich," he told her, "I'm gonna get a big loft and just walk from one window to the other, checking out the view. You wait."

"We could all share a loft, even if we're not rich," Annie said.

"Oh, bullshit, Annie." Justin lit one of her cigarettes, even though he almost never smoked. "We're never all going to live together again. Don't you know that?"

"People do," Annie said defensively. "They get out of school, live together, and share lofts."

"I'm not going to need to share my loft; and, anyway, I don't want to all live together." He took a long drag on the cigarette and looked at her. "You can come over for my incredible parties."

Annie laughed. "O.K., as soon as you get rich, let me know."

He smiled at her and winked. Knowing Justin, she figured it would all probably happen just like he said it would, but she didn't quite believe that he would really call her when he hit it big.

"You and Sam," she said, looking out the window at the sky, which was pearled in the east with the first gray light. "You're both gonna get rich quick."

Justin laughed to himself.

"What is it?" Annie asked.

"Oh, nothing. Just a dumb game we used to play."

"What?"

"Me and Nick and the girls. We'd pick some name out of the phone book and call it up—" He put on an announcer's voice. "Hello, are you ready to play the 'Get Rich Quick Show'? They'd say 'yes,' or 'what?' or something, and then we'd go: 'Well, I hope you get rich quick!' and hang up." He started laughing.

"That is *so* stupid!" Annie said.

"I know!" Now he started shaking with laughter. "Nick would cut out pictures of televisions and sofas and shit from magazines and *send* the pictures to these people. You know, a little envelope would arrive . . ."

He couldn't talk he was laughing so hard. Annie started giggling, and she lay back against the soft cushion of the front seat.

Every time the laughter would slow down, one of them would start up again.

"Stop!" Justin said finally. "I can't drive!"

When they hit the early morning commuter traffic coming into Riverdale, just north of the city, Justin put on his Springsteen tape. Annie drifted off in spite of herself, and when she woke up they were cruising down the West Side Highway, back in Manhattan at last.

"I'm sorry," she said. "I didn't mean to fall asleep."

"That's all right," said Justin. "I was thinking, watching you sleep there, it was like we were some old couple or something. Like we'd been together forever, coming back home from a road trip."

Annie looked at him. "Why do you say stuff like that?"

"I don't know. Why not? It's just something I was thinking."

"Yeah, but . . . we're not together or anything."

"I know that." Justin started laughing. "Of course we're not, stupid. It was just a thought—'cause you were sleeping and I was driving, you know? Like people do when—"

"I hate it. I hate you saying things like that. As if you gave a shit."

Justin stopped laughing. "I'm sorry, Annie."

She wasn't quite sure if he was being sincere, and she felt herself blush. She shouldn't have said anything. She was with Liz now, so what did she care? Justin kept his eyes on the road. Annie kept trying to think of something to say, but her mouth tasted like glue from coffee and cigarettes, and she felt as if she had nothing in her head at all. He dropped her off early, at the deli on the corner near school. She had two dollars and wanted to buy some strength with fresh coffee and a buttered roll.

Justin was in a hurry by now, and she could tell he was worried about making it downtown in time for his first class.

"Bye," she said as she jumped out. "Would you be up for going again?"

"I don't know," he said, brushing his hair back and looking at himself in the rearview mirror. "Hey, get me a coffee—black, two sugars—I'll wait out here."

Annie walked into the deli feeling self-conscious. Mrs. Grossman, the lady behind the register, had known her for years, and now she leaned around the corner of the sandwich counter to try and get a look at the boy in the car. Annie figured she looked like she felt, so she said good morning, but left it at that, refusing to answer the knowing smile from Mrs. Grossman today. She brought the coffee out to the car and leaned in the driver's side window.

"Thanks," Justin said, smiling after he had had a sip. He looked at the rows of younger girls walking to school in their uniforms and shook his head. "It's gonna be a fuck of a day, isn't it?"

"It already is," Annie said. "So, pretend you're my boyfriend for a minute and kiss me for the lady in the deli who's watching."

Justin gave a quick look into the deli, where Mrs. Grossman stood peering at them. "If she leans out over that counter any more she's gonna have an accident," he said. Then he pulled Annie's head down and kissed her briefly on the lips. "There," he said. "As if I gave a shit."

"No," Annie said. "You'd be a better kisser if you gave a shit."

He grinned at her and she grinned back. "Fuck you, Annie," he said, and she knew that everything was O.K. again.

"Give me a call," he yelled out the window as he pulled away. "When you hear from them. Give me a call."

"I don't even know your new number!" she shouted back.

But he kept driving, and she watched until the green Dodge had disappeared into the horde of cars and taxis streaming down Second Avenue.

Annie took the bus up every weekend that fall. She and Justin spoke a few times on the phone, but he would only say that he would drive up "soon," never that weekend. She hated to admit that she had hoped for more from him again and hardened herself against her disappointment by not calling him after the second time. If he wanted to know how things were going, he could call her. That he actually did call a couple of times surprised her, but he didn't offer to drive up again.

So Annie learned how to navigate the Port Authority bus terminal, walking quickly through the long underground tunnel that led from the Seventh Avenue subway. The tunnel gave her the creeps, and when it was empty she allowed herself to run from one end to the other, as if she was just about to miss her bus. The whole bus station smelled of urine and cigarettes, and after the first few trips Annie began to recognize the street people who lived there. They had their corners marked out with coats and newspapers, and though they didn't bother to hold out empty paper coffee cups to Annie for money, they eyed her in a way that stripped away her streetwise bravado and made her hurry past them.

Annie read while she waited for the bus and did homework as she rode out of the city through the Friday afternoon traffic. It was a four-and-a-half-hour bus ride, more than twice as long as it took to drive because the bus stopped in every little town on the way. Since Annie had nothing else to do on the bus but study, her grades had never been better. Luke was pleased and talked about how glad he was she hadn't changed schools. This made Annie smile, for she had never felt more absent at school. School days were to be endured, semiconscious, while real life began up in the country with Tessa and Liz.

Justin's plan was working so far. The local high school had accepted the girls with very little commotion after they had spoken to Peter and Marie on the phone to confirm that they weren't runaways. The schoolwork was easy for them, and they were both pulling down straight A's, which kept the teachers off their backs. No one at the new school suspected that Tessa was pregnant. She had fabricated an ankle injury to escape P.E., and no one paid much attention as long as their grades were so good. Liz said that they pretended to be shy and boring; so not only were they the new kids, but they were "brains" who had no social life. Annie thought Tessa looked bigger every time she saw her, but in the oversized sweaters and skirts they bought at the St. Vincent de Paul thrift shop, Tessa just looked pale and overweight. And no one in high school looked twice at overweight girls, no matter where they came from.

Weekends were strangely peaceful up in the country. Tessa luxuriated in not having to hide her belly at home, and she pulled up her shirt so they could all watch the baby as it began to move around, rippling and bulging out through her skin. Tessa giggled as it swam inside her and said that she couldn't describe how it felt, but it made her hold her breath for a moment and then laugh. They ate mostly pancakes, popcorn, and spaghetti and played hearts for hours. The game began on Friday night and finished on Saturday night, with long tallies kept on slips of paper. Tessa kept careful track of everyone's score, since they decided to make it a tournament that would last through Christmas. Tessa and Liz were always vying for the lead, as Annie was lousy at cards—but she didn't really care what they were doing, as long as they were together.

The future was carefully left out of their conversations, though now Tessa was sure the baby was a boy, and her belly was becoming enough of a presence that they called it "Dean" in honor of Dean Moriarty, their favorite character in *On the Road*. As they played cards they fantasized about driving cross-country next summer. So baby Dean would be part of it, somehow, and Annie started to think that maybe it would be all right to have a baby along on the road trip. It would make them feel more like a family anyway.

"Just a typical American family," Annie joked with them one night. "We'll go take pictures at the Grand Canyon."

"Four girls and a baby," Liz said. "We're gonna hit those scenic overlooks, and nobody's gonna believe it."

"Four?" asked Tessa.

"Sam will come," Liz said. "She's read the book too, you know."

It was hard to talk with Liz and Tessa about Sam because Liz was so defensive and Tessa was so mean about her. Annie felt that she had come up against a barrier; the three of them were sisters, and she wasn't. She was only allowed part way in. But Annie couldn't believe that Sam hadn't come up to visit them yet. She made so many excuses that by mid-October Annie stopped calling her to tell her when she was leaving. Sam spoke to Liz and Tessa a couple of times a week on the phone and always said that she might be able to come up the next weekend, but after a while no one took her seriously. Annie had gone downtown a couple of nights in September during the week, but Sam didn't want to talk about Tessa and would change the subject quickly after a few sarcastic remarks about the "unwed mother" or the "right-to-lifer." If Annie persisted, Sam would spend most of Annie's visit on the phone with her friends, so that Annie left late at night having spent more time with Marie than Sam.

Marie always wanted to pick Annie's brain about Liz and Tessa and why they had wanted to leave the city. These conversations were becoming more and more elaborate and uncomfortable for her, as Annie theorized with Marie about every possible reason but the truth. Marie had announced that she was coming up for Thanksgiving, and as the time approached, Tessa got more and more nervous. Finally, after talking to Annie, Sam agreed to come up with Annie and Marie so that Liz and Tessa wouldn't have to be alone with her. Liz and Tessa thought that they could hide the pregnancy from Marie through the visit, but Annie agreed with Sam that it would be almost impossible. But Marie was determined to see them, and though Annie wished that the girls would just tell Marie and get it over with, she wasn't sure she wanted to be there when Marie actually found out.

The only real scare they had before Thanksgiving was one afternoon when Tessa went into town by herself to go to the drugstore for cigarettes, and the woman behind the counter asked her when she was due and was she taking good care of herself—seeing a doctor regularly.

"I was wearing the wrong clothes," Tessa said to Liz and Annie later, back at the house. "I was in a hurry when I left. I mean, I wasn't going to school or anything, just to the drugstore."

"What did you say?" asked Annie.

"I told her everything was fine, and I bought some prenatal vitamins. Look, this little bottle was ten dollars, can you believe that?"

"Maybe she just wanted to get you to buy the vitamins," said Annie, but Tessa wouldn't even smile.

"I just never really thought of going to the doctor if nothing was wrong," said Tessa.

"Right," Liz said. "Nothing *is* wrong, Tess."

"We were just going to go to the emergency room when I went into labor, you know. I mean, I don't have any money for checkups."

"Yeah, I know. It's not your fault." Annie wished that she knew whether it was important to see the doctor a lot when you were pregnant. "But I haven't done anything different except eat a lot," Tessa said, shifting around on the couch so that her belly could rest more comfortably. "What if I've totally fucked up my own baby."

"Tessa, listen," Annie said. "My mom had a nervous breakdown when she was pregnant with me. I was so drugged up that I was born asleep! But I'm O.K." She smiled at Tessa. "I mean, mostly."

Tessa smiled a little. "Yeah, I guess," she said. "But that does explain a few things."

"No shit," Annie laughed. "So Dean's gonna be O.K. too. You haven't done anything like that. I mean, just look at you. Nothing is wrong with you."

"O.K., but I'm going to the Holy Name Clinic on Monday," Tessa said. Holy Name was the only hospital in the area, seventeen miles away.

"I guess . . ." Liz said slowly. "I mean, they said the hospital stuff is free if you really don't have any money. But you'd better make sure they don't tell the school."

"Or call your parents for money," Annie said.

They talked about it all night as they lay on the bed that they had dismantled and moved into the living room for warmth earlier that day. There were blankets tacked over every doorway now, and still it was cold. Finally, Liz agreed that it was better to go to the hospital, even if they told the school, than not to get a checkup at all.

"Doctors aren't supposed to tell on anybody," said Annie. "They take an oath."

"Yeah, but we're underage. I don't know . . ." Liz chewed on a fingernail and looked at Tessa. "You're still feeling good, right?"

"Look, I just want to talk to a nurse or something. Make sure he's O.K.," said Tessa.

When Annie left that Sunday, she made them promise to call her Monday night and tell her what happened. But when they still hadn't called by midnight, Annie called them.

"We didn't go," said Liz, who answered the phone. She was whispering because Tessa was asleep in the bed beside her.

"Why?" asked Annie. She found herself whispering too, even though she knew Ellen had taken one of her sleeping pills and wouldn't wake up.

"We were too scared they'd tell Mom and Dad. It's only a couple more months. Tessa's feeling good."

"What about Dean?"

"She took the vitamins."

They were silent for a moment, then Liz whispered, "I don't really want to go to the hospital until she's having the baby. We've been so lucky. I mean, it seemed like asking for it. Child welfare agencies, Christian organizations, I don't know. Sometimes I feel like Pippi Longstocking staying out here, and I don't want to get busted."

Annie didn't say anything.

"Annie?"

"Yeah?"

"What do you think?"

"I think Dean's going to be O.K. I mean, we were all healthy, really, and *our* mothers . . . but I don't know about after it's born. I guess babies have to go to the doctor too, sometimes."

"Yeah, well. There's programs. Food stamps. I don't know, I guess we'll figure it out."

"You'll be back in the city then."

"Right."

Neither of them spoke for a long time until Liz whispered, "Annie?"

"Yeah?"

"I'm scared shitless about afterwards."

"Yeah, me too."

"But I love you."

"Me too."

It was cold, and the dirt was frozen into ruts in the driveway when they all arrived at the house that Wednesday night before Thanksgiving. Tessa and Liz had both come to the bus station to pick up Marie, Annie, and Sam, and so far everything seemed fine. Tessa was dressed in bulky clothes, and Marie didn't seem to think anything of it. She was so excited about finally seeing Janis's country house that she didn't pay much attention. As they drove toward the house their breath steamed up the inside of the car windows quickly since the heater hadn't worked for years. Peter had never bothered to fix it, for it had always been the summer car. Annie rubbed out a clear circle on the window next to her and looked out at the trees and hills, which seemed so completely devoid of life that she couldn't imagine the summer anymore. There had been snow already that year, and there was a stillness in the air. The last time Annie had walked down to the stream that she and Justin had walked through during the game, thin sheets of ice had covered the deeper pools. Everything about the summer weekends she had spent up here seemed locked away in the hardened earth. It was an act of will to imagine the color green ever overcoming this landscape of brown, gray, and black.

Marie had brought up roast turkey sandwiches and mashed potatoes from Katz's deli, along with briny pickles as big as your fist. The feast made everybody happy, especially Tessa, who craved deli food. They slept late and ate their sandwiches on a blanket outside in the thin winter sun. Now that they were here, Annie couldn't tell that Tessa was nervous at all. Everyone seemed to be getting along, and Sam was at her best, funny and sweet, even to Tessa. Marie wanted to see everything, since she had to go back to the city on Saturday, so, after eating, the girls led her down to the pond, where the cattails held themselves high and the reeds near the shore showed bright green against the black water. Next they showed her Janis's garden, carefully put away under hay and plastic for the winter. Marie liked the place, and though she made a few remarks about Peter, she clearly enjoyed getting to look at the world he had shared with Janis for ten years. There was something almost triumphant in the way she spoke about Peter and Janis's divorce, and Annie could tell immediately how much it bothered Liz. But everyone seemed determined to get along for the next two days, and Tessa was acting so intimate with Marie that Annie caught herself wanting to talk about the pregnancy in front of her more than once. But Liz stayed close by Annie, being unusually quiet. Annie noticed and tried to follow her lead.

On the first night the girls gathered on Tessa's bed after Marie was asleep, and Annie asked how Marie could possibly not know about Tessa. She was wearing baggy clothes, of course, but still, Annie wondered if Marie wasn't letting on.

"No," said Liz. "Definitely not."

"Mom wouldn't stay quiet about it if she knew," Sam agreed, yawning and stretching. "First she would lose it completely, then she would try to take over."

"And I've been this heavy before," Tessa said. "Just not recently."

"I guess you're right," Annie said. "But what if she's waiting for *us* to tell?"

"She's not looking for it," said Liz. "If it crossed her mind she would know in a second, but it hasn't even occurred to her. The minute it does we've had it."

"Well, even if she doesn't know now, she'll find out someday." Annie looked at Tessa.

"Yeah," said Sam. "I can't believe you've still got two and a half more months to go."

Sam reached out and put her hand on Tessa's stomach. "It's so hard." She was surprised.

"Wait," Tessa said suddenly, reaching for Sam's hand and holding it in place against her belly. "Feel that? He's kicking."

Sam's face went still and gentle as she felt the baby move against her hand. Tessa's body rippled across the front as the baby shifted, pushing out a foot or an arm. Nobody said anything until Tessa shifted uncomfortably and pushed back vigorously into her stomach.

"Hey, Dean, that hurt," she said. "That's enough out of you."

They all laughed, and Tessa said half dreamily, for they were all getting tired now, "I wish Mom could feel that."

Annie looked up quickly, wanting to say that she could if only Tessa would tell her. But Liz caught her eye and Annie lay back again and said nothing, wishing for a moment that she were the one with this baby inside of her. This secret to hold alone and decide whom to share it with. Of course, if it were my baby, she thought, looking again at the turgid globe under Tessa's shirt, it would be an abortion.

Marie's visit surprised everyone by how smoothly it went. Elise, who actually had been checking on them once a week as Janis had asked, came by on Friday, and she and Marie got along well. And why not, Annie thought, watching them drink coffee together. Marie doesn't know that the reason Elise is so interested in her is because she was fucking Peter too. Elise reassured Marie that Liz and Tessa were doing fine, and that the school wasn't bad; her own kids went there. So Liz and Tessa were glad of Elise's visit, and Annie never told them what she knew.

Then on the last night Marie looked at them before they had cleared the dishes away, while they were still smoking their after-dinner cigarettes, and said, "I've got something I need to talk to you about."

Annie kept her eyes averted from Marie, knowing that she always had a guilty face whenever something was going on. She felt the other girls hesitate and didn't dare look at them.

"What is it, Mom?" Tessa asked, still sounding perfectly innocent.

"Well, I've been wanting to talk to you about this for a while. Sam, you probably have some idea of what I'm talking about."

"Uh huh . . . ," Sam murmured noncommittally. Annie wondered what Sam knew that the rest of them didn't and gave her a sharp look. Sam stayed concentrated on picking at her fingernails.

Marie paused and looked at everyone for a moment. Nobody spoke. "I'm seeing someone," she said with a shy smile. "And I think it's serious."

"Oh, Mom, that's so great!" Liz said enthusiastically. So enthusiastically that Marie was suspicious.

"Well, yes, it *is* great," she said, looking around at the smiles and giggles that were erupting around her. Annie found herself unable to stop laughing at Liz's response, and Sam kicked her under the table. Marie looked at them all oddly, then she smiled. "Sam told you, didn't she?" She paused and looked at Sam. "I knew you would figure it out."

"Well, of course, Mom," Sam said, grinning. "You haven't come home except to change clothes for the last two weekends!"

Marie laughed. "That's not exactly true," she said. "But, yes, his name is Dennis, and even though he's a little bit younger than me, and another musician—I think you'll like him. He composes mostly and plays bass. Jazz." Marie stopped and looked around. "You'll meet him soon, I hope. Maybe over Christmas. But I wanted to tell you now that we're all together. I'm hoping . . ." She stopped and lit a new cigarette, frowning briefly. "I'm hoping this will really work out. I think we have a shot at it anyway, this time."

"I hope so, Mom," Tessa said. "He sounds really nice. Where is he from?"

"New York," Marie said. "Actually he grew up in the city." She stopped for a half-second. "And I should tell you, he's black."

"He's black?" Sam said. "Wow. I mean, no big deal and everything, but wow. You're pretty cool, Mom."

"Oh, come on, Sam," said Liz scornfully. "That's just as prejudiced as anything else. Why is she cooler because she's seeing a black man?"

"Oh come off it, Liz," Sam grinned. "It is *way* cooler to be seeing a black man. It just is."

Marie laughed. "Well, I'm glad you think I'm cool, Sam. And I really hope everyone likes Dennis. He's nervous about meeting you. I warned him that we're usually a den of women on Cornelia Street."

Marie's news took care of the rest of the visit. She was happy to talk about Dennis, and the girls wanted to know everything. It wasn't as if Marie had never dated before, but she had never announced it like this, and they all thought that meant she and Dennis were going to stay together for a while. On Saturday morning Sam, Marie, and Annie rode the Greyhound bus back down to the city, and as they settled into their seats Marie waved through the window at Tessa and Liz until the bus pulled away.

"I think they're doing really well," Marie said to Annie. "Don't you? Maybe getting out of the city, a new school . . . I miss them, but they seem happy up here, don't you think?"

Annie spent most of Christmas taking the bus back and forth across the park, and then the subway up and downtown. She had spent the first part of Christmas Eve with her father and Jill at the ballet for a performance of *The Nutcracker.* Jill was due only a few weeks after Tessa, and she was dressed in a chic maternity dress that billowed gracefully around her. Luke held her arm protectively as they went through the crowded lobby at Lincoln Center.

They had been married in a civil ceremony that Annie had not attended, and by September they had moved to a new apartment on Central Park West. It turned out that Jill's family had money. Annie hadn't spent much time in the new apartment, where there was no actual bedroom for her. Jill spoke generously about the extra bed that was in the small maid's room off the kitchen, but Annie got the feeling that she wouldn't be allowed to put any posters on the wall. They had already decorated a room for the baby, however, and clean white furniture sat waiting inside on a red-patterned rug. Brightly colored mobiles turned gently in the air above the crib and the changing table. Annie hated it.

There were lots of young children at *The Nutcracker,* of course, and Annie felt conspicuously older. She hunched down in her seat next to Luke.

"You've come here every year?" Jill asked Annie as they waited for the orchestra to begin playing.

"Uh huh."

"That's so great," Jill said, looking around her. "Look at all these kids coming to the ballet. We'll have to do that with your brother as well."

"Boys don't like it as much," said Annie. "Unless they're fags."

"Oh, come on, Annie," Luke said sharply.

"What?" she said. "What's wrong with being a homosexual?"

Luke looked away.

"There's lots of little boys here tonight," Jill said, completely unruffled. "And don't forget the Prince."

"I know the story," said Annie.

Then the orchestra began playing the prelude, and Annie forgot about being too old for *The Nutcracker.* She loved the music and the set, with its huge Christmas tree, and the Magician, with his array of magical toys and the nutcracker itself. She forgot about everything else for a little while and became the little girl, Clara. As she watched the smallest children running through the legs of the adults in the Christmas party scene and then the dancing between the adults and the children that took place afterward, she was surprised by the longing she felt. She shook her head against the tears she hated herself for having, and she was glad of the dark, so no one could see her. But just then Luke reached over and took her hand, which made it almost impossible not to cry. She tried not to look at him, and the feeling had passed by intermission.

During the second act she watched dispassionately as the snow fell thickly on the Sugar Plum Fairies, and she wondered how cold it was up in the country that night. Liz and Tessa were staying up there for Christmas. Marie had wanted to go up there with Dennis and Sam and do a Christmas at the house. But then Dennis had gotten a gig for Christmas night at the Blue Note, and everyone was going. Everyone meant Justin and Nick as well, because Marie wanted to make a party of it. She had told them to come. Nick was in town for Christmas vacation, and Sam had seen both of the boys and said they would be at the Blue Note that night. Sam was excited about going; they all knew they wouldn't be carded if they came with Dennis and Marie.

As soon as Tessa heard that Nick was going to be there, she refused to go to the city for Christmas. She hadn't spoken to him all fall while he was away at St. John's, and nobody even brought up the idea of her telling him anymore. It all seemed too far gone for discussion at this point. Sam had tried to talk Tessa into coming down to the city anyway, and of course Liz wouldn't leave her up there alone, but Tessa wouldn't even consider it once she found out about Nick. Annie reminded Sam that Tessa really shouldn't be anywhere near her mother right now if they still wanted to keep the pregnancy a secret; but Sam said she didn't care, she just wanted to have them home for Christmas. Peter was out of town. For the first time in ten years, he had gone to visit friends in Vermont for the holiday and had sent all of the girls sizable checks, with a card that promised he would take them all to dinner soon. The girls knew he would never come up to the country to visit and that Christmas with Peter would have to wait for their eventual return. Annie was planning to go up to the country the day after Christmas, and Sam had said she would go with her, but Annie doubted that she was really going to come.

As the heavy red and gold curtain came down on the stiffly smiling cast of *The Nutcracker,* Annie straightened up and sighed. The night before Christmas had never seemed so long. Last Christmas Eve she had gone downtown after the ballet to help the Shanlick girls steal a tree. Buying a tree on the street was too expensive, so the Shanlicks had always waited until midnight on Christmas Eve to get their tree. They would drink steadily for a few hours, then go out to Sixth Avenue, where the tree sellers lined the pavement, and pick out a tree from what was left behind. The sellers often abandoned their leftover trees to the sidewalk. Nobody was going to buy a tree after Christmas.

It was fun to be out late on Christmas Eve, half drunk and dragging a huge tree home through the streets. They always got a tall tree since Marie's apartment had fourteen-foot ceilings, and last year they had to cut the bottom off to make room on top for the star. Annie had told Sam that she was willing to help if she was going to do it again this year, but Sam said that she didn't want to do it without Liz and Tessa. Marie had said that they could buy a smaller tree this year. Annie thought about the long subway ride just to decorate a tree that was already bought and paid for, and found herself without the heart to go downtown.

Annie went home to Ellen's house right after the show instead. Luke hailed a cab for her and pressed the money to pay for it into her hand as a Christmas treat. After Ellen went to bed, Annie made popcorn and watched television in the living room until late that night. Christmas lights were blinking over and over in apartment windows across the street, and the late-night newscaster declared that it was a night full of wonder and miracles, but when Annie went to the window to smoke a last cigarette before bed, she had to admit that it still didn't feel like Christmas; whatever that meant anymore.

Christmas morning was spent with Ellen. They had each stuffed a stocking for the other, and they opened them together sitting on Ellen's bed. They ate chocolate before breakfast, and Ellen made kippers with eggs and brewed a pot of the strong English tea that Annie had bought for her. Annie had been given a tape player as her present from both of her parents, and she played her favorite tapes as they sat at the kitchen table over breakfast. It was comfortable to be sitting in their nightgowns until noon; Ellen loved Christmas.

"I don't know why Christmas always makes me happy," she said to Annie as she poured another cup of tea and lit her first cigarette of the day. "I always sort of dreaded Christmas as a child." She took a long drag and looked out the window at the gray, snowless day. "Our parents would give us wonderful presents. I mean, piles of presents under the tree and stockings with silver dollars in the toe. Every year a silver dollar—"

"Just like you did for me when I was little," said Annie, wishing Ellen hadn't stopped doing that and trying to remember when she had. "Why did you stop?"

"I didn't," Ellen said mischievously. "It was Santa Claus, and you stopped believing in him."

"Mom!"

"Oh, all right, next year I'll try and remember. Anyway, we had these kind of storybook Christmas mornings when I was a kid. But then, after all of the presents were opened, our parents would ask us to choose one of our presents to give to a poor child for Christmas. Something for 'the Poor,' as they said. And, you know, you were really supposed to pick your favorite present to give away or you wouldn't be sacrificing anything. So, it sounds like a good and noble idea, and all of that—but actually, as a child, it was horrible, because no sooner had you opened up the present you had always longed for, than you knew that you would have to either give it away or be responsible for ruining Christmas through your selfishness."

"Which did you do?"

"Both. I would usually fall into selfishness and ruin; Aunt Sophie was always the good one. So, I had the toy, but I could never really enjoy it for the rest of the year because it would just remind me of what a disappointment I was to my parents."

"Ugh." Annie bit into an apple and tipped back in her chair so that she was resting on the two back legs. "It sounds awful."

"It was," Ellen said, giggling. "I don't know why I still like Christmas, but I do."

"Maybe 'cause you don't have to spend it with them anymore."

"Maybe."

"Is that why we never spent Christmas with Mums and Grandpa?"

"Oh, there were lots of reasons." Ellen's face changed just slightly, and Annie immediately wished she hadn't asked. "What time do you have to be at your father's house?"

Then Annie's day of commuting truly began. She had to take the bus across town to Luke's apartment, where he and Jill were hosting a Christmas dinner of "strays." Annie was the only person under thirty at the dinner table. After living through that she went downtown to the Blue Note. She was let in after they found her name on the guest list, and she saw Sam, Marie, and the boys sitting at a table near the front. There was a girl sitting with them, and from the way Nick introduced her Annie knew she was his new girlfriend. Her name was Sally and they had met at St. John's. She was very pretty, with honey-colored hair that fell perfectly straight to her shoulders. She seemed nice, but Annie couldn't help wanting to dislike her out of loyalty to Tessa. She caught Sam's eye after they were introduced, but Sam just shrugged. She was more interested in flirting with Justin than paying attention to Nick and Sally.

The music was good but very loud, and after the initial hellos nobody really tried to talk until the break. Justin was friendly to her, and Marie gave her a big hug, but Annie felt chronically separated from the group. After two drinks Annie went to the bathroom and then, after one look back at the table, she slipped out the door without saying good-bye. She was feeling hazy, neglected, and sorry for herself. As she rode the near-empty subway back uptown she thought about all of the Christmases she could remember. Maybe I'll be like Mom, she thought, maybe I'll like Christmas when I'm a grown-up.

Justin called her the next morning and woke her up.

"Sam says you're going up today."

"Yeah, I am. There's a one o'clock bus."

"Want to drive instead?"

"Really?"

"Yeah. I'll pick up Sam around noon and then we'll come get you."

Annie didn't believe that Sam was really coming until she saw her sitting in the front seat with Justin. She jumped into the backseat, cramming her bag into the mountain of Justin's and Sam's stuff. Sam smiled at her as they pulled away from the building, and Annie felt a surge of happiness.

"All right!" she said. "All right, we're all going to be up there together."

"All except Nick," Justin snorted. "He wanted to come, you know."

"Oh, my God." Annie looked at Sam, who rolled her eyes.

"He was going to come until this morning," Justin said. "Then Sally called and invited him to Vermont."

"Skiing with her family," Sam said. "Can you believe that? Her family owns some lodge up near Stratton, or something. One of those places."

"Forget a lodge. Her family owns the whole fucking ski resort, Sam!" shouted Justin.

"Yeah, well, all those rich kids go to St. John's," said Annie. "Half my class went there this year."

"Nick said—get this—" Justin turned onto the West Side Highway and began heading north. "He said that all of these St. John's kids had a bonfire the night before winter vacation, and they burned all this expensive ski equipment, stereos, all that shit. They call it a 'potlatch.' "

"What? Why?" Annie asked.

"I think it's because they're showing off how much they've got," Justin said, shrugging his shoulders.

"Maybe they get new stuff for Christmas every year anyway," said Sam. "They've gotta make room in their closets."

"Maybe . . ." Annie was quiet. Even at her own school she had never heard of anything like that.

"Sally's not like that. She's all right," Justin said. "She's gorgeous too, which isn't so bad." He paused for a moment. "I don't know if Sally burned any of her own stuff. Nick just said that they were there and saw people doing that."

"And Nick gets to go to Vermont and ski for free," said Sam.

"Everything for free," said Justin.

"Yeah, well, who cares?" asked Annie. "Who the fuck wants to go to Vermont anyway?"

"I wouldn't mind," Justin said. "Vermont, or the Bahamas. Seems like everyone who isn't going skiing is going to the Bahamas. It sounds pretty good to me."

"You've just got to fuck your way to the top, Justin," Sam said. "Like Nick."

"Yeah, well, it's not like I haven't tried," he muttered. "But that's not the only way to get there."

"You can go to the Bahamas when you're rich and leave your loft empty for the winter," said Annie.

"It's not gonna be a loft," Justin said. "I changed my mind. I'm gonna get a huge apartment on Fifth Avenue. Like, eleven rooms facing the park."

"How come?" asked Annie. "Lofts are so great for parties."

"Fuck the parties," said Justin. "I want a doorman."

"All right." Annie laughed uncertainly. "Live wherever you want. But I don't know about Vermont. The whole state is like a walking L.L. Bean catalogue."

"Yeah," said Sam, turning around from the front seat and smiling at her. "I'd rather go up to our place—I mean, Janis's place—in the country anyway."

"Have either of you ever even *been* to Vermont?" asked Justin.

"No," Annie admitted. "But I know what it looks like from the catalogue."

They all cracked up, and Annie was still smiling when they hit the

Saw Mill River Parkway, and she lay down in the backseat to sleep. It felt good to be lying there with nothing to do but watch the treetops flying past against the white sky. For the first time since Christmas Eve, she felt safe.

It was getting dark when they arrived at the house, and as they turned down the driveway, Annie was surprised to see colored lights strung under the eaves.

"They put up Christmas lights!" said Sam.

Justin laughed. "Keeping up with the neighborhood. Good thing Mom can't see it."

"Why?" asked Annie.

"Oh, she's just a snob. She hates Christmas lights," said Justin.

"I'm glad they put them up," said Sam. "I don't care if they're tacky. They look pretty."

They pulled up to the house and Sam jumped out first, running to greet Tessa and Liz.

"I wanted to warn her," Annie said to Justin, watching them from the car. "Tessa's a lot bigger than she was at Thanksgiving."

Justin shrugged and then opened his door to get out. "It'll be all right," he said, winking at her. "Sam's not as bad as you think. Let's get the stuff out of the car."

Justin was right; things were all right. Liz and Tessa had put up a Christmas tree, so they sat around the living room eating spaghetti and drinking a cheap bottle of wine that Justin had brought up from the city. Tessa and Liz had bought lights, but they didn't have any ornaments for the tree, so Sam thought of cutting out pictures from magazines for decorations. They pulled out old magazines and perched photos of rock stars, models, and even cars onto the branches of the tree. Annie and Liz found Janis's sewing kit and strung popcorn in long strings.

"This is so ridiculous," Annie said, looking around. "I feel like I'm in a scene from *Little Women.*"

"I know," Justin said. "Norman Rockwell's Christmas with a pregnant teenager under the tree." But he was smiling at Tessa and she laughed.

"At least I don't have to keep it a secret when I'm home," she said, rubbing her belly. The baby was due in mid-February, and Tessa looked so pregnant that Annie couldn't believe they were still hiding it at school. But nobody had said anything to Tessa or Liz since that day at the drugstore, and they had never shopped there again.

"They ignore me at school," Tessa said. "They think I'm the fat brain."

"Yeah," said Liz. "Everyone there is either a 'jock,' a 'head,' or a 'brain.' We get good grades, and we try to be boring as shit, so . . ."

"You've always been boring as shit, Liz," said Justin without missing a beat, and that started it.

Liz threw a pillow at Justin, which hit his wineglass, spilling red wine down his shirt. He took one look at his shirt and threw the remains of his glass onto her, splotching her T-shirt in the middle. Liz screamed, grabbed the bottle for more ammo, and the fight was on. Annie threw her wine at Justin, who took Sam's and dumped it right over Annie's head. Sam slipped on the slick magazine cuttings and fell down in the center of the room, dragging Liz and the bottle down with her. They were laughing and pushing each other when all of a sudden Justin looked at Tessa. She was sitting back in her chair, but Justin threw another glassful right onto her belly.

"You're in this fight, too, Dean!" he shouted. Tessa scrambled up, laughing, and wiping away at the big red stain.

"You jerk. You asshole!" she said, but Justin knew that she wasn't really mad. Justin had told them that he thought the whole thing about Dean Moriarty was stupid, and he had hated *On the Road;* but now he was also calling the baby Dean, and that made her happy.

"Well, that's the end of the wine," he said, holding up the empty bottle.

"And look—we're all tattooed," said Sam. Everyone had wine on their clothes.

"These'll be like our T-shirts from a concert," said Annie, looking around.

"Yeah!" said Justin. "I Got Stained: Christmas, '75. Let's get another bottle." He got up and headed into the kitchen.

"Justin!" Liz said. "Forget it!"

"Not to throw around," he called back to her. "To drink."

"But you said Janis would be pissed if we drank anything here," said Tessa.

Justin paused, leaning on the doorjamb. "I'll tell her *I* drank it," he said. "No—I'll tell her Nick did it. I'll say he stopped by with Sally." He leered at Tessa, who made a face at him, then he walked into the kitchen. "She never minds anything if Nick does it," he called from the kitchen. "Though knocking you up might upset her a little, I guess."

They heard the sound of bottles clanging together in a cabinet.

"He's drunk," Annie said matter of factly. "He drank way more of that bottle than we did."

"Yeah, but—"

"And he was drinking beer on the way up," said Sam. "We both were, while you were sleeping."

Justin came back in with a bottle of bourbon. "There's no more wine," he said, smiling. "So, I'm moving on to whiskey." He put five glasses down and sat on the rug. "Anybody else want a glass?"

"Justin," Liz said. "Isn't Janis going to kill us?"

"Maybe," he said, filling his glass halfway with whiskey and raising it in a mock toast. "Fuck her if she can't take a joke."

No one said anything. That was what they had always said last summer, right after the divorce. Whatever they were talking about, in the end it always came down to: Fuck 'em if they can't take a joke. Nick had said it the most and always with perfect timing to make them laugh. They had stopped saying it after Justin and Nick had gone away to the country and Nick had never really come back. Tessa had hated the phrase after that, and the girls had stopped using it. It was kind of stupid, anyway, Annie thought to herself as she watched Justin taking a long sip, but it was their code.

Now Tessa leaned forward and picked up a glass. "Fuck 'em," she said, grinning at Justin, and he filled it up for her.

Everybody got drunk that night, and Justin got drunker than anyone. By the time they finished the bottle of whiskey, Sam had apologized to Tessa and Liz for never coming up to visit, and then she passed out. Tessa had cried about Nick, and Justin had promised to be the best uncle the baby could ever have. While Tessa and Justin were still making plans for Dean, Liz pulled Annie upstairs and started kissing her just out of sight of the living room.

"Come on," she whispered, "let's go to bed."

"Liz," Annie said between kisses. "They'll see. Justin will see."

"I don't care," Liz said, and Annie realized that she was just drunk enough not to care either.

They stumbled up the stairs holding hands, falling into the double bed they had first made love in last spring. They made love roughly, drunkenly, pulling into each other heedlessly as if they didn't have much time. They threw off the covers even though the room was cold. Liz's body was dark on the smooth white bed, and Annie pulled Liz toward her in one hard movement, biting and kissing the inside of her thighs and wanting nothing more than the smell and feel of Liz's sex on her mouth. She dug her fingers into Liz's buttocks, raising her up from the bed and holding her there, finding her sex again and again. Liz crooned to her in half phrases that meant nothing, and neither of them cared how much noise they made.

Much later, Annie woke to feel a weight on her body and something strong pressing between her legs. She didn't remember falling asleep, and she arched her pelvis back without opening her eyes. Then she sensed an unfamiliar movement and willed herself awake. It was Justin on top of her. His pants were down to his ankles and he was rubbing himself against her; she could feel his hard-on between her legs. His fast breathing, next to her neck, smelled rancid. She froze, halting her responsiveness, and realized as she focused her eyes that she was still drunk.

Liz was still sleeping with her back to them on the other half of the bed. Annie pushed her hands against his hips from underneath, breaking his rhythm. "Justin, cut it out," she whispered.

He didn't say anything and pushed harder against her. She shoved him and managed to get halfway out from under him. "Get off!" she said louder, pushing at him with her leg to make him move.

"Oh, come on, Annie," he whispered, raising himself up on his arms and looking at her. "Just for a little while."

"No." Annie felt her nakedness suddenly under his eyes, and everything felt disconnected to her. How could Justin be here, she thought drunkenly. It's not his room.

"I heard you," he said. "I heard you in here and I think it's disgusting what you and Liz are doing. It makes me want to fuck your brains out, Annie. I'm going to fuck you so hard you won't ever want girls again." He pulled her down and edged his way gently back on top of her again, pressing his sex against hers. "I heard you," he said again. "It turned me on."

He entered her and Annie inhaled with the suddenness of it, but whether it was because she was still half-drunk or just hadn't had time to think about it, it didn't hurt this time. For the first time it didn't hurt, and Justin moved slowly inside of her. She was so surprised by her pleasure that she forgot to resist it and allowed him to pull her along into a perfect, intuitive rhythm that tugged at her from the inside and gathered her tightly to him. She didn't know how it was that her nipple was in between his lips and her legs were wrapped around the middle of his back and she was coming against him as he quickly pulled out, coming onto her breasts and belly as she shuddered at the force of their confluence.

They said nothing to each other. His breath was so strong as he breathed hard next to her ear that she tried not to inhale, and she felt the taste of vomit in her mouth. Annie was suddenly completely sober. She was stunned by what had just happened, what she had done. She hated him for his arrogance and his ability to arouse and shame her. She looked at Liz in the bed next to them and hoped that she had been drunk enough to stay asleep, that she wasn't just feigning. Justin's breathing had changed and his body felt heavier. He had slipped into sleep as soon as he had finished. Now his body felt like a trap, and she hated herself for allowing it to come to this, pinned under him and her desire for him, that now seemed foreign and repulsive.

"Justin, wake up." He murmured impatiently at her but woke up, rolling off of her and lying on the very edge of the bed. He stared at the ceiling without moving. "Get out of here," Annie whispered. "I'm with Liz, now. You're drunk. Go to bed."

"What do you mean you're *with* her?" he asked.

He's drunk but he's going to remember this, Annie thought.

"I mean—we're together, for now. You know."

"No, no, I didn't know," Justin said, and for a minute he didn't seem drunk at all. "Not until tonight, when I heard you girls doing it up here, as if nobody would ever notice."

"Get out of here, Justin. Leave me alone," Annie said. "And fuck you for listening to me and Liz."

"Yeah, well, it was hard not to hear." He was still lying beside her and he looked right into her eyes. "And 'fuck you,' Justin, for fucking me so good? What about that part, Annie?"

When Annie didn't say anything he slowly got up and pushed off the edge of the bed to get upright. Then he leaned down and pulled her head up, cradling her face in his hands so that her hair fell between his fingers and her ear was close to his mouth. "I know all about you, Annie," he whispered, and then, letting her go, he clattered out of the room, reaching for the doorjamb to swing around the corner toward his bedroom.

She got up and closed the door behind him, got back into bed, and looked at Liz. She had rolled over toward Annie and her eyes were open. She had been awake all along. Annie waited for her to say something, but she didn't. Annie grabbed a blanket from the floor and held the covers close to her chin. She stared out the window opposite the bed, with no words to speak first. When Annie started to cry, Liz curled her body around her and rocked silently against her back. "I'm sorry," Annie said at last, and then she said it again and again, until Liz told her to shut up.

"Being sorry doesn't make any difference," Liz said. "And I don't feel sorry for you." But she didn't pull away from Annie as her crying ended. For the second time that night, Annie didn't remember falling asleep.

The next morning everyone was crabby and embarrassed. Justin avoided Annie and Liz, and Annie wondered what anyone else in the house had heard last night. Liz had gotten up first, and she seemed to be avoiding Annie as well, keeping silent as she drank cup after cup of coffee. Tessa lay on the couch looking puffy and angry. She was ordering Sam to pick up the glasses, bottles, and ashtrays from the floor. Sam cooperated sullenly, and they wrangled back and forth the whole morning.

Everyone was relieved when Justin announced that he was driving back to the city that afternoon, instead of waiting until the end of the weekend. Sam immediately perked up and grabbed at the chance to go back home, promising Liz and Tessa that she would be back soon, "before the baby comes." Justin didn't make any promises, though he gave both Tessa and Liz hugs before leaving and even put a twenty-dollar bill on the kitchen counter to help out with groceries. He shrugged when Annie said she was going to stay up in the country with Liz and Tessa. Liz had been carefully neutral about it when Annie asked if she could stay. Annie felt like she only really started breathing again after she watched the Dodge climb the hill and disappear onto the main road.

They did nothing for the next five days. Eating, sleeping, and playing hearts was all they could manage. Tessa was declared the winner of the tournament, and on New Year's Eve they tuned in a fuzzy picture on the black-and-white TV to watch the ball fall in Times Square. But even on that night they went to bed early. Annie and Liz hadn't made love again, and though the tension had lessened, there had been a complete absence of desire between them. They hadn't talked about it. Liz clearly wanted to avoid talking about it, and though Annie was too tired to think, she still thought about it all the time. She hated herself and Justin, and as the days went by with neither forgiveness nor rejection from Liz, her shame turned into a constant, dull depression. She wondered if Liz only wanted her around to help her through this time with Tessa, and she was afraid that once the baby was born Liz simply wouldn't want Annie around anymore. Annie tried to be the same as she had ever been to Liz, but in fact she felt lifeless from the waist down and welcomed the chance to be left alone.

On New Year's Day Annie took the bus home, finding it hard to believe that she was only halfway through the ninth grade and an entire semester stretched out ahead of her. She had never felt more acutely that her real life was elsewhere, and five days a week were spent watching the time pass slowly from eight-thirty to three o'clock. She took the bus back up for only one weekend in mid-January, and Tessa was tired and irritable all weekend until they agreed that by now she was so pregnant that she shouldn't even go to school. The baby was due in four weeks, and they decided that it was time for Tessa to come down with mononucleosis, something that everyone they knew in high school had been sick with. Once that was decided, Tessa cheered up a little, but Liz was afraid of leaving her home all day alone, in case she went into labor.

"I'll be O.K.," Tessa said. "And I can always call the school office and get you to come home."

When Annie left that Sunday she wasn't sure if she could make another visit that month and she made Liz promise to call her the minute labor started. "I'll get up here somehow," she said. "It doesn't matter about school."

It was four A.M. on the first Wednesday in February when Liz called. Annie had a phone next to her bed, and she picked it up on the second ring. She was wide awake, as if she had never been asleep.

"Annie, it's me." Liz sounded scared. She was whispering.

"Is it happening? Has she had it yet?"

"No. No, but she's in labor."

"But, wait—It's too soon."

"The books said it could come anytime within two weeks of the due date, remember?"

"Is she O.K.?"

"I guess. I mean, sort of. We're gonna go to the hospital pretty soon I guess."

"When they're five minutes apart."

"Right."

"Are they?"

"I don't know, my watch broke. There's a clock in the stove that works, but I hate having to leave her alone to go look at the time."

"I'm coming up."

"We might be at the hospital already."

"I know."

"How will you get there from the bus station?"

"I'll figure it out."

"O.K."

There was a pause.

"Are you O.K.?" Annie asked.

"Yeah. I gotta go."

"I'll be there as soon as I can."

"O.K." Liz hung up.

Annie could tell that Liz had been about to cry. Liz was never the one who cried. Annie lay still for a moment. The apartment was quiet; if Ellen had heard the phone, she had gone back to sleep. Annie looked at the clock, then dialed Justin's number.

"Hello?" Janis answered the phone. She was half-asleep.

"Is Justin there?" Annie hadn't heard Janis's voice since last summer. It made her pulse jump, and she gripped the phone tightly to keep it from shaking.

"Justin? Who is this?"

Just a friend, Annie wanted to say, and some phony names floated through her head. "Janis, it's Annie," she said.

"Annie? What the . . . Annie, it's the middle of the night."

"I know. I'm sorry, Janis."

"Is there anything wrong?"

"No, no. I just need to talk to Justin. It's important."

There was a silence. Annie felt frozen.

"Well, all right. Justin!" Annie heard her mumbling something angry to Justin before he got on the phone.

"Hello?" He sounded asleep too. Annie felt embarrassed for having called. It was four in the morning, and now everyone would know something was happening.

"Annie, what is it? You woke Mom up, you know."

"I know. I'm sorry." She felt as if all of the words were leaving her. "Justin, you gotta take me up there. Tessa's having the baby."

"Oh, shit," he said. "Shit, shit, shit."

Annie waited a moment. "Justin, please. If you drive we can be there in two hours—"

"Two and a half."

"Well, the bus is four and a half; and the first one doesn't even leave until seven."

Justin didn't say anything. She could feel how angry he was.

"Justin, this is the last time. It'll all be over after this."

"Yeah, until she comes home."

Annie said nothing. She could imagine Janis standing there in her robe, waiting for Justin to get off the phone to ask him what was going on.

"All right," Justin said. "All right, I'm coming." And he hung up the phone.

Annie got dressed as if she was going on a camping trip. She wasn't sure when she would be back, and she packed some extra clothes in her backpack, along with her diary. She counted her money—seventeen dollars—and wrote a note to her mother. She knew that she was going to get into trouble for leaving in the middle of the week, and missing school, but all that seemed far away. She paced in the kitchen while she waited for Justin to get there, aware of every second passing by. She thought of calling Sam and decided against it. Let Liz call her, she thought. I don't want to deal with Marie. Finally she got so impatient that she went downstairs to the lobby and watched the street change color from black to gray as the sky slowly lightened around the upper edges of the housing project across the street.

When Justin's green Dodge pulled up Annie ran out to meet him. Justin reached across to open the passenger door for her.

"Hey," she said, as she got in, throwing her pack into the backseat.

"Hey." He didn't look at her and gunned the car away from her front door.

Annie felt the old fear start up again, but she bulled through it. "Thanks for doing this, Justin. Really."

"Yeah, well." His eyes narrowed as he took a corner and swung around a pothole. "It's the last time."

"I know. They'll be coming back after this."

"No, I mean—I'm done."

"Done?" Annie felt her throat closing up. She didn't know what he was talking about.

"Done with the girls, the whole thing."

Annie stared at him. "What do you mean? You can't just—I mean, they're your sisters."

"No, they're not!" Justin shouted and pounded the wheel with his fist. The car lurched and swung toward a parked car. He regained control of it then shot through a stop sign and turned onto the West Side Highway. "They're not my sisters, and they're not yours either."

"I know that," Annie said. "Tell me something I don't know, Justin."

"You think Peter Shanlick is so great? Like having him and the girls join our family was so fucking fantastic?"

"I don't know."

"Their dad fucked my mom over, O.K.? He blamed everything on her; he screwed around on her, they both fucking hated each other, and now they've finally gotten smart enough to end it. Do you think I mind? Like I'm sad, or something? Shit, no."

They had reached the tollbooths on the bridge leading out of the city, and Justin threw his quarter hard into the white plastic basket so that it rattled around the rim before rolling down. The bell rang and the tollbooth arm raised in perfect rhythm. Justin stepped on the gas and tore up the empty road through Riverdale. Annie didn't say anything; the blood in her ears sounded like the entire Atlantic Ocean was trapped inside her head.

"You think all those parties they used to have on Great Jones Street were so cool, don't you? Well, it sucked there, Annie. Sometimes there was no heat and no hot water and nothing but beer in the house. Great fucking artists. Good luck to the rest of us. You don't know Jack about it. You just came down for the parties, like everyone else. And Marie's place is the same fucking shit. A bunch of drunks sitting around all night talking about ideas and hoping to get laid. The girls can do it, but I'm not gonna hang around that crap anymore. I'm sick of all of them."

"You're sick of us too?" Annie heard how young that sounded as soon as she said it, and she held her breath, wishing it hadn't come out of her mouth.

"Yeah," he said, sighing. All the fight seemed to go out of him at once. "I am. I'll help you out today, you know, with Tessa and everything, but it's not like I'm obligated, all right?"

Annie couldn't speak.

"We don't have the same parents. We just grew up together, like you and me. It doesn't mean anything."

Annie pulled out her pack of cigarettes, and Justin held out his hand for one without taking his eyes off the road. She lit both of their cigarettes, and they drove in silence for a while. Annie opened her window partway; the early morning air smelled of cut grass and water.

"I got into the University of Michigan," Justin said suddenly. "Early admissions, with a good scholarship. I figure I can get a student loan for what's left over."

"You're gonna go to Michigan?" Annie turned in her seat so that she was facing him.

"It's a really good school, Annie. What do you know?"

"Nothing, but . . . it's in the Midwest."

"Yeah, so?"

"I don't know. What about NYU? I thought you were applying to NYU."

"I applied early admissions to Michigan. That means if I get in, I'm going. And I got in."

"I can't believe you're gonna live in Michigan."

"Yeah," Justin said, almost to himself. "I just found out yesterday. I got the letter."

Annie couldn't think of anything to say. He wants to go, she thought, trying the words out without speaking them aloud. He really wants to go.

Justin drove too fast, gunning the car past the speed limits through the little towns. Annie didn't say anything. She didn't care if they got a ticket; all she could think of was Liz up there alone with Tessa. She wondered if they had gone to the hospital yet and imagined Liz driving up that long driveway with Tessa beside her; or maybe she would be lying down in the back. She closed her eyes but couldn't sleep, so she smoked too much and stared out the window at the towns that were now deep in the mud and slush of an unexpected February thaw.

"Let's go straight to the hospital," she said to Justin as they drove into town. "It's been two hours since Liz called, and she was already in labor. I hope she hasn't had the baby yet."

"Why not?" he asked. "Isn't it better if she gets it over with faster?"

"Yes," Annie said, as she watched the square blue signs for the hospital get more frequent. "But I want to be there."

Justin parked on the street, and they got out of the car for the first time since they'd left New York.

"I gotta take a wicked piss," Justin said, running his hands through his hair. Annie decided not to look at herself in the rearview mirror and grabbed her backpack. She walked ahead of Justin into the main entrance of the small hospital. It was about seven in the morning, and everyone else in the lobby looked fresh. The woman behind the main desk was fully made up, but she was wearing a sweatshirt with a big heart on it. There were heart-shaped candies in a plastic dish on her desk, and Annie remembered with a frown that Valentine's Day was coming up.

The woman looked up at them with a smile that was so bright it made Annie wince.

"We're looking for the maternity ward," she said hesitantly. "Tessa Shanlick."

The woman's smile became more forced when she noticed Justin at Annie's side. We must smell bad, Annie thought to herself, and she wished she had brought a toothbrush.

"And where's the men's room?" Justin asked, his voice sounding hoarse and tired.

"The maternity ward is on the third floor," said the woman after a quick glance at him. "But they only allow immediate family." Neither of them said anything. "The restrooms are down the hall past the elevators," the woman said, before looking back down at her desk dismissively.

Annie followed Justin down the hall, and they both went to the bathroom. She splashed water on her face and tried to comb through her hair with her fingers. I look about thirty years old, she thought to herself as she looked at her eyes in the mirror. Outside the bathroom Justin was pressing his nose against a huge fish tank in the hall.

"Look at this," he said when Annie came up to him. "Look at

these guys." Two big white fish slowly circled as an unseen motor quietly bubbled a jet of air in the corner of the pristine tank. "I wish I lived in there," Justin said.

"I know," Annie said. Now that they were here she didn't really want to go upstairs either. Just the idea of Tessa being in an actual maternity ward seemed to separate her from them. "Come on, Justin." She touched him gently on the forearm. "We'd better go up."

"Yeah," he said, heaving himself off the glass with an effort. "God, I hate hospitals."

They walked down the hall without speaking. They had just passed the hospital gift shop when Justin said suddenly, "Let's get her something," and Annie followed him into the store. The store was filled with perversely cheerful chotchkes: lots of china statuettes of children with sappy expressions on their crudely painted faces. There were also stuffed animals with plastic hearts strung around their necks like licenses that read GET WELL SOON, or CONGRATULATIONS.

Justin picked up one of each and smirked at Annie. "I just can't decide which one to get her," he said.

"How about flowers?" said Annie.

They walked back to the small cooler filled with bouquets. The flowers were mostly daisies dyed a variety of colors and red and white rosebuds.

"Let's get her a rose," Annie said quietly. "Everything else is so ugly."

"The roses are six ninety-five each," the woman called from behind the counter where she had been eavesdropping.

"What a rip-off," Annie said to Justin. "Maybe . . ."

"No, let's just get it," Justin said quickly. "I'll pay for it."

He picked out a white rose and brought it up to the counter.

They walked slowly to the elevator; Justin carried the rose, and Annie read each sign they passed out loud, as if they were going to get lost. When the elevator came they had to squeeze in next to an old man on a gurney who was being moved somewhere by an orderly. The man was dressed in a white-and-blue-checked hospital gown, with paper slippers perched loosely on his long feet. The old man didn't move his head when Justin and Annie came in and stood beside him, but stared up at the ceiling without expression, breathing regularly and heavily. Annie wondered if he was dying. If this was what dying people looked like. His face was unevenly shaved and had patches of white bristle along the jawline. A sudden nausea came over her and she leaned against the back of the elevator, closing her eyes for a second and trying to breathe through her mouth. The smell of ammonia was overpowering.

The door opened with a two-toned ring, and Justin stepped out. Annie followed, opening her eyes again and hoping that he hadn't noticed anything. There was a main desk directly ahead of them, and all along the hall were photos of babies and mothers. In a corner just past the desk was a plain white statue of the Virgin Mary with a brightly colored rosary hung around her neck.

As they approached the desk, Annie suddenly felt terrified, and just as the nurse looked up expectantly her stomach heaved, and she turned and vomited onto the floor.

Justin yelled something and jumped away from her as Annie tried to steady herself on the edge of the desk. The nurse came around almost immediately and held her shoulders.

"There, there," she said, handing Annie a bundle of tissues. "Are you all right, dear?" Annie nodded her head as she breathed in and out slowly. Tears had come to her eyes, and her stomach clenched again but subsided.

"Come and sit," the nurse said. "Eric! Could you come here please?" she called over her shoulder, and Annie saw a young man come around the corner with a mop and a bucket.

"I'm sorry," Annie said. "I'm so sorry. I didn't mean to—"

"Of course not," said the nurse, putting her into one of the plastic chairs that lined the hallway. "But if that's morning sickness I think you've gotten here a little too early. We don't do prenatal here, dear, just labor and delivery. Are you the father?" she asked, turning to Justin.

"No!" he said. "We're not. We're friends. We're here to see my sister."

"Oh, your sister." The nurse looked at Annie. "Get her a glass of water," she said to Justin. "There's a water cooler just past my desk."

"I'm not pregnant," Annie said unsteadily. "We're just here to see someone."

"Are you sure?" the nurse asked her quietly. "Honey, if you are—"

"No," Annie interrupted vehemently. "No, I'm sure."

The nurse smiled at her, a little puzzled, and handed her the water Justin had brought back to them. "Drink," she commanded, and as she watched Annie swallow, she said, "It's nice to know that some girls your age aren't active yet. I don't see much of that here, of course."

Annie held out her cup to Justin for more water. She knew better than to look at him. She was feeling better now, and she smiled at the nurse. "Thank you," she said. "I'm O.K. now." She looked at the floor and saw that it had been mopped clean. "I'm really sorry."

"That's O.K.," the nurse said, going back behind her desk. "You just sit there until you feel better." She looked at Justin, who had brought Annie another cup of water and was standing there looking as if he wanted to be anywhere but there.

"What's your sister's name?" she asked.

"My what?" he said. "Oh, yeah. Well, she's my stepsister actually, kind of . . . her name's Tessa Shanlick."

The nurse raised her eyebrows but only repeated "Shanlick" and began to look through a big book that sat on her desk. "Oh, yes. She was admitted through the emergency room last night."

"The emergency room? Is she all right?" Justin sounded scared.

"Yes. Oh, she's fine. And the baby's fine too."

"The baby?" Annie got up and stood next to Justin.

"Yes." The nurse looked behind her at a chalkboard, where Annie suddenly saw the name "Shanlick" written in sloppy cursive. "The baby was born just about an hour ago. A baby boy. A short labor, so it wasn't too hard on her."

"Oh, my God. Oh, my God," Annie said, and she reached for Justin's hand involuntarily. He didn't pull away.

"A boy," he repeated. "Where is it? I mean, can we see it?"

"Can we see her?" asked Annie.

"The baby's in the nursery," the nurse said. "And I'm not sure if— there's her sister, in the waiting room." She looked at Annie. "Are you her other sister? She talked about you."

"No," said Annie.

"Yes," said Justin simultaneously.

The nurse stared at them without smiling this time.

"We're steps," Justin went on. "I mean, *I'm* their stepbrother, but *she* is their real sister." He pushed Annie forward a little.

"It's kind of complicated," Annie said after a beat.

"Yes. It certainly must be," said the nurse. "We only allow the immediate family to visit right away, but if you're her sister . . . why don't you both go down to the waiting room and see the girl she came in with. I believe she's a sister also."

"Yes," Annie said. "That's Liz. Thank you."

She and Justin walked down the hall together.

"I can't believe you threw up," Justin whispered.

"It wasn't my fault," Annie whispered back. "It's not like I meant to do it. It was the smell I guess. That guy in the elevator."

"You're a fuckin' weirdo, Annie," Justin said. Then he smiled at her and shook his head. "You all right now?"

"Yeah."

The waiting room was a windowless room painted yellow with a pink stripe around the top molding. Liz was lying on the floor with her sweatshirt bundled under her head like a pillow. She was snoring. Annie and Justin looked at each other. She looked like a little girl with her mouth half-open, and they knew how embarrassed she would be if anyone heard her snoring. They watched her for a moment, then Annie knelt down and shook her shoulder. Liz pulled away at first, then she opened her eyes and turned toward them with her eyes still full of sleep.

"Oh . . . you came." She smiled at them. "He's here. Do you know? The baby's here."

"Yeah, yeah, we know." Annie gave her a hug and sat next to her on the floor. Liz looked up at Justin and smiled. "He's beautiful."

"Can we see him?" Annie asked. "And Tessa, will they let us? Is she O.K.?"

"She's good. She's sleeping, I think. Or she was. What time is it?"

"About eight," Justin said. He laughed. "We drove really fast."

"She had the baby really fast." Liz got up with a huge smile and pulled Annie by the hand. "Come on, you gotta see him."

She led them down the hall to the nursery. There was a small window set into the wall, and through it they could see rows of identical plastic bassinets with a tiny body bundled up in each one. "There he is," Liz said, pointing to one of the bundles.

A plastic card, inserted in the end of the bassinet facing them, read: "Shanlick, D." The baby was sleeping with his head away from them, and Annie could just see a bit of a red face wedged between the hospital blanket and a little blue striped hat.

"Look at him," Annie said quietly. "It's little Dean. She really named him Dean."

"Dean Shanlick," Liz said.

The three of them stared for a moment in silence.

"Isn't he incredible, Justin?" Liz asked without taking her eyes off the baby. "It's our nephew. We've got a nephew."

Justin didn't say anything; he just looked and looked.

"I think he looks a little bit like Nick," Liz said after a minute. "Don't you?"

"I don't know," said Justin. "Maybe." He peered around trying to get a better look at Dean. "He looks a lot like the other ones if you ask me."

Liz and Annie looked at each other and laughed.

"Oh my God," Annie said again. "Look at him."

The baby opened his mouth and started moving his head around. He started crying, though they couldn't hear anything through the glass.

"He's crying!" Justin said. "Hey, come on, he's crying, aren't they gonna do anything about it?"

Liz laughed again. "They will, Justin. Don't worry."

One of the two nurses in the room came forward and picked Dean up quickly and professionally. Seeing the three of them standing there, she held him up to the window for a moment. His eyes were squeezed shut and he looked like he was really howling now.

"So what happens? Aren't they going to feed him?" Justin asked. "Is he all right?"

"They said he's perfect," Liz said. "Seven pounds, three ounces."

"God, he's so tiny," Annie said as she watched the nurse take him away. "I can't believe he's an actual person."

They stood there for a little longer even though they couldn't see Dean anymore. There were about ten babies in the nursery. Some were much smaller than Dean, and on the far left there was a large, pink baby with a shock of red hair sticking up on its head.

"God, they all look so different," Annie said after a minute.

"I was thinking they all looked the same," said Justin. "Tessa better make sure she's got the right one."

"Can we see Tessa?" Annie asked.

Liz looked around; there was no one else in the hall. "Yeah," she said. "She might be sleeping, but let's just go down to her room."

"Was it O.K.?" Annie asked Liz as they walked. "I mean, the birth? Was it O.K.?"

"They say it was," Liz said, yawning. "I thought it was horrible, on the way here. I mean, she was crying and yelling. I've never seen her like that. But then they took her right in from the emergency room, and they wouldn't let me stay with her while he was born."

"Why not?" Annie asked. "She had to be alone?"

"They wouldn't let me," Liz said. "But I guess they knocked her out anyway, or something."

They got to a door and Liz walked in without knocking. Justin and Annie followed her. There were two beds in the room with a green checked curtain separating them. In the first bed was a middle-aged woman who was eating her breakfast. Her bed was surrounded by bouquets of flowers, and Annie recognized some of the stuffed animals from the gift shop. She saw Justin noticing that too and realized that he was still holding his rose for Tessa.

The first woman smiled at Liz. "I think she's still sleeping," she said.

"We'll be quiet," Liz said. "We just want to peek at her."

They pushed the curtain aside and went in. Tessa was lying on her back, with a tube in her arm. Her hair had been pulled back into a half-unraveled braid and her face looked pale and puffy. Her body was a nondescript lump under the sheets. The breakfast tray sat unnoticed on a small table near the bed. Liz went right next to her and Tessa stirred, then opened her eyes. She stared at them for a minute, as if she didn't know where she was, and then a slow smile spread across her face.

"Hi." Her voice sounded weak and hoarse, and there was a burst blood vessel in one eye that showed a bright red trail through the whiteness.

Annie went up next to Liz and reached for Tessa's hand. "How are you?" She was afraid to hug her, but Tessa squeezed her hand hard. Something about Tessa's face was different, and it wasn't just her eye or that she was so puffy. She's a mother, Annie thought. She's somebody's mother now.

"I'm totally destroyed, but I'm fine. Did you see him?"

"Yeah. He's great, Tessa. He's so . . ." Annie couldn't say anything else. She and Tessa just stared at each other, smiling so hard Annie thought her face would crack open.

"Justin," Tessa called, and Justin came up to the bed.

"Hey, congratulations," he said roughly, and handed her the rose. "I brought you this."

"Thanks," Tessa whispered, and suddenly none of them were able to speak, even Justin.

"Little Dean," Tessa said eventually. "He's here."

There was a rustling of the curtain and a nurse came in noisily.

"Oh, hello. I see you've got your family here." She smiled at them. "I'm Nurse Blaine," she said.

Annie noticed immediately that the nurse's name tag also read "Adoption Services," and she stiffened.

"Nurse Blaine was there when Dean was born," said Liz to Annie.

Tessa smiled at the nurse. "And she was great."

"*You* did a great job once we took care of that pain," Nurse Blaine said briskly. "Well, I'm here to take your vitals. Everything looks fine, and the baby's doing great." She began to move in toward Tessa, and the three of them stepped back. She looked at Justin pointedly and said, "You three may want to wait outside while I check her."

Annie wanted to shout at her to get out. She hated her nurse's smile, as if she knew more about Tessa than they did. But Tessa smiled at her, and Liz murmured something polite and led Justin and Annie out of the room.

When they were back in the waiting room, Annie exploded. "What is that cross on her name tag? Is she trying to get Tessa to give him up? What's up with that?"

"Annie, shut up!" Liz hissed back. "She's fine. She was here last night and she was great." She checked to see if anyone was in the hallway outside the waiting room. "Look, you weren't here, you don't know anything about it."

"O.K., O.K." Annie sat down and tried to lower her voice. "But, Liz, has Tessa changed her mind?"

"No, she hasn't. Nurse Blaine just works here, Annie, and at the adoption center I guess. For fuck's sake she's a good nurse, all right?"

"What about the adoption?" Justin asked.

"She brought it up." Liz held up her hand to stop Annie from interrupting. "She did bring it up, but Tessa said no, and I don't think she's said anything about it since."

Annie was quiet.

"It's her job to do that," Liz said.

"Why? Why is it her job?"

"Because Tessa is sixteen, why do you think? Because there's no father around, and our parents don't even know about it."

"Did Tessa tell her all that?"

"I think so." Liz sighed and sat down in a chair opposite Annie. "That nurse is an O.K. person, Annie, even if she is a Christian."

"What *is* going to happen?" Justin asked.

"What do you mean?" Liz said.

"I mean. What's Tessa gonna do? She can't hide out up in the country forever. Mom'll find out. Someone will find out. And she has to tell Nick."

"I know she does," Liz sounded exhausted. "It's gonna be bad, Jus."

"She's bringing him back down to the city, right?" Annie asked. "I mean, you guys aren't going to stay up here, are you?"

"I don't know, I don't know," Liz put her head down on her arms. "Everything's different now that he's really here."

"Did you tell Sam?" asked Annie. "Do you want me—"

"I called her." Liz smiled. "She's excited, actually. I'm supposed to go down to the city tonight to pick her up."

"Pick her up tonight? Can't she just get on the bus?"

"Of *course* she can." Liz laughed. "I want to go get her. Me and Tessa talked about it before. I'm going down to spend the night and see how Mom is doing—"

"Are you going to tell Marie?"

"No. No way. I'm just going to see her. Then Sam and I will come back up, get Tessa and the baby, and then the three of us are going to tell Mom together, with Dean."

"Sam agreed?"

"Yeah. Tessa wants her to come up here first."

"She should've just come up with me and Justin," Annie said.

"You didn't call her. She didn't know." Liz looked at her. Annie looked away, and Justin slouched back in his chair, letting his hair fall over his face. She couldn't tell if his eyes were closed.

"Did you?" Annie asked. "Did you call her?"

"Not until it was over," Liz said. "I couldn't."

"But you called me," Annie said quietly.

"Yeah, well." Liz looked at her with a slight smile. "I knew you would come."

"When are they going to let Tessa leave the hospital?" Justin asked.

"Maybe today," Liz said heavily.

"Today?" Justin sat up. "But she doesn't look so good. You know, there's tubes in her and shit."

"Yeah, but I guess she's doing well." Liz shrugged. "I don't think they let the public assistance cases stay very long."

"No shit," Justin said, and his face darkened. "Typical."

"Can you guys stay with her tonight?" Liz asked. "So I can go get Sam?"

"Of course," Annie said quickly. "We can stay, right, Justin?"

"Yeah, O.K., we'll stay," he said. But he sounded far away. As if he's already gone to Michigan, Annie thought.

They discharged Tessa in the late afternoon. She was wheeled to the car in a wheelchair, with Dean wrapped up in hospital blankets on her lap and piles of paperwork. She looked big and awkward in the wheelchair, and everybody was scared as they tried to get into the car. Justin was angry and kept muttering about how could these people send her home if they didn't think she could even walk to the car. But she could walk, really; at least she made it from the curb into the back of the Dodge while Liz held Dean, and Justin held her arm. But she walked very slowly, as if her limbs were made of glass. Liz climbed into the back, holding the baby, and Justin and Annie got in front for the drive home. The baby was quiet, and Tessa gasped a little with every bump and jolt. When Annie asked her what was wrong, she said simply, "Everything hurts."

They drove to the bus station first, so that Liz could catch the late-afternoon bus down to the city. Liz's eyes were hollow and dark with lack of sleep, but she looked bravely at Tessa as she handed Dean over to her.

"I'll be back tomorrow," she said. "With Sam. It'll be O.K., Tess." She gave her a kiss, and touched the baby gently with the tip of her finger. "I don't want to wake him up," she said, and then looked at Justin and Annie. "I'll call when I get there." She leaned forward and gave Justin and Annie each a quick kiss on the cheek. She's treating us exactly the same, thought Annie, and in that instant she knew that it was absolutely over between her and Liz. Annie felt herself panicking. She tried to hold Liz's gaze for an extra moment, even reaching out her hand to hold onto Liz's arm as she was getting out of the car. But Liz shook her head just slightly, as if to say that this wasn't the time to talk—which it obviously wasn't, Annie knew, but still—then the door slammed shut, the baby started crying, and Liz was gone.

As Justin drove away, Annie stared straight ahead and tried to talk herself out of what she already knew. That Liz's brief kiss was the moment of good-bye. But everyone else was there, and the baby, and what should she have said? Sometime soon she and Liz would be able to talk about it for hours, she thought, but she knew that Liz was never going to be her lover again. Maybe I'm crazy, she thought, I'm too tired. It was just a little kiss, and there's so much else going on. And I don't even know if *I* want to be lovers anymore, she said to herself, but she still felt as if something kept collapsing inside her chest over and over again.

The baby wouldn't stop crying. He cried for the rest of the car ride, he cried as they carried him into the cold house, and he kept crying even after Justin had made a fire and Annie had made a nice bed in a bureau drawer that they emptied and brought into the living room. Tessa had all of this equipment to deal with: a rubber ring to sit on when she went to the toilet; pads for her breasts, which were leaking and swollen and painful; bottles of formula for feeding the baby if he didn't want to breast-feed; pads for her bleeding; bottles of pills for pain, pills to keep her from getting an infection and pills to soften her stools. There was even a strange plastic spray bottle to rinse her stitches with after she went to the bathroom. She and Annie both looked at this last item in total bewilderment. Neither of them had ever used a douche or even sanitary napkins since the sixth grade.

Tessa sat in an armchair holding the baby, with all of the hospital supplies and piles of literature spread out around her on the floor. Annie started reading things out loud, yelling over Dean's crying about symptoms of colic and what to do for infected nipples. Tessa was sure hers were infected or they wouldn't hurt so much. Every time the baby sucked on her breast, Tessa started crying also because it hurt so much. Then she would pull the baby away, and he would start screaming again. Justin sat awkwardly next to the fire, feeding it bits of wood and looking as if he wished he spoke a different language the more Annie read about vaginas and nipples and blocked milk ducts.

Time became fluid, as if they were in a dream born of lack of sleep and the strangeness of everything. At one point Justin brought in a pot of spaghetti, and they all ate right out of the pot while Annie and Tessa took turns holding Dean. They made a bottle, but it was too hot, and then he wouldn't take it again. Dean's little body would almost relax and then it would suddenly go rigid again and the crying would begin. Tessa finally managed to nurse him for long enough to satisfy his hunger, but she cried through the whole thing and said that her belly was cramping, her nipples hurt, and the pain pills weren't doing anything. She lay on the bed and let her breasts hang out in front of Justin. She didn't want anything to touch them, she said, not even a T-shirt. They were much bigger than usual, taut and veined with milk, and when Tessa asked Annie to put warm washcloths on them to ease the pain, she felt how hard and hot they were. They didn't feel or look like anything sexual, and Annie didn't know if they were infected or not. Tessa lay on the couch while Annie brought the washcloths to her and Justin took a round of walking with the baby.

After a while the three of them stopped trying to talk to each other, and Dean's crying was the only sound throughout the house. He would slow down and almost stop, and whoever was holding him would pause for a moment in their walking, to see if he was falling asleep. Then, just as everyone had begun to relax, the crying would begin again. Tessa finally fell asleep on the couch, and Justin passed out in the bed, while Annie walked back and forth between the kitchen and the living room for a long, endless period during which she tried to get Dean to take the bottle and she willed herself not to look at the clock. They were all long past the point of singing to him or even talking to him, and Annie walked in a daze while he cried and hiccupped on her shoulder. It was on one of these rounds that she suddenly realized it had gotten quiet. He had stopped crying and was finally sleeping with slow, shuddering breaths. She eased herself into an armchair in the living room and sat leaning her head back, longing for nothing more than sleep. If I can only put him down, she thought, if I can only put him down I could lie down and sleep.

Her neck and shoulders were aching from carrying him, and she moved silently to the little bureau drawer that sat waiting full of blankets for the baby to sleep in. She shifted him in her arms, cradling his head, and gently, gently, lowered him down into his bed. She no longer marveled at his delicate hands and tiny nose, which looked pushed in like a pug's. Please, please, she whispered to the baby, please let me sleep. He settled onto the blankets, and Annie froze there for a moment, her hands underneath him, still cradling him. Her back was aching and the blood rushed to her head, making her dizzy. She carefully began the process of removing her hands, and Dean shifted like a fish, slithering suddenly from her grasp so that he was lying spread-eagled on his back, but he didn't wake up.

Annie breathed at last, and without a backward look at the baby, she crawled into the bed next to Justin without even taking her shoes off. She grabbed a pillow and closed her aching eyes; it must be around four in the morning, she thought. Jesus Christ. Just then, Dean started crying again. It began as a few little whimpers, and Annie dug her head under the pillow, praying that he would go back to sleep, but instead his cries became howls, until Annie knew that all three of them were lying there awake, but nobody was moving.

"Where is he?" Tessa asked at last.

"In the bureau drawer," Annie said. "He's safe, anyway."

Justin pulled the pillow over his head and rolled to his other side. Tessa was just lying on the couch, unmoving. The light was still on in the kitchen, and the harsh, white, fluorescent overhead illuminated the living room from the open doorway.

"I can't do it again," Annie said to Tessa. "I'm sorry, but I just can't. I thought he was asleep."

"Isn't he ever going to sleep?" Tessa asked dully, but nobody answered. Dean's crying sounded worse and worse, and finally he began coughing.

"Tessa, come on," Justin said at last. "Nurse him or something."

"Yeah," said Tessa darkly. "Here I go."

She heaved herself up on one arm, and then, finally, breathing heavily through the pain, she got herself onto her feet and over to the drawer. Annie watched her bend over slowly, as if she was an old woman, and pick up the baby.

"I'll take him in an hour," Annie said to Tessa. "Wake me up."

Tessa made no response as she walked into the kitchen with Dean in her arms, her breasts hanging out of her open hospital gown and a blank look on her face. I should get up, Annie thought. I should help her, but her body wouldn't respond and her eyes were aching too much to keep them open.

Annie woke up with a start to a silent house. The baby wasn't crying, and the light was gray outside the windows. It was so quiet she could hear birds: one, two, then three chattering at once. Annie sat up. Justin was still asleep, but the couch where Tessa had been was empty. She stumbled out of the living room, suddenly afraid, wondering how long it had been since she lay down. Tessa was sitting at the kitchen counter stirring a cup of tea. She didn't turn to Annie when she walked in and leaned on the doorjamb.

"Where is he?" Annie asked. "He's not crying."

"He's sleeping," Tessa said, gesturing to the floor without looking at Annie. "He fell asleep about fifteen minutes ago. Finally."

Annie saw that Tessa had dragged the drawer into the kitchen, and she looked inside. Dean was lying on his stomach with his head turned to the side, his little back rising and falling quickly like the rib cage of a bird or a lizard.

"Thank God," Annie said, hitching herself up onto the counter next to Tessa. "Oh, thank God he's sleeping." Then looking at Tessa she saw that she was staring out the window. "What is it, Tess? Are you all right?"

"I called Nurse Blaine," Tessa said evenly. "She's coming over."

"What do you mean?" Annie was suddenly completely awake.

"She's going to take him for adoption," Tessa said, and she turned to Annie at last. "Please don't hate me."

"I don't, I don't. Tessa—you called her?"

"I can't do it, Annie." Tessa looked down at her teacup, stirring it vigorously though there was no milk. "I'm not a good mother. I don't feel right. I don't even know if I love him, Annie. All I kept thinking was what'll happen when we go home. Mom and Dad . . . and Nick." She looked at the baby, and then back at Annie. "All I really want is for him to leave me alone." Her voice broke then, and she reached for her teacup. "So, I called. And that's why. You can hate me if you want."

"Tess," Annie paused. "What if it's just one bad night, you know? Maybe—"

"No. If I'm gonna do it, I have to do it now," Tessa said. "Before anyone finds out." She looked out of the kitchen window at the fox fire rising up from the field in front of the house. "Before I start to love him."

Annie could think of nothing to say. She looked at Dean, sleeping in his white hospital blanket printed with bears and beach balls; his hand was curled into itself like a tiny red leaf, and she wished she could hold him without waking him up. But she could think of nothing to say.

"Did you talk to Liz?" she asked at last. "Or anyone else?"

"No," Tessa said. "It's my baby, Annie. Not ours, not Nick's, mine. Are any of you guys gonna live with me for the next twenty years? Really? I mean, Annie—in twenty years I'll be thirty-six. We'll all be old. No one's gonna want to stick around that long."

"Why?" asked Annie. "Where are we gonna go?"

"Places." Tessa tugged at a fingernail with her teeth. "Everybody goes places."

A white van turned in at the top of the driveway. The headlights shone through the patches of early morning mist like searchlights.

"That's her," Tessa said without moving. "She said she'd be here soon. She was on duty at the hospital."

Annie watched the van bouncing down the dirt driveway. "I'm going to wake up Justin," she said. Tessa didn't say anything; her face was expressionless as she watched the van approach the house. Annie went to the living room and shook Justin awake. He woke as suddenly as she had, jolting into awareness.

"Justin, it's Tessa," Annie said. "Wake up. You gotta wake up. This lady's coming over to take the baby."

"What?"

"To adopt him, you know. I mean, to take him to be adopted. Anyway, wake up."

Justin sat up on the edge of the bed and blinked. They had all slept in their clothes, and he pulled his shirt down from where it had hitched up over his stomach. The back door opened, and they heard Tessa saying hello.

"She's here right now?" asked Justin, stopping himself mid-yawn.

"Yes, I told you. Tessa called her. Come on." Annie went into the kitchen.

"Hello," said Nurse Blaine, looking very stark in her uniform and white shoes. There was another woman with her, a plump, middle-aged woman wearing blue slacks and a purple sweater, with a gold cross displayed prominently on a chain around her neck. "I was just telling Tessa that this is Mrs. Hawthorn, from the Extended Hand

Christian Services," she said to Annie and then turned back to Tessa. "That's our adoption agency, as you know."

"This is Annie," Tessa said to Mrs. Hawthorn as Justin walked into the room. "And this is Justin." They all shook hands.

"Are you the father of the baby?" Mrs. Hawthorn asked.

"No," he mumbled. He saw the baby lying in its bed on the floor and leaned over to get a better peek. Then Justin looked directly at Mrs. Hawthorn. "I'm his uncle."

"Uh huh," she said, looking from him to Tessa and back again. "And is the father of the baby here?"

"No," said Tessa. "He doesn't know."

"Well, legally, in the state of New York, he doesn't have any rights to the child since you are underage and unmarried. So it's no problem for you to sign the adoption papers yourself."

Mrs. Hawthorn put a paper folder on the kitchen counter, moving some teacups aside to make room. Annie suddenly saw the house through their eyes and thought what it must look like. Three teenagers living alone in a house, with the kitchen a mess and the living room beyond filled with blankets half-thrown onto the floor. She hated these women for coming here. We're not so bad, she thought to herself. We didn't hurt the baby or anything.

Nurse Blaine had walked over to the drawer with the baby in it, and she leaned down and adjusted the blanket more snugly. "There," she said. "He looks just fine. But I guess you had quite a night of it."

Tessa leaned her head on her hand. "He didn't go to sleep until right after I called you," she said. "It was like he knew."

There was a pause and then Nurse Blaine said briskly, "I'm sure he just wore himself out, poor thing."

"Yeah," said Tessa, unconvinced. "I guess he did."

"Now, Tessa. I want to remind you of some of the things we spoke about in the hospital," she paused and looked at Annie and Justin, who were both standing there silently. "Would you like to go to the other room to discuss this, or—"

"They can be here," Tessa said. "They're my family."

Nurse Blaine smiled at Annie and Justin. "All right," she said. "Now, you remember that list you made up in the hospital, for and against adoption. Do you still have that list?"

"Yes," Tessa said. Annie stared at her. Neither Tessa nor Liz had said a word to her; she wondered if Liz knew.

"You remember that there were many reasons on that list for choosing adoption. That it may be the best choice for the baby, as well as for you. Do you remember that, dear?"

Tessa nodded her head, but she didn't say anything.

"By choosing adoption you are going to be sure that he is going to have a stable, loving family who want, more than anything, to bring up a child. We screen all of our families very carefully at Extended Hand, so you don't have to worry about that. Mrs. Hawthorn here has all the literature for you."

"All right," said Tessa.

"And you will be able to continue your education and pursue your career goals. I really want you to know that though this is a very hard choice, I think it is the best one, Tessa, for you and the baby."

"Can he keep his name?" Tessa asked.

"No, I'm afraid not." Nurse Blaine looked sympathetically at Tessa. "His birth identity and your identity will be kept in sealed records at our agency, and unless there is a medical emergency, those files cannot be unsealed once you sign the adoption papers. I'm sure you understand that the adoptive parents need to feel that it's their baby once they adopt. Do you have any unusual medical history that we should know? Or does the father?"

"No," said Tessa, and then she looked at Justin.

"No," he said. "No history."

"Do you have any other questions for us, Tessa? And do you feel clear about this?" Nurse Blaine asked. "This can be a very emotional time, we know. And you've already been through a lot." She smiled at Tessa and touched her hand.

Tessa didn't smile back, but she looked at Nurse Blaine for a long moment, then at Annie and Justin. "No," she said. "But, I mean, what about when he grows up?"

Nurse Blaine held her hand. "He will have a good, safe home to grow up in, I can assure you."

"No, I mean," Tessa's voice dropped to almost a whisper, "I mean, could I ever see him?"

"You give up all legal rights by signing the adoption papers," Nurse Blaine said gently. "That means that you no longer have the responsibility of raising a child when you still have so much of your own life to live, but it also means you have given up your rights to him. The papers will be sealed, as I said. This is for the protection of the adoptive family, and, we believe, better for the child. He shouldn't be confused about who his parents are."

"But what if he knows," Annie broke in. "What if he just knows he's not theirs?"

"We counsel all of our families to tell the children that they have been adopted," Nurse Blaine said pleasantly. "An adopted child is still a wanted child, you know, very much wanted. He just won't know who his biological mother and father are, and we have found, research has found, that it really is better that way. Better for the child. We're really trying to do what's best for him as well as for you, Tessa."

Tessa didn't say anything. Annie looked at Justin, but he was looking at the baby, as if he wanted to memorize him. He's not going to say anything to stop this, she realized.

"Tessa," she said, "don't you want to talk to Liz first?"

"We already talked about it," Tessa said, and she looked up at Annie dry-eyed. "You guys thought this was a good idea, remember?"

"Yeah, but . . ." Annie looked at her hard. "But now it's different."

Nobody said anything. The quiet of the country settled into the kitchen for a moment, the sound of the stream and the highway merging together with the sound of a bird outside the window. It was a small black-and-white bird, Annie noticed, that jumped lightly from branch to branch, calling in counterpoint to the highway drone.

Mrs. Hawthorn cleared her throat expectantly, and Nurse Blaine took her hand from Tessa's.

"Are you ready to sign the papers, dear?" she asked. "It's your decision. If you don't want to that's fine."

"But you came all the way out here," Tessa said.

"Oh, that's all right," Nurse Blaine said. "We do this all the time. We just want what's best for you and the baby."

"Yes." Tessa looked at Dean, who was still sleeping quietly. "It's all right. I mean, I'll sign. Where are they?"

Mrs. Hawthorn passed the papers to Nurse Blaine, and Tessa signed quickly on each line the nurse pointed out. Annie wanted to leave the room, to grab the baby, to do anything but stay. She stood there in silence.

Mrs. Hawthorn gathered up the papers efficiently and patted Tessa on the shoulder. "I really think it is the best thing," she said. "It's hard now, I know. But you be sure to keep that list and look it over. It will help." She looked at Justin and Annie. "You know that this is going to be a hard time the next few weeks, and she's going to need your help."

"We're not going anywhere," Justin said quietly. Annie just nodded.

"Would you like some time alone with him," Nurse Blaine asked, "before we go?"

Tessa nodded and Nurse Blaine looked at Mrs. Hawthorn. "We'll wait outside for a few minutes," she said. "But it's best not to draw this out."

The two women let themselves out of the kitchen and stood outside on the patio. Tessa looked at Annie and Justin, then she got up and looked down at the baby.

"I don't want to wake him up," she said uncertainly.

"It's O.K.," Justin said. "I mean, if he wakes up."

Tessa reached down and picked Dean up. He wriggled for a moment then gave a small sigh and stayed asleep. She smiled at him, and then brought her face very close to him for a moment, breathing hard. When she brought her face away she was crying. "I just wanted to smell him," she said. Then she held him out toward Justin and Annie. "Do you want to?"

Annie moved in and brushed his hand with her cheek. His skin was like paper, and his fingernails were long and feathery on the tips of his fingers. She felt herself starting to cry as she looked up at Tessa, and she moved to her, putting an arm around her waist.

"Let me hold him a minute," said Justin. Tessa handed him the baby, and he held it against him for a long moment, staring down at his face. The bundle of blankets dwarfed Dean's body, and he was no longer than Justin's forearm.

"It's all right, little Dean," Justin whispered. "You're gonna be all right."

Then he looked up at Tessa and Annie, and they saw that he was crying too. He couldn't brush the tears away because he was holding the baby, and his face twisted.

"Do you want me to take him out?" Justin asked Tessa. "Or do you want—"

"You do it," Tessa whispered. "I can't."

Justin nodded and walked out the door. Tessa and Annie watched through the window as he handed the baby to Nurse Blaine, who held him gently and securely as she got into the back of the van. Justin stayed outside for a long time, watching the van lumber back up the driveway and turn toward town. It was a perfect winter day, cold and clear, the sky an enamel blue. Annie took Tessa's hand and walked outside with her to Justin, the mud frozen under their bare feet. Justin turned to them and wrapped his long arms around both of them, hugging them hard until Tessa's heaving changed to a slow quiver and Annie leaned her head on his sleeve as he pressed his cheek against Tessa's, the wind whipping their faces clean.

. . .

Justin and Tessa thought that Annie would go back to Cornelia Street with them, but when they drove past the Christopher Street subway station, Annie wanted to get on the train and ride it all the way uptown. She wanted to go home. They said good-bye quickly, while they were waiting for the light to change. Tessa had called Liz and Sam from the country and told them not to come up, that they were coming down to the city today, and they would talk when she got there. Annie hadn't spoken to Liz because she knew she couldn't say anything without telling her everything, and Tessa wanted to do it in person.

"Call us later," Tessa said, as Annie reached for her backpack and opened the door.

"It's already later." Annie smiled, her eyes red and narrow with exhaustion.

Tessa was too tired to smile, and Justin was staring into his side mirror, watching the traffic. But he reached out a hand to Annie as she pulled her bag past him, and when she paused he smiled at her without saying anything. Then the light turned and she slammed the door shut, while the cars behind them honked and Justin gave them the finger out the open window.

She caught a train that was just pulling into the station, heading north toward Fourteenth Street. The swaying of the subway was hypnotic, and Annie tried not to fall asleep. It was midday and the other subway cars and stations were relatively quiet. She got up and walked to the very front of the first car, where the small window looked out on the tracks leading straight on into the lights of the next station or veered around a corner lit by narrow strings of blue lights, punctuated by an occasional red or green miniature traffic signal.

At Ninety-sixth Street she got out and began to walk the long blocks home. Annie felt as if she was walking slower than everyone else she saw on the street. The white stone Virgin in front of the church on the corner of Amsterdam was the same, with its metallic gold halo like an enormous Chinese wok suspended over her head. "Our Lady of South Harlem," Luke had always called it. The ground was strewn with leftover firecracker wrappers, red and gold labels: "Black Cat" and "Gypsy Woman." Annie could tell there had been firecracker wars in front of the stone Virgin last night.

She walked past the bank on the corner of Columbus that had a big clock in the window, which her mother had used to teach her how to tell the time—it was one-thirty-five. She jumped up and ran along the top of a low cement wall. The wall bordered the front of an apartment building and enclosed the dirt covered by more landscaping bark than flowers, though not many weeds had managed to gain a foothold on West Ninety-sixth Street.

The lobby of her building was deserted except for an old woman leaning on her walker and staring at the cars rushing by. The apartment house smell was there again. She could detect different smells as well as voices from the apartments on her hallway, which was mostly quiet except for the news radio that the Lowensteins across the hall had turned on. Annie had never been in her building in the middle of a weekday before, and before going into her apartment she leaned back against the wall for a moment. There was the hum and clank of the elevator as it went from the main floor up and back again. Down at the other end of the hall a man and woman started arguing—a quiet insistent harangue. Liz is wrong. I'm never getting married, she thought; kids, maybe, but never married.

She turned the key in the lock of her apartment and felt an outdoor breeze coming from inside. She closed the door quietly behind her, and looking around into the living room, she saw that the glass door to the terrace was open, and Ellen was standing out there in her nightgown; the afternoon wind lifting it up and swirling the silky material around her knees.

Annie held her breath for just a moment, watching. "Mom?"

Ellen turned around, surprised. Then she smiled, and Annie saw that she was holding a cup of coffee.

"Good morning," she said, pulling awkwardly at her nightgown. Then she saw Annie watching her and gave up, laughing and letting it fly up around her again as she hugged her. "I went to bed late; I just got up."

Annie hugged her tightly without saying anything.

"What are you doing here?" Ellen asked. "I thought you were staying up at the country another day. Your note said that Liz was really sick."

"Liz is better. She'll be fine. I wanted to come home," Annie said.

Ellen looked at her and her smile became gentler. "Good," she said. "And school?"

"It's too late to go today. I'll get the homework from somebody. It'll be O.K." She leaned against the balcony rail and looked out at the street. The ugly apartment buildings around them were comforting somehow, and the sameness of the street below.

"You just got up?" she asked her mother.

"I couldn't sleep," Ellen said, yawning and having a sip of coffee. "So I finally gave up and stayed up until about eight; then I called in sick and went to bed until one." She looked around and took a deep breath. "It's such a nice day, I'd rather be up."

"Yeah." Annie walked back into the apartment and lay down on the couch, suddenly feeling that every part of her was aching for sleep.

"Hey," Ellen came inside and perched next to her. "I have an idea. What if I make us some cinnamon toast?"

"Really?" Annie smiled. It was her favorite thing.

"Why not? Wait here."

Annie lay unmoving and listened to her mother rustling in the kitchen. Cinnamon toast was one of the few things Ellen actually cooked, but she did it very well. She heard the refrigerator door open and close and the clatter of the metal baking pan sounded loud in the quiet apartment. She half-dozed, and as the smell of sugar and cinnamon filled the room, she wondered if she had come home and dreamed all this; it seemed so unlikely that her mother would be home in the middle of the day, and cooking.

"I thought we could eat out on the balcony," Ellen said, right next to her ear, and Annie realized she must have drifted off. Ellen had hauled the beanbag chair from Annie's room onto the balcony, as well as several large cushions from the living room. Annie nodded and followed her out there, pulling the blanket from the couch on top of her as she walked.

Ellen had made a huge pile of cinnamon toast and more coffee for both of them. Annie ate as if she couldn't stop, and Ellen laughed at how hungry she was, then told her to eat more.

"Everything tastes better outside, doesn't it?" Ellen said, taking a deep breath of the air that somehow smelled cleaner at this time of day.

Small brown birds with light tufts of feathers on the backs of their heads filled the sparse branches of the trees on the street below them, and every now and then a clutch of sparrows would swarm up and dip miraculously around a streetlight or shift direction for no apparent reason before dropping back to the rooftops, all the time singing.

Annie leaned back into the cushions and pulled the blanket up to her chin. She was just beginning to lose the chill that had begun as they stood in the driveway outside the house. The morning already seemed as if it had happened a long time ago, to another person. Ellen reached over and stroked her hair, tentatively at first, as if she was afraid Annie would push her away, but Annie stayed there without moving, until eventually Ellen's hand came over her forehead and gently brushed her eyelids closed just as she used to do when Annie was a baby. Annie let herself be soothed by Ellen's familiar hands—the scent of lilac and tobacco—and pretended it was forever.

Rebecca Chace is an actress, playwright, and author of the memoir *Chautauqua Summer,* which was a *New York Times* Notable Book for 1993. She has contributed to the *New York Times Magazine* and the *New York Times Book Review,* among other publications.